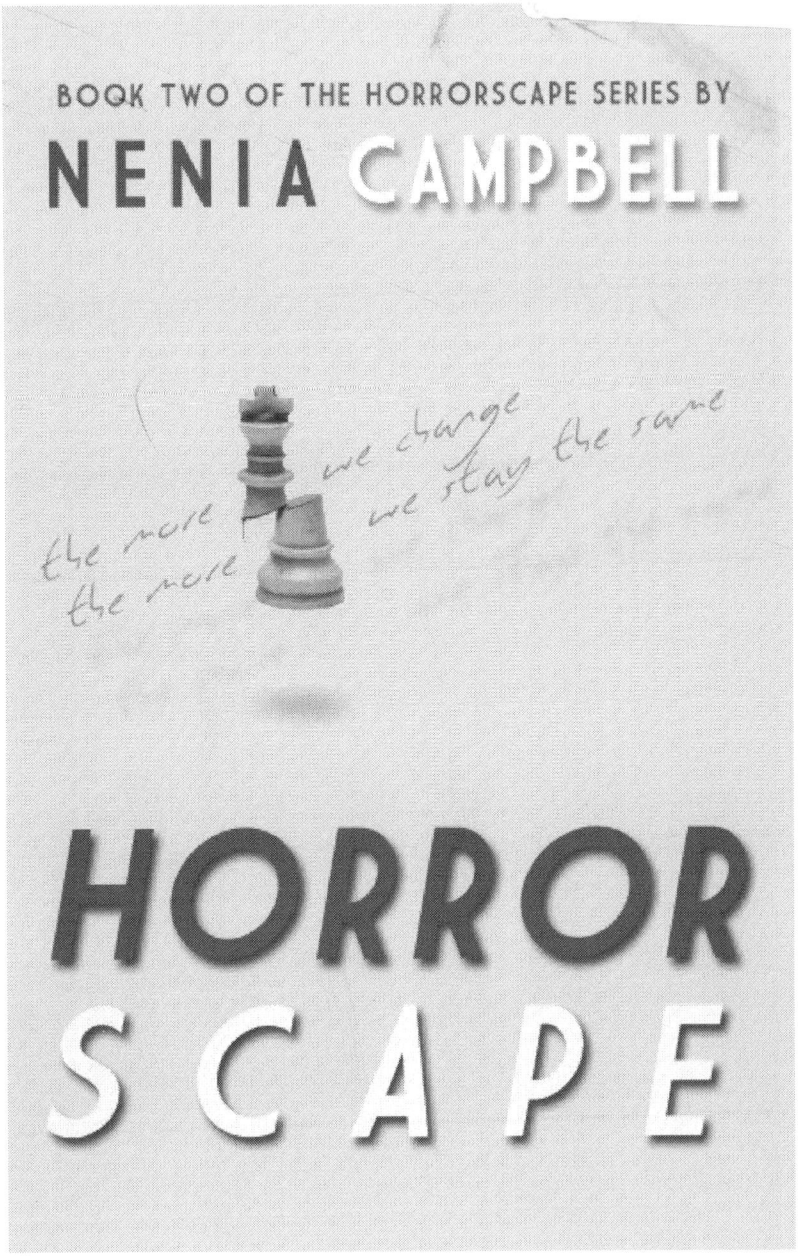
BOOK TWO OF THE HORRORSCAPE SERIES BY
NENIA CAMPBELL
the more we change
the more we stay the same
HORROR
SCAPE

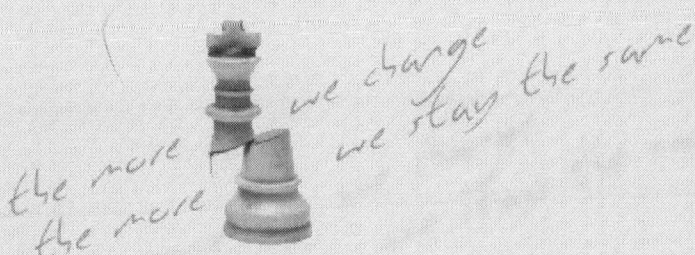

HORRORSCAPE by NENIA CAMPBELL

Horrorscape by Nenia Campbell

Horrorscape by Nenia Campbell

Copyright © 2012 Nenia Campbell
All rights reserved.

Horrorscape by Nenia Campbell

DEDICATION

Put your name here: ___Saskia___ .

Thank you so much for purchasing this book.

Horrorscape by Nenia Campbell

Table of Contents

Prologue

1. OPENING

2. DECOY

3. WAITING MOVE

4. ANTIPOSITIONAL

5. UNDERMINING

6. CAPTURE

7. HANGING PAWN

8. COMPENSATION

9. EXCHANGE VARIATION

10. WILD

11. EN PESSANT

12. SHAM SACRIFICE

13. BREAKTHROUGH

14. ATTRACTION

15. CASTLING INTO IT

16. TRAP

17. DOMINATION

18. VACATING SACRIFICE

19. TREBUCHET

20. COUNTERPLAY

21. THREAT

22. OVERLOADED

23. RELATIVE PIN

24. PASSIVE

25. CHECKMATE

Epilogue

Horrorscape by Nenia Campbell

Prologue

There was something delightfully intimate about the relationship between predator and prey: the careful dance, neither party quite willing to make the first strike or reveal their true intentions. In many ways, it was a courtship ritual—a ritual that continued until the whole game was brought to climax, and the predator reaped his just reward.

He was fascinated with predators of all kinds. Wolves. Hawks. Lions. Creatures that had been known throughout history for strength, nobility, and the ability to inspire fear. Symbols of power. Symbols of conquest. Symbols of evolutionary superiority. He felt he, himself, embodied many of these traits. He even had his prey—oh, yes—and her name was Valerian Kimble.

She wasn't beautiful in the classical sense but he enjoyed looking at her nonetheless. He liked the subtle curves of her willowy form, with its awkwardness that belied her athletic ability. How quickly she could run.

He liked how dark her eyes got, downcast in fear. How the light could morph them from jade to evergreen. Most of all, he liked her hair, and the way it flared like a bank of glowing embers in sunlight, and her lovely mouth—as sweet and as soft as the crushed petals of a rose.

He felt her, even in sleep.

He lowered his eyes to the desk, though there was

nothing meek in the gesture. Several sheaves of paper lay before him. Most of them were crumpled, others had been tossed aside in rejection. He toyed with the fountain pen in his hand for a while. Then he sighed and closed his eyes.

For a long time, he did not move at all. His face was as solemn as one in the midst of prayer. But it was not God of whom he was thinking, and his thoughts were far from holy.

Damn her. He got up abruptly, disappearing into one of the upstairs rooms. There was a click as the door closed and locked. Silence.

Minutes passed, hours. Somewhere in the depths of the house a clock struck six. The door opened, and he emerged wearing a pair of black sweatpants. He sat down at the desk again, freshly inspired. All thanks to dear, dear Val.

A work of art: a work in progress. Not quite ready for the showcase. She possessed a number of flaws he intended to paint out. Weaknesses of character aside, the most nettlesome of these was her boyfriend and the sheer defiance he represented on her part.

Dull. Wholesome. Hardly a worthy adversary. He was nothing more than a bully who, like many of his type, had found an outlet for his adolescent aggression in sports, and while he might be able to kick a ball around a field, he wouldn't be able to dodge a bullet or a blade. And if it ever came right down to it, he wouldn't be able to protect Valerian from one, either.

Perhaps that was why she had chosen him; perhaps she enjoyed feeling in control. *Is that it?* He wondered, a cruel smile marring his face. *Well. I'm afraid that's about to change.*

Horrorscape by Nenia Campbell

Chapter One

Opening

Val walked out of Conceptual Physics in a daze as her best friend, Lisa Jeffries, babbled about the latest in her most recent line of conquests.

She'd gotten another one of those phone calls this morning, asking her if she liked to fuck dangerous men, that girls like her were "proof that some women were asking for it." Just when she finally thought they had stopped, too. *But then isn't how it always goes?*

Tears stabbed at her eyes and she set her teeth, refusing to blink and let them spill. Not here at school.

Suddenly, powerfully, she wished her mother were here to hug her, to hold her in her arms and tell her everything was going to be all right. She felt it like an ache in her chest.

"What about you, Val?"

"Huh?" She swiped at her eyes with the back of her hand, faking a yawn.

"Your thoughts," Lisa said, dryly.

"I can't wait for the three day weekend."

"Why? Do you have *plans*?"

Val gave her a half-hearted swat.

"What was that for? I only asked what you were doing this weekend?"

"We both know what you really meant."

Lisa rolled her eyes. "Seriously, though. What are you doing?"

"Probably nothing. We're getting the house remodeled. Everything's getting ripped up, torn out...I'm probably going to end up shut in my room with my computer for six-odd hours."

"So the usual for you, then." She dodged another swat. "No hot date with James?"

Val shrugged and adjusted her messenger bag. "Guess not."

"You guys have been dating for four months. You haven't gotten hot and heavy yet?"

Val flushed. She looked away. "No."

"Has he—you know—*asked*?"

The redness moved down her throat. "That's none of your business," she said stiffly.

"He has! He has, hasn't he? And you said *no*."

Val closed her eyes. All her ambivalence from earlier returned full-force. She felt faint. "I'm not ready. He doesn't understand."

"Of course he doesn't. You're holding out. There's no other explanation necessary; you're the evil one."

"James isn't like that. I told him about...what happened. He knows why I can't—"

Horrorscape by Nenia Campbell

"Val, I hate to burst your bubble, but even if he's pretending it's no big deal, it is. All guys are secretly like that. Sex-obsessed, I mean. Whether they show it or not is just a test of character—and any guy who says otherwise is either a liar, a cheater, or both. You just wait until the honeymoon period is over. Then you'll see."

"No, I won't. Because that's just not true. And anyway, it's none of your business so discussion is *closed*."

Lisa sighed. "It's completely beyond his control."

(control can be)

"What's beyond whose control?"

(a powerful aphrodisiac)

Val stumbled. Two warm arms caught her and she found herself staring up into a pair of sea-foam green eyes. "Whoa, steady on there, Clumsy. You're taking 'falling for you' to a literal level, aren't you?"

(it's hard to resist)

And far too easy to give in.

James frowned at her. "Hey, you're shaking. You okay?"

She smiled weakly. "No. I mean, yes, I'm fine. I just tripped."

Lisa jumped in. "We were just talking about—"

"How great the break will be. Right, Lisa?"

"Oh, that's right, all right," Lisa said. She gave Val a devious smile which she didn't trust for a minute.

James was still frowning. "Your parents still doing the construction thing this weekend?"

"Unfortunately."

His face fell. "So we can't hang out at your place."

"Probably not. I'm sorry." Val wished he wasn't doing this in front of Lisa, and her too-sharp eyes.

James shrugged. "Too bad."

"Why do we always have to go to my house? Yours is bigger than mine."

"Because my brother's an ass, who acts like an even bigger ass when you're around." James snorted, glancing at Lisa. "He has the biggest crush on her, it's not even funny." He turned back to Val. "You wouldn't understand, you're an only child. But he seriously makes me want to punch him in the face sometimes. That's why."

Val tried to laugh it off. "Hey, he's fifteen. *I* don't care."

"I do."

She tried not to flinch. His voice was pleasant enough but she still felt a tug of anxiety. She'd had to blow him off a lot recently. First because of football season (she was in band, and had to travel to various other towns for competitions, as well as play at all of the major home games), and then again because of midterms. James was a senior, like her and Lisa, so he should have understood her problems. Especially since his classes were much, much difficult than hers.

She would rather go out with him than do stupid homework or practice her clarinet. It was only the threat of failure and post-apocalyptic parents that had kept her on track and out of her boyfriend's house on weekends. Well, that, and the fact that lately, it seemed like he tried to jump her whenever they happened to be alone.

"Well, maybe we can do something else. Go out for once." She smiled timidly. He returned the smile with markedly less enthusiasm.

"Maybe."

Great, Val thought, as he and Lisa fell into a discussion about the football game this weekend. A discussion that conveniently excluded her. *He's mad.*

"We can all go to the game," Lisa suggested. "It's close enough that you'll be able to help out if your parents need you, right Val? I mean, you have a cell phone."

"Val's parents are kind of overprotective," James said, before she could even open her mouth.

Now *she* was annoyed. "They are not!" She paused and added in a sour voice, "And considering what happened before, I wouldn't really blame them, even if they were!"

She gave him a look.

"Sorry, Val," he muttered, pulling her into a hug made awkward by the bulk of their backpacks. He smelled like Old Spice, and his sweatshirt was so soft and cuddly she had to resist the impulse to nuzzle her face against his chest. She was still angry at him; she didn't want to give in so easily.

"What?" Lisa sniffed. "No apology for me?"

Val glanced at her over James's shoulder. "Why should I apologize to *you*?"

"For snipping at me earlier."

"I'm *sorry*, Lisa."

"Next time don't sound so sarcastic and it'll be perfect."

James glanced at his watch. "Better get moving, ladies." He released Val. "Bell will ring any minute."

The three of them walked to the 600 hall, where their lockers were. From the way the halls were filling up, Val guessed it was more like a matter of seconds.

Only forty-five more minutes of class and I can go home.

Val grabbed her math book. Hopefully she'd be able to pay attention today. She was starting to feel a little sick.

Did I remember to take my medication?

The bell rang, shattering her thoughts like brittle glass.

Horrorscape by Nenia Campbell

I feel so strange.

James walked her to class. His Calculus class was only two down from her Geometry classroom. "Why do you take it?" she asked. "Isn't it hard?"

"I like being able to do things other people can't do."

And he kissed her. On the mouth. In school.

She knew she should feel pleased, but all she felt was that same shapeless worry. *Is that why you kept asking me out?* She wondered suddenly. *Because I kept saying no?*

"Later," he said, pulling away with a smile and a wave.

Seeing him smile—just for her—should have brought a feeling of indescribable happiness. He did make her happy. Sometimes. She just couldn't be passionate with him; the moment he got too close, he made her want to run away.

This was so not functional.

Part of her yearned for the early days of their relationship, when they were still too shy with each other to be anything but platonic. He'd tried harder back then, too. And he'd been wittier. More engaging. He still invited her over to his house. Now, she wondered.

Does he love me?

Do I love him?

That was unpleasant to think about, though, so Val pushed the thoughts away.

Horrorscape by Nenia Campbell

■□■□■□■

The Geometry classroom was dim and stifling. The old blinds were stuck fast, and nearly impossible to get open. Mr. Giles had made a show of going to the thermostat and fiddling with the various knobs and switches, making it quite clear that changing the temperature was an exercise in futility itself.

Hot and sniffy, Val glared down at her math problems for a long time. She thrust her arm into the air. "I need help."

Yes, you do, someone whispered.

"What do you need help with?" said Mr. Giles.

"The proofs." Val pointed. There was a nervous squeak in her voice. She cleared her throat. "I don't get them."

"What about them don't you get?"

"The *proofs*." She stabbed an accusatory finger at a picture of a triangle. She was beginning to feel like she was in the middle of one of those old Abbot and Costello routines her dad thought so hilarious. "I know I'm supposed to explain them using theorems and postulates—"

"—*And* the definitions."

"Yes, and those," Val agreed impatiently. "But I

don't know when to use them. I mean, I can barely solve the problems themselves."

"You're supposed to have the definitions memorized," Mr. Giles said. "Which you obviously haven't done, judging from some of your quizzes, Valerian. Perhaps if you actually did the homework you would have an easier time in class."

She didn't imagine it; somebody definitely laughed.

"It's hard," she said, feeling hopeless. She was just another slacker to him, trying to weasel out of work. "I can't think logistically."

"Logically," the teacher corrected, with a sigh. "You can't think *logically*."

"What good is logic?"

"Well, in chess, for example, logic is very important."

A shiver snaked down her spine. "I don't play chess."

Mr. Giles blinked, startled by her vehemence. "It might improve your scores. Chess can be very remedial for math."

(care to make a little wager?)

She was saved from having to respond by the crackle of the intercom. "Valerian Kimble to the administration office, please. Valerian Kimble to the administration office."

Horrorscape by Nenia Campbell

She'd been in high school for four years, and they'd never paged her before. It couldn't have happened at a better time. She glanced at her teacher.

He waved her off. "You had better go. We'll discuss your homework when you return."

Oh, boy.

■□■□■□■

While a welcome distraction from proofs, the administration office was a dark and gloomy place with ugly wallpaper that hadn't been changed since the sixties. A vague smell of disinfectant hung loosely in the air. It probably came from the nurse's office down the hall, but seemed prominent everywhere else, too.

Mrs. Fields was on duty that afternoon and she gave Val an unimpressed look as she walked in through the door. Behind the Bride of Frankenstein makeup, she looked tough. Not surprising, considering her name, and the fact that it was an open invite for jokes pertaining to cookies and her unfortunate girth.

"Can I help you?"

"Um, you called for me on the intercom?"

"You're Valerian, are you?"

"Val, yes."

Ignoring her, the secretary reached behind her desk

and pulled out an olive-green planter box. "This came for you." A leafy green plant was growing out of it, speckled with little pink flowers. "And this," she added, dropping an envelope on top of the plant, crushing the fragile blossoms. "It your birthday or something?"

"No." Val stared at the flowers. She had never seen anything like them before.

"Better get back to class. Do you need a pass?"

Val shook her head. "Who is it from? Who sent it?"

"I don't know, he didn't say. Now get back to class."

He?

Val left the office, puzzled and a little too warm. Why would a boy be sending her things? Or was it a man? She stopped outside to set the flowers on a bench so she could read the card.

They couldn't be from James. He would have made a point of mentioning it, of dropping heavy hints. He would have gone with the more traditional roses; they were safer.

She wished she'd thought to ask the secretary what the sender looked like, but it was too late now. She was dealing with an angry-looking parent now, sheepish child in tow. She could see the drama unfolding through the window.

She returned her attention to the card. The paper was grainy and left her hands feeling dry. She licked her finger before sliding it under the flap and slicing it open with her nail. The paper inside was plain and off-white, like parchment. It smelled expensive.

Frowning now, she unfolded the stationery, revealing inky black writing. A few flower petals, pink like the ones growing on the plant beside her, fluttered to the ground at her feet.

I've been watching you for some time. I know you're passionate about the things and people you love—an disinclined to do things that don't suit your interests. In that aspect, you remind me of a powerful predator, a hunter. But in many other ways, you are a lower-scale being. The hunted. The prey.

I have singled you out because you have potential. I want to play with you. I want to play suicide chess with you. You with your pawns, and me with mine. Together, we will level the playing field. And do you know what else? I know you'll do it. Because the same passion that fuels your affections drives your curiosity. You like a good challenge. I think you'll find me <u>quite</u> a challenge.

In all regards.

Even now, I know you're looking for me, wondering who I am. Where I am. How I know what I do.

These questions will be answered over the course of my game, although when the time comes, you may no longer desire the answers.

Are you frightened? Do I frighten you? I should. Because

first you must play the game for more than you can afford to lose. Sacrifice everything. Learn true fear.

Only then, will you win the game.

I am the Grandmaster. I look forward to playing against you, my dear.

X

P.S. The flowers are valerians. Your namesake—quite appropriate, I thought, although not as beautiful as you.

Her heart was throbbing when she finished the letter.

(I wonder what makes her blood race—lust or fear?)

Val sank down on the bench. The letter was full of masked emotions, yet bore a harsh, clinical quality that chilled her. Games, flowers, prey, predators? It was more than her mind could comprehend. Distantly, she remembered that a 'grandmaster' was a high-ranking chess title. Gavin had taught her that, but she nipped that thought in the bud, as she did with all thoughts of him.

Somewhere, someone at this school was watching her. *Stalking* her. *Hunting* her.

Val shivered in spite of her sweatshirt, which she pulled more tightly around her. Gavin? Was it Gavin? She wondered, and the wind blew more fiercely around her, echoing her unease.

Horrorscape by Nenia Campbell

Are you frightened? He'd asked. *Do I frighten you?*
Yes, he did. Yes, she was.
(You should be)

Chapter Two

Decoy

It had taken Val years to feel safe again. For weeks, months, she had lived in constant terror of Gavin's return. The smallest things had set her off: the sound of a creaking floorboard when she was home alone; the smells of sandalwood and roses, or of paint and sawdust; the searing, bittersweet taste of peppermint.

Over time, her skin had thickened. With the aid of medication she learned to force herself to evaluate the situation from a logical standpoint, and respond to potential threats accordingly until they stopped seeming like threats. It even worked a little.

But in her Health notebook, which she had kept from freshman year, she had copied out his messages to her, along with the dates and times they were sent. She had stared at his words until they had been branded into her memory. She could have recited them in her sleep. She knew his style, his speech, his overly familiar mannerisms.

This man, the letter writer, acted like a stranger.

And yet—there were distinct similarities. The chess. The references to predators and prey. The desire for fear.

She had received several copycat letters and phone calls, some of them quite disturbing, from people in town who blamed her for the entire incident. She had been called a "whore" and a "slut," a "terrorist" and a "psychopath." She had been denigrated and chastised, propositioned and persecuted—to the point where Gavin started to seem like a minimal threat by comparison.

Maybe this was another one of those. Another sick freak who wanted to torture her, to punish her for things beyond her control. Val thought about showing the letter to her mother and asking her advice, but the thought made her feel nauseous. Her mother always overreacted, causing Val to become so stressed out that she needed to pay an additional visit to her therapist.

Even if he didn't return, he had left his mark upon her. She was cursed, God help her.

■□■□■□■

The contractors had come early, just as Val was departing for the football game. Her parents had caved, since it was only the junior varsity game, which ended earlier than varsity, with the proviso that she was to call before coming straight home. Val's father had added, "You tell that boy of yours that if anything happens to you, I have a Remington and a shovel."

She had laughed weakly, knowing it was expected of her, even though his lame attempt at humor nothing to lift her mood. Her heart was heavy as she waited for the bus to come to her stop. It was a gray, chilly day, with the promise of rain hanging in the air like a thinly-veiled threat. The letter was folded away into a pocket of her sky-blue parka, the strange words weighing her down as heavily as a block of lead. She couldn't get them out of her mind, and that bothered her.

Was it possible that he *had* come back after all these years? He was insane, yes, but not stupid. Far from it. A brilliant chess master, he had a mind that could analyze games many steps in advance, predicting an infinite number of both defensive and offensive moves, as well as their respective counter-moves. From what she knew of him, those abilities translated at least in part to real life. Val had a hard time believing he would come to a town where people had a fair chance at recognizing him and turning him into the police or, worse, delivering their own brand of rough justice.

He had said it himself best: he was always the hunter, never the hunted. If he did allow himself to be chased, it was only so he could spring a trap, rather like the queen sacrifice he had used against her when teaching her how to play chess years ago.

(you thought you had me; but the only trap you were springing, my dear, was upon yourself)

Warm breath. Warmer body. A room lit by a single naked, swinging bulb. The cloying smell of paint chips mingling with the smell of sandalwood, and a darker, animal scent that was inherently his.

The memories slammed into Val so powerfully, it

felt physical. This, combined with the potent blend of emotions they elicited, made her stumble backwards.

She imagined she could feel his lips against her neck and clapped a hand to her tingling skin, drawing in a shaky breath. *Not real,* she told herself. *Not* real.

The bus pulled up to the curb, splashing filthy water. Val found herself taking an unsteady step to the side as the door opened and several young children disembarked, accompanied by their parents—some of whom shot her vaguely unsettled looks, hurrying their offspring along that much more quickly.

The driver was the same woman who had been driving her to the high school for the better part of three years, now, and she smiled in recognition. "Good morning! Cold out, isn't it?"

Val nodded. "It's supposed to rain, I think."

Her hand shook as she dropped her fare in the box. Neither of them noticed.

"I remember my grandmother used to say that being in the rain washes bad luck away." The driver laughed fondly. "Didn't seem to work too well, though. I always just ended up catching cold."

Not five seconds later, raindrops began to splatter against the windows with an unpleasant pattering sound, causing Val to jump in surprise. The clouds were darker now, almost black, and reflected her present mood perfectly. With a tight smile, she took a seat before she could embarrass herself further. Why was she so jumpy?

(These questions will be answered during the course of the game, although by then you might not want the answers)

Never mind. That was a stupid question. A better question was: What was she going to do about it?

(Part of me wants her to run)

Val dug her knuckles into her forehead. She wished the driver hadn't brought up superstitions. Both the letter and the inclement weather seemed to be omens that something was going to happen soon, something bad.

"Have a good day, young lady!" the bus driver called after her. "Don't get too wet!" The doors were closed when Val got it in her head to turn around.

Thanks a lot.

James was waiting at the bus stop and talking to one of his friends. When he heard the screech of the bus's brakes, he looked up. "Val!" He was speaking and moving animatedly, practically glowing with excitement. "Oh, and this is Mark," he added carelessly, gesturing at the friend.

"Hey," she greeted him, trying to figure out why he was so pleased. "Did the freshman team win?"

"Freshman?" James blinked, taken aback. "I don't know. Why are you asking me? Didn't you come to see the JV play?"

Horrorscape by Nenia Campbell

I came to see you.

Really, he could be so completely oblivious.

The friend wasn't. Oblivious, that is. He took one look at Val and said, "Hey, I gotta go, bro."

"Later. Oh—Val, did you get a letter at school yesterday?"

"...What?"

Impatience flicked across his face. "I asked if you received a letter. In your locker. At school."

How had he known? She hadn't breathed a word about the letter; she'd been too busy trying to decide what to do about it herself, whether it was even *real*.

Was it from James? Was there a darker side to him than she had imagined? She'd been surprised that way before. But James had about as many faces as a two-dimensional drawing. There had to be another explanation.

James snapped his fingers in front of her nose. "Val? Valentine? You listening to me?"

Val started, aware she had paused long enough to draw suspicion. "Yes," she said slowly, her hand slipping into her pocket to touch the folded square. "I did. Why?"

"Well? Are you going to go?"

"Go where?"

"You know," he said, looking at her very strangely.

"The party."

Val blinked. "Party?" Her initial panic was giving way to confusion but hadn't entirely subsided yet. She still needed to know. "What party? What are you talking about?"

"Lisa and I—and Blake, for some reason—got letters in our lockers after school," James explained, apparently not picking up on her hesitation, or else pretending not to. "They're invitations to a party this weekend."

"Oh," she said. "I see."

"That's why I asked if you got a letter." James ran a hand through his tousled hair, which was on the verge of being totally soaked. Hers probably looked worse. She hadn't had time to wash it this morning. "Didn't you get one?"

She breathed out slowly. "My letter was…a little different."

Now he looked confused. "Different? Different how?"

"In wasn't an invitation." Val hesitated. "It was a personal letter. A—" *love letter isn't the right phrase. Whatever emotion the person who wrote that was feeling, it certainly wasn't love* "—strange letter. And it was all about me…and some twisted game."

"Don't worry about it," he said, smiling, "Probably from some freshman secret admirer."

"Secret admirer?" Val was wary of all secrets now,

especially those pertaining to identity. People who hid things about themselves did so for a reason; the innocent had nothing to hide. "James, it was creepy. It wasn't admiring at all. It was—" she faltered, struggling to recall the word that had been in her SAT-prep book. "It was condescending."

"All right." He shrugged. "So the guy sucks at writing love letters. That's what you have me for."

"James, it isn't a joke."

"Well, not with that attitude, sure."

"I mean it. The letter reminded me of…Gavin."

(I am a genteel hunter. I capture, not kill.)

Was it from him, though? She couldn't decide. The tone was…similar, but not quite right. Then again, it had been three years. Three years was a long time to change.

James stared at her. "Gavin…. You mean the weirdo from freshman year? Hit List Guy? Why would he do that?"

Because he was obsessed with me? Because he wanted to own me? "Because he wants to be pen pals, James. Why do you think? You warned me away from him. You knew he was dangerous, even back then. So why not now? Why wouldn't he want revenge? I almost got him sent to prison."

She wanted to hit him when he laughed. "Revenge? Jeez, Val, have you been watching too many horror movies. I wouldn't worry too much about it," he added, almost as an afterthought. "Probably some asshole playing a trick. Remember all those phone calls you used to get?"

"I still get them."

"Well, there you go."

Val looked at him sharply. She was annoyed that he hadn't asked to see the letter, which is what she would have done if their positions had been reversed. Didn't he care that it was from another boy? He was her boyfriend, for God's sake! She wasn't keen on possession types but she didn't want to be *ignored*. Plus, it just didn't make sense. Why would James be jealous about his little brother's cute little crush on her, but not this creep's? And why on earth would he bring up the phone calls? He know how much she hated talking about them, or even just thinking about them.

(I hear you like to fuck dangerous men, isn't that right?)

She shuddered, massaging her temples where a massive headache was in the process of forming.

(if you rat me out to the cops, I'll slit your throat)

"If you didn't get an invite, I'll invite you. Don't worry, I'm sure one more can't hurt."

Val fought the urge to snap at him for being so selfish. He was obviously thinking of her or he wouldn't have brought it up at all, even if it was only because he wanted a date to some stupid party.

"I have to ask my parents."

"I'm sure they'll let you go. They wouldn't want you getting in the way while the construction crew was working."

Val toed a puddle forming at her feet. "I don't know.... What if they need my help with something?"

"What could they need your help with? You told me you'd be stuck in your room all day."

"They might need—something, I don't know. Look, they get weird about things like this. You know they do."

James was unfazed. "It's at a big house over on Eastwood. There's no reason your parents wouldn't let you go. Have you seen the security on those houses?"

I thought the same thing back then, with him.

But inviting her friends—but not her? That was odd. Why would Gavin do that? It wasn't like him. *So maybe it's not him.* She could have convinced herself of it if the eerie feeling she'd gotten on the bus had disappeared, but it hadn't; it had intensified to the point where she felt invisible eyes boring into her back.

Her letter, her friends' letters—were they connected somehow?

Coincidence.

Right? *Right?* "I'm not so sure I should go," Val said falteringly. "This is too weird."

"No, weird is staying at home, alone."

"My panic attacks have been getting worse," she whispered. "What if I have one at the party? What if I go to pieces right there with everyone watching?"

"If you stay at home, you're letting him win. Be strong, Val. Don't let him get to you."

How could he tell her that? *Be strong*. As if it were so simple. As if she was supposed to hold up the ceiling of her sanity even as the walls came tumbling down all around her.

"What did *your* letter say?"

"'You are cordially invited to attend a party like no other,'" he said, deadpan.

Val breathed a sigh of relief. They were nothing similar.

Still; she had heard stories about some of the situations Eastwood kids got into at parties. Bad situations covered up by their rich families. Way out of her league.

"What time is it?"

"Uh." James delved into the pocket of his jeans and produced a slightly crumpled piece of black paper. This discrepancy in colors between their two respective invitations made her feel a little better, as well. She'd been afraid that his would be in cream, too. "This says it starts around eight but there's no end time. Probably not past midnight, though."

She gave him a look. Her curfew was at midnight.

On the dot. No exceptions.

"Come on, Val," he pleaded. "It'll be good for you."

If James was there to protect her and Lisa was there to supervise him, she might be able to persuade her parents into extending it by an hour or so.

Maybe.

If she even wanted to go.

"All right," she conceded, "I'll ask."

Horrorscape by Nenia Campbell

Chapter Three

Waiting Move

When Val returned home, she found her parents in terrible moods. The contractors had made a mess, tracking plaster and wood splinters throughout the house in their work boots, ruining one of her mother's favorite wool rugs. They were arguing with each other about the cost, and whether they ought to switch to another company.

Val hovered in the doorway and picked at a cuticle. If she wanted a positive outcome, she'd do best to wait until tomorrow morning when they were less annoyed. On the other hand, if she did wait until Sunday she would probably lose her nerve—and part of her, a fairly big part, didn't want to go at all, and *wanted* them to say no.

She stepped into the living room, sidestepping the bits of plaster that dusted the floor like powdered sugar. "Hey...um, Mom? Dad? Can I ask you something?"

"Not right now, Val," her father said.

"What is it?" her mother said.

"I kind of got invited to this party on Saturday."

As she expected, the news was not received with much enthusiasm.

"Where is it?"

"In Eastwood."

"Eastwood?" her mother repeated. "Who do you know in Eastwood?"

Val shrugged. "I don't. James invited me."

"How long is it? What kind of party is it going to be?"

If either parent were likely to cave on the issue, it would probably be her mother. But the years had made her more conservative and she had never quite forgiven herself for letting Gavin come so close to ruining Val's life.

"It starts at eight, and will probably end around one," Val recited. "Probably. I think it's a theme party."

"Do you want to go?" her mother asked.

"I don't know. But James, Lisa, and Blake will be there, and they all seem to think I should."

"How are you planning on getting there?" Mrs. Kimble said, just as her father asked, "Who's Blake?"

"James would probably drive all of us." Her father raised an eyebrow. "He's a good driver."

Her father looked offended. "I didn't say anything. Now tell me who this Blake character is."

"He's not a character. He's a good friend of James and he's on the honor roll."

"Well, if he's on the *honor roll*," Mr. Kimble muttered. "Wasn't that other boy of yours on the honor roll, too?"

"Robert!" Val's mother squawked.

Gavin was never mine, she wanted to snap. *There wasn't enough of him there to give. Besides, his teachers were afraid of him, too. Nobody in their right mind would ever be afraid of Blake.*

Her mother was eying her with a worried expression. "Blake sounds like a nice boy, and of course it should be safe if Lisa and James are both going."

Val's heart sank a little; this was not what she had been hoping to hear. Outright refusal would have been nice.

"Besides," her mother continued, in a light voice, "Eastwood is a wealthy area. Val might meet someone nice. And she'll have her cell phone."

"*Mom.* James and I haven't broken up yet!"

Yet? Where did that come from?

Luckily, her mother didn't pick up on it. "Sorry, honey. But you won't be dating James forever. You should keep your options open, that's all I'm saying."

"Val's not a gold-digger," her father said sternly. "We didn't raise her to be that way."

"I'm not saying she is. I'm just saying it would be nice for her to meet some new kids—especially after what happened—and if one of them happens to be a boy, well…"

"She's a big girl now," her father said, surprising

her. "She should be able to go to a party. God only knows, most kids her age have already gotten into drugs and sex, both. Val's a good girl with a good christian sense of right and wrong. She'll be able to take care of herself."

The unexpected praise brought color into Val's cheeks. On impulse, she hugged him. "Thanks, Daddy."

"Of course, Bunny," he said, patting her back.

"But what about you, Val? Do you want to go? You said you weren't sure."

"I've been getting the phone calls again—and yesterday, a creepy letter."

"In that case," her mother said. "It might be good for you to get out, to be with friends."

"Really?"

"It's far better than being alone. Your father and I might be going out that night, too."

"Just make sure you take your phone," her father said.

Neither of them went into the incident in greater detail, tiptoeing around it like a sleeping dragon instead. Val was relieved. Her earlier conversation with James had left her drained; she was grateful not to relive it.

"I guess," she sighed. "And I'll call if I need a ride."

"And tell that boyfriend of yours that if you don't return safely, I have—"

"Robert, give the Remington a rest. She gets the point."

My first party.

Back when things were normal, she had been to her friends' local affairs but had always known most, if not all, of the guests, whether they were acquaintances, friends-of-friends, or just people from track. Then the invitations had stopped. It was as if the incident had left her contaminated and everyone was afraid of catching what she had by association. Sophomore year had been a very lonely year.

This would be different. The party was in a different neighborhood, with different kids: kids who wouldn't know her as Psycho Girl, or Psycho Slut. She'd just be an ordinary girl, one of many. She wouldn't know anybody there except for her own friends.

Val paused. Funny. She didn't think that was supposed to be so fearsome.

■□■□■□■

The phone was silent: a sleeping predator that could be shaken awake at any second. Soon, very soon, it would be. The call he was expecting was a very important one.

He lay beside the phone on his bed in the darkness, calmly breathing in the musty air. The house, and most of its belongings, had been obtained at a moment's notice from used stores—or from the goodness of his many brothers' and sisters' respective hearts.

Blood is thicker than water.

A shadow passed over his face. How true that was. No matter. He'd set the stage to his liking. All he had to do was wait for the opening scene.

He toyed with the stem of the rose, letting it slide through his fingers until he was cupping the bloom in his palm. As glorious as the chase was, sometimes a gentler touch was required, grasping with a silk glove, not letting the intended feel the iron beneath until it was too late.

His fingers contracted and the fragrant smell of crushed petals filled the room. A few slipped through the cage of his fingers and fluttered to his bare chest.

Soon.

The phone rang.

He blinked lazily and turned over to reach for the phone, snapping it open.

"Hello?"

"Yes?" He was pleased to note a pause.

"This is James—James Lewis. You sent me an invite."

"Ah, yes. I did."

Another pause.

"Well, I got it."

"And you'll be able to come?"

"Yes. And so can Blake, Lisa, and Val," he said, lumping her name in with all the rest.

"Val?" Enjoying the way her name sounded in his voice, rich and full and rounded, like blood, or a finely aged wine. "Hmm. I don't recall her name being on the guest list."

That would defeat the purpose of the game, wouldn't it? The boyfriend's ego wouldn't let him attend a party alone and Val—well, he wanted her skittish, but not so spooked that she would be too afraid to go to his little soiree.

He had spent a long time on that letter, toying with the words, playing with them like a cat with a mouse. He wanted her to suspect, yes, but not to be certain. The unknown was far more deliciously terrifying than the known, and she did look so arousing when she was afraid.

Do you like roses, Val? What about white jasmine?

He'd been too eager before, in his foolish youth. Now that he had matured he was better able to rein in his impulses and appreciate the delay of gratification. Delay could be savored and seductive in and of itself. What was the hunt, after all, if not a delay of the capture?

An annoying voice jerked him from these pleasant

thoughts. "No. I guess she wasn't invited."

"Pity."

There was another silence, longer this time. "Does that mean she can't come?"

"No, no, bring Val if you want to—just make sure she wears all black."

"All black?" His voice was wary. "Why? That wasn't on the invitation I got."

"I wonder why. It must have slipped my mind."

"Is this some kind of theme party?"

"You might say that."

This time, when he spoke it was no longer a front of bravado but curious, inquiring, and—unless he was mistaken—perhaps a little frightened? His smile grew. *Yes.*

"Who are you, dude? How do you know us? Do you go to our school?"

"All will be revealed in good time," he said softly. "Goodbye, James."

"What? How do you—wait—"

He hung up the phone carefully and pushed himself up to a sitting position. Unruly black hair fell back against his neck and shoulders as he stretched, closing his eyes like a cat. A candle was burning on his desk and the flame danced as he moved closer. He picked up the remnants of the rose he'd been toying with and slowly fed it to the flames, watching as they greedily consumed the flower.

Finished, he expunged the flame, filling the room with blackness. He went back to bed, this time to sleep. Everything was coming together so nicely.

But first, a taste.

■□■□■□■

The *Macarena* chimed noisily from the confines of Val's backpack. In the quiet of her room, the sound was loud and frightening, especially after the way her nerves had been thoroughly unfurled by the business of those letters.

She rooted through old homework until she found the phone beneath some crumpled sheet music. "James?"

"Hey. I just got off the phone with our host."

"You actually spoke with him?" *What did he sound like? Did he sound like Gavin?*

"Yeah. Somehow he left you off the guest list." Val frowned as James quickly added, "He says it's still all right if you come, though."

How nice of him. "What's his name?" She found it difficult to believe someone would remember all three of her friends' names and still manage to overlook her. More than that, it was hurtful, so much so that it might as well have been an intentional slight. Maybe it was.

"That's the thing," James was saying, "he wouldn't tell me. His name, I mean. His voice didn't sound familiar, either—certainly not like anyone I know."

A bad feeling brewed in the pit of her stomach. This time, it took more effort to quash. "Don't you think it's a little weird he wouldn't tell you who he was?"

"I guess." James seemed annoyed by her probing. "He said it was a theme party, so maybe it's an attempt at mystery. The theater geeks do stuff like that."

"What's the theme?"

"No idea. Look, it's lame, but at least he's *trying*."

"James, I'm not really comfortable with this—"

"Oh, that reminds me. He wants us to wear all black. Can't believe I almost forgot."

"Why—"

"Don't ask, I've got no idea. Theme party, remember?" James let out a deprecating laugh. "I gotta go, Valentine. Pick you up tomorrow."

"But I don't—"

He hung up before she could finish the thought. She set the cell phone down roughly on her nightstand. He seemed to be doing that a lot lately, cutting her off before she could get the last word in.

For a moment, she considered calling him back and telling him point-blank that she didn't want to go. She even scrolled down to his name in her contacts list. Then she put down the phone and sighed.

What was the point? She'd already decided to go. Calling him back now would just make her try to weasel out.

She considered James's last instruction. Wear all black. She wondered why. Black was a color associated with the occult, wasn't it? It *was* October, true, but still too early for Halloween. Good God, what if he was a satanist?

This isn't a horror movie, she reminded herself sternly. She laughed bitterly. *Satanists? Really? That was silly thinking, even for you.* Far more likely to be harmless eccentricity. Rich people were allowed to be a little crazy.

"I don't even want to go," she muttered.

"Val? Did you say something?"

"No, Mom. Just—just talking to myself." Did she own anything black? She shuffled over to her closet. The mirrored surface of it reflected her too-pale face. She tugged open the door and began to rifle through the hangers. *No, nope, no—aha!*

Val tugged free a black lace shirt she had completely forgotten about. She wasn't sure she'd even had a chance to wear it; a price tag was still dangling from the arm.

Pretty, but not really her style. Too dark. Dark satin, with lace screening, it was set in a design that looked like dead flowers. Carnations, maybe, or peonies. Her mother must have bought it for her. She hoped it still fit. She'd gained some weight since quitting track and couldn't remember when her mother might have bought the shirt.

The phone chimed again from the desk.

Val draped the shirt over the back of her desk chair. James? No—it wasn't his ring tone. A text message. Well, that explained it. She didn't recognize the number, though, and the area code was from out of town.

Please, not another prank call.

She selected 'read' from her phone's menu. There was a second as the message loaded. Val's eyes widened.

Open game.

Chess, she thought. *Oh, God, no, please, no.*

She punched the buttons so hard her fingers hurt. *Is your name Gavin?*

The response was almost instantaneous: *Gavin who?*

(Checkmate)

Horrorscape by Nenia Campbell

Chapter Four

Antipositional

Dying sunlight filtered through the gauzy blinds, filling the parlor with a dusty glow. He picked up one of the glittering glass chalices from the buffet and carried it with him into the bedroom where he poured in it a garnet wine whose bouquet evoked images of iron and berries and passion. Very primordial, it was not enough to dull his keen senses. Quite the contrary—it made him feel more alive.

The wine was rich and heavy on his tongue. Thick, viscous, metallic and tart. Easy to see why red wine was used to represent blood in Communion. The similarities were striking. "Cheers," he murmured.

As the alcohol burned a path through his blood, he relaxed further. She had him keyed up. He enjoyed feeling the anticipation of the fight, but the time was not yet right. If she knew just how much he enjoyed her resistance, how it pleasured him to know how superior his strength was to hers even at her most desperate, how he could still remember the taste of their commingled blood in his mouth, she would be—he smiled—very alarmed.

She was already imprisoned. He had bound her to him long ago, the moment she unwittingly revealed her weaknesses to him. She just couldn't see the chains. Not yet.

Horrorscape by Nenia Campbell

Soon, he reminded himself. *Soon*. He picked up an antique gold pocket watch, polished to a shine for the occasion. Glanced at it. *Very soon. It's almost time.*

First impressions were everything.

This was the standard he employed as he did a final walk-through of the house. He needn't have bothered—he knew he had prepared sublimely—but it gave him satisfaction to admire the effect of his own handiwork.

Yes, he was quite pleased, he decided, taking another sip of the wine. Quite pleased, indeed.

His other guests had responded mere hours before. They had taken a bit more of his resources and persuasion, but their jaded disaffection would provide an interesting dynamic.

He stepped into his white pants and began to button up his black dress shirt, all the while keeping his eyes on his reflection. Over the shirt, he added a white dinner jacket, and a white cravat to hide the silver chain he wore around his neck. Italian black boots completed the ensemble. He looped the watch chain through his belt loops, slipping the watch into his front pocket.

Ready or not, here I come. He drained the glass of wine and went back downstairs. *Come play with me, Valerian.*

■□■□■□■

Horrorscape by Nenia Campbell

Val tugged the lace shirt over her head, adjusting the hem over the top of her gray stone-washed jeans. She didn't have any black ones and was quickly coming to resent the cheery pastels of her wardrobe as she searched in vain for a solid black sweater.

I could swear I owned one, she thought, shoving aside hoodies and t-shirts. *The one Nana gave me, with the beaded flowers on the back. It would be perfect.* But that sweater had gotten a hole in it. She had thrown it away last year.

I'm losing my mind.

She stared at her reflection. The transparent sleeves and sweetheart neckline weren't at all suitable for an October evening. James would be annoyed—when he stopped staring down her decolletage, that is.

I shouldn't be going to this stupid thing. Look at me. The shadows beneath her eyes were darker than ever, the color of an angry bruise. *I'm a wreck.*

And afraid. So afraid. He had left his mark on her. She could still hear his voice in her head, even now.

(*Redheads bruise so easily ...*)

Would her therapist have been content to let Val rely solely on her medication for solace if she knew how his words haunted her still? She grabbed the jar from her bedside table and shook out two small yellow oblongs. *Probably not,* she thought, choking the pills down dry.

(*Don't make it so easy for me to take advantage of you*)

What other choice did she have? Spend her life

hiding in the shadows?

"Mom, do you have a black sweater I could borrow?" Val tugged at the neckline, trying to see if she could get more coverage by making it drape lower in back.

"None that would fit you," her mother called. "And don't yell through the house, Val!"

"Sorry."

She called Lisa. Lisa had tons of clothes, and most of her wardrobe was black. She claimed it was slimming. "Yeah, I can lend you a sweater," Lisa said. "No problem."

"Oh my God, can you?"

"Jesus, don't freak, Val. It's just a sweater. Do you think a dress is too dressy for a high school party?"

"I don't see why it would be."

If Lisa was wearing a dress, Val was in trouble. The number of little black dresses *she* owned was zero.

"What kind of dress is it?" Val pressed. "Formal? Because I'm wearing jeans…."

"You'll be *fine*. I'll probably be overdressed as is. Whatever. It was on sale at the mall and fits like a dream. I'm going to wear it to the party since Thomas never called me back about the invite. Asshole. He is going to be *so* jealous when he sees the Facebook photos."

"Thomas?"

"Yeah. The guy I was telling you about. On Thursday? He totally blew me off—go away, Mom! God, when the door is closed that means don't bug me! I swear, she's been buzzing around me all day, like she thinks she's going to get invited, too." Lisa went on in a lower voice, "And she would go. That's what scares me. She totally would."

The thought was, indeed, terrifying.

"Oh, James is here. Speak of the devil." Her voice got faint for a moment as she held the phone away from her mouth. "I got it, Mom! *Mom.* Dammit. Sorry, my mom is hitting on your boyfriend. This is officially creepy. Gotta go. I'll bring your sweater—see you soon."

Val looked at the mirror a moment longer, and sighed. *I look like I'm going to a funeral.* She brushed her red hair and added a dab of lip-gloss. *Or a cult. Or like I'm very strung-out.*

Luckily her parents were in the kitchen and not sniffing around her bedroom door like Lisa's mom. She was able to walk right on by without them commenting on her clothing.

(I'm surprised your mother let you come out to play with the big bad wolf)

"Have fun, Val!" her mother said, when she heard the front door open.

"Remember what we talked about," her father added.

How could I forget?

"I will!"

James picked her up in his dad's '97 Honda. Val's nervousness grew when she saw what her friends were wearing: all black, no gray, and so formal. Lisa was wearing a strapless; Blake, a collared shirt and shorts; James, the same debonair slacks and shirt he'd worn to homecoming just last week, minus the tie.

When she sat in front, Lisa passed up a cropped chenille sweater which she tugged on. She tied the ribbon around her waist, and it made her bust look too big for her own liking. *Lisa would.* Having pulled the edges of the sweater as closely as possible, she gave up and fastened the bow making a mental note not to bend over.

"Am I under-dressed?"

"You look fine. That top is gorgeous with that sweater. *You* look gorgeous."

"Yes, you do," James agreed, glancing at her—at her chest, anyway—before returning his eyes to the road.

"But these jeans are more of a gray." She pinched the denim. "A *light* gray."

"Val," James cut in, "Chill. He's not going to bar you entry just because you're a couple shades off."

"You look very nice," Blake agreed shyly.

Easy for them to brush off her concerns when they

were all wearing black. Val leaned back in her seat. The drive was not going to be a short one; she had plenty of time to bask in her uncertainties.

Lisa and Blake chatted about a mutual teacher neither of them liked, with James inevitably barging in every few seconds or so with a joke or some inappropriate remark that made them all burst into laughter. None of them made any especial effort to include her, and her mood sank further. Was all night going to be like this?

On the other side of the window, the sky was pitch black, even the stars occluded by the banks of heavy clouds. It was a new moon, too, with shadow lingering where there should have been silver. Val remembered reading somewhere that seeing the new moon for the first time through glass was bad luck. *Stop that. You stop that right now.*

The distance between the houses was growing and the houses themselves had started increasing dramatically in size. Even the buses didn't venture out this far.

James glanced at the invitation, which was taped to his dashboard, and parked in a circular dirt clearing. It was empty, except for a few other cars. Val held her breath, releasing it only when she saw that a '77 Camaro was not among them.

"Here we are…I think," James announced, sounding out of place amidst the moonless sky and the silent, dusty road. *Unwelcome.*

Val turned her attention towards the house. It was very large. Tudor-style, with intricate brick patterns inlaid in the white walls. Rose bushes fronted the porch and she counted several different colors, including yellow, coral, and white. *God, it's like something from a storybook*, she thought.

But was it the prince's castle, or the witch's cottage?

"See any witches?" Blake murmured and Val jumped, looking over at him, both startled and oddly pleased. At least one other person was on the same wavelength.

"Not yet," she said gratefully.

James opened the door for her and Lisa, who giggled uncouthly and declared how *impossible* it was to exit a car decently in such a short skirt. Val rolled her eyes. Blake helped himself out. The four of them started towards the front door but James paused in front of one of the rose bushes. As he bent, his intent became clear.

"James, don't! Leave them alone."

Too late. He had snapped the stem. "They won't miss one measly little rose."

"They might." She watched, helpless, as he twirled the yellow flower in his awkward hands. Wasn't there a fairytale where everything was set in motion by a single stolen rose?

"Look, it's your favorite color."

Horrorscape by Nenia Campbell

He remembers. She tried to look stern. "James..."

"A rose for a rose." Carefully, he tucked the flower into her red hair and this time she couldn't help smiling. She glanced down at his hand, twined with hers, and it faded.

"You're bleeding!"

"He probably pricked himself on a thorn," said Blake.

"It could get infected. Anybody have some antibiotic cream? A bandage?"

Lisa looked pointedly at her tiny clutch. "What do I look like? A pharmacy?"

James shrugged and brought his hand to his mouth to lick the blood away. Val winced and something—no, it was gone—some ragged scrap of memory gusted past her, and for a moment it was nearly close enough to touch.

"Yellow must mean caution," he muttered.

"Actually," a new voice said, "Yellow means infidelity."

A man was leaning against the ivy-covered trellis. Leaning back against the frames as he was, his legs seemed to go on forever. He had to be well over six feet tall.

He was looking at them directly, giving Val an unobstructed view of his face. His eyes were a pure, pale gray that seemed to hold no color at all, and his hair was as black as their clothing: a sharp contrast to his light eyes and lighter skin. Val swallowed hard. *He looks an awful lot like …*

No. No, the face was different. Everything was, really.

The resemblance was uncanny, though. Enough to make her mouth run dry. It had been years since she had seen him last, and she supposed he could have changed, or her memory had, but—

No. Gavin had worn glasses.

Maybe he got corrective surgery, or contacts.

But that couldn't be it, because his face had been different.

Faces can change with age.

Do you want it to be him? She wanted to scream at herself. *Is that what you want? You want a rehashing of what went down freshman year?* She couldn't take her eyes off him.

Blake studied her with a quick frown, and she made herself look down at her shoes. *It's not him*, she decided, and now that she had torn her focus from his face, she noticed his clothing and a new worry coursed through her. Hadn't their host told them to wear black? All black?

"Infidelity?" James was saying.

"Oh yes," the man who looked disconcertingly like

Gavin said, still smiling. "Cheating, you know. Or dying love." And she could have sworn that he was looking right at her when he said that—and that he winked.

She met his eyes angrily, trying to ignore the panicky way her heart was trembling inside her chest, or the memories surging from the dark places whence they'd been banished for all these years, and wondered what he was implying? That she would cheat? Or that James would?

Or that he wants me to cheat with him?

The thought came out of nowhere, and nothing she did could banish it. She felt almost as guilty as if James had caught her in *flagrante delicto*. That was another thing, she just realized. Gavin's body hadn't been quite so…fit.

"Who the hell do you think you are?" James blustered.

He smiled coolly, and his face lost some of the friendliness but none of the amusement, and her conviction wavered again. Gavin would have reacted quite differently, she was sure. He was fire—blazing, unpredictable, and ruthless. This man—he was ice. In a voice as chilly as the morning frost, he said, "I'm your host."

■□■□■□■

Horrorscape by Nenia Campbell

The interior of the house was sophisticated. Oriental carpets and a myriad of vases in candy colors lining the window sills where they were sure to grow in sunlight. The man's pace was brisk, keeping them from taking everything in, but Val caught enough to know the family was well-off.

"I'm sorry," James began, "I didn't—"

"Quite all right," the man said, without turning around. "I accept your apology."

Who is he?

He led them right into a sitting room where several other kids were waiting. There were three, about the same age as Val and her friends: one girl, two boys.

The girl was wearing a white shirt, left unbuttoned to reveal a lacy chemise beneath. She was also wearing a frothy skirt that made her look a bit like a bride, especially with her freckled youthful face and bright blue eyes.

She glanced at them, eyes flickering over James and Blake, before settling on Val with a look of condescension. The disdain on her friendly-looking English-country-girl features was as disconcerting as a rabbit baring its teeth.

"Who does that girl think she is?" Lisa hissed into Val's ear, "She's not even wearing black—idiot."

Val nodded her silent agreement and studied the two boys. One was tall and thin, with blond hair and brown eyes. His face was unusually shaped, angular, with too much sharpness on its planes to be handsome, but he was interesting-looking and not unattractive.

The other boy was shorter and more solid, with the kind of physique one would expect from a wrestler or a linebacker. Both boys were dressed similarly to their host, although they seemed more uncomfortable in the formal wear than he did. As Lisa pointed out, all three of them were wearing white.

Did James get it wrong?

It wouldn't be the first time.

"You can sit," their host said, gesturing at the chairs. "We'll have introductions a little later." A movie was on, though nobody appeared to be watching it.

James put his hands on his hips. "Who are you?"

"For now, you can just call me GM."

"Gee-Em?" James repeated. "And what does that stand for?"

"All in good time." He produced a remote and muted the movie. It was a monster movie, judging from the amount of blood. The characters' mouths continued to move onscreen, caught in a silent scream.

"Pretentious, huh?" James said to her.

"The movie?" she asked, startled.

"No. His name. I bet it stands for God's Gift to Man."

"No, because then it would be GGM," said Lisa, who

had overheard. "Maybe Grand Misfit? No—Gory Masochist!"

Blake smiled, ducking his head.

Val said nothing. She couldn't think of any humorous additions to add to the joke, and she didn't want their host to overhear her. She focused on GM himself, who raised his hands, as if calling for attention. Well, okay, *that* was a little pretentious.

"Welcome," he said grandly. "I'm so glad you all could make it. We'll have introductions shortly. There's a table in the back set up with food and the like, and of course you're welcome to watch the movie and get to know each other. I'm certainly looking forward to getting acquainted with all of you."

(I want to see more. Know more. Know you.)

There was a pause. No one seemed to want to make the first move. Finally the girl in white stood up and there was a clatter of chairs as everyone rushed to follow suit. Val smiled uncertainly at one of the boys, who glanced away and quickened his pace.

Val found herself walking beside Blake. "Am I being paranoid, or did that guy just stiff me?"

"I guess he's a snob. This is a nice neighborhood."

Val nodded her agreement. *But not very nice people.*

"You know, my dad wanted to buy a house in this area when we first moved here."

"Oh?"

"They'll set you back several mil, and they attract the wrong kind of people."

Val nodded absently. The rude kind, she was sure.

The table was weighed down with sandwiches, crackers spread with unfamiliar toppings, cheese, fruit, and something that looked like wine but proved, on closer inspection, to be a bottle of sparkling cider.

GM, or whatever his name is, really outdid himself.

"Wow," said Blake. "He's even got sushi. I've changed my mind—I *like* this guy."

"What's this pink stuff?"

"Salmon." James appeared beside her. Blake took his cue and left to go talk with Lisa. "I was just talking to that GM guy and he said it's some kind of pâté."

Val set the container back down. "'That GM guy'? Does that mean you two kissed and made up?"

"What the hell is that supposed to mean?"

She blinked. "Well. You did shout at him earlier. He's not so bad. Kind of strange, though, don't you think?"

"I guess." James's mouth was full of salmon pâté. She resisted the urge to tell him to chew with his mouth closed. "The stuff about the roses was weird, but I know guys with weirder interests and hobbies." He shrugged.

"I meant that he won't tell us his name."

James laughed. "Maybe it's supposed to be part of the game."

"How?"

"I don't know." He picked up another cracker and spread it thickly with the salmon. "Guess the name and win a prize? Rumpelstiltskin!"

"Hmm." She chewed on her lip thoughtfully. "How's your finger?"

"It just a cut." His eyes lighted on the green bottle. "Is that wine? Sweet."

She turned away to help herself to a sandwich. He had cucumber and dill, with cream cheese. Her favorite. She took a bite, and rounded back on James just in case it really was wine that he'd found, and suddenly found herself in the presence of GM. Startled, she took a step backwards and nearly lost her balance.

"Careful." His hand closed lightly on her shoulder.

"Oh…hi." She looked down at his hand on her shoulder and he let it drop. "Thanks."

"I didn't mean to frighten you." He had the tact not to comment on her *faux pas*, or the fact that she sounded like a horny schoolgirl with strep. *Maybe he's truly oblivious.* It was possible, but hard to believe. Someone like him?

He's even better looking up close.

She glanced at James, who was frowning with

disappointment as he poured himself a glass of what apparently was just harmless apple cider.

"Do I...know you from somewhere?"

He arched an eyebrow but didn't blink. "I should think you'd have remembered me."

"So no, then."

"I never said that." His eyes flicked over her in appraisal. "I like your shirt."

Is he...is he flirting with me?

"Thanks." She folded her arms, then realized that made it look like she was flaunting her breasts and quickly lowered them. "I didn't even realize I had it, until I looked in my closet. I suppose it's one of those rare cases when impulse shopping pays off." *You're babbling.*

"Impulses usually do that. Pay off, that is."

He's definitely flirting—and not subtly, either.

(I can be suppressed no more effectively than a tiger can be leashed)

"Black roses are my favorite flowers," he continued, though he was no longer looking at her. He was staring off at something in the distance.

Val frowned. "There's no such thing as a black rose."

"Precisely."

She had no idea what to say to that. "You know a lot

about flowers." Had Gavin? She couldn't remember.

"Yes. Every flower has a meaning."

"My name is a flower."

"I know."

"You do?"

"Valerian," he said, and she turned towards him, inquiring. "It means love, sleep, purification…protection." He tilted his head towards her, offering a lazy smile. "Sound like you?"

"No," she said, made uncomfortable by the sheer intensity of the gray of his eyes. "Not at all."

"Is that so?" he said, lips twisting into a—well, it was almost a sneer.

She was taken aback at his mercurial change of attitude. Angry, too. No wonder James had shouted at him; she had half a mind to start shouting at him herself.

"I think I know whether I fit my own name, GM. What would you know about names, anyway? You won't even tell us yours."

"You'd be surprised," he said, in the same low tone as before, "by just how much I know, my dear."

The skin of her spine prickled. "I am *not* your dear."

"Perhaps not," he agreed, and a bolt of ice pierced through her insides as she had a horrible epiphany.

GM.

"GM wouldn't stand for...it wouldn't stand for Gavin Mecozzi, would it?"

"I'm afraid not," he said. "No. No, that's not what it stands for at all. Nice try, though."

"What, then?"

"All in good time, my dear. You've had your guess."

(A gentleman never tells)

"Stop calling me that, and answer the question."

"No."

"I'm serious."

His polite smile turned slightly feral. "As am I."

(In fact, I really don't think you want to fuck with me at all)

Feeling sick, she decided to go find James. She had already turned away when she heard him speak again. "Have patience, and endure, my *dear*. Both you and your boyfriend seem to be in dire need of it." He laughed. "Patience, I mean. Don't be in such a hurry to ask questions whose answers you will not like."

Is that a threat? She turned around to ask exactly how did he come to know so much about her—and why—but paused, brow furrowing. He was...gone. Vanished.

Chapter Five

Undermining

Vanished? Val cut her eyes across the room, glossing over the other guests. She was relieved to find GM chatting with the brunette girl in white just a few paces away—*You see? There you go. People don't just disappear. Stop trying to freak yourself out*—but her relief was short-lived. How had he known the meaning of her name, with such encyclopedic precision too, without skipping a beat? How did he know that James was her boyfriend? And why had he called her his *dear*? If he had known that James was her boyfriend that should have discouraged him from flirting. Because that was what he was doing.

(*I can assure you, my dear, that I am no garden-variety reprobate*)

And just like that, her conviction that he wasn't Gavin crumbled. Again. The strange, archaic speech patterns—the unusual coloring—surely that was too great a coincidence.

The brunette laughed at something GM said, taking a step closer to him. He smiled back but the smile did not reach his eyes and through a series of movements too coordinated to separate and individually identify, he managed to simultaneously dismiss her and excuse himself, seamlessly polite the entire time. Before Val could even blink, he was talking to the heavier of the two boys in white while the girl's expression flickered between annoyance, hurt, and anger.

If it was Gavin, though, he had changed in more than looks alone. The Gavin she remembered was sober and brooding, lacking in social graces but making up for it in sheer intensity.

She was tempted to ask Lisa's opinion. *She* knew the unwritten rules of social conduct better than anyone else. But Lisa was talking to the other boy in white, the blonde. *He* was talking, anyway. Lisa was nodding in all the right places but her eyes were turned away from him—*searching for escape*, Val thought. They made eye contact and Lisa mouthed, "Help me."

What am I supposed to do? Drag her out by the ear?

No thanks. She didn't want to get involved. Not because she was afraid of the tall boy—not much, anyway—but he *was* creepy, and gave her an icky, slimy feeling. She didn't want a scene. She didn't like confrontations.

Val felt her friend's eyes bore into her back when she turned away. The beginnings of a headache burned behind her eyeballs and she thought, *I'm going to pay for that later*.

"Val?" James said, walking over with a glass of golden liquid. "What are you doing here all by yourself?"

She turned towards him, grateful for an excuse to look away from Lisa and GM. "I got ditched."

"So I saw." He took a sip of cider, frowning at the taste. Or maybe at her. "What were you guys talking about?"

"My name."

The glass paused a few centimeters from his lips. "Your name?"

"That, and other things. He knew what it *meant*."

James shrugged and took a sip. "What does it mean?"

"The *flower*. The symbolism. Love, sleep, something, something—I can't remember the rest." She almost added, *he knows a lot about flowers* but that would have sounded like she was defending him, or parroting what he'd said before. "It was creepy, like he didn't even have to think about it."

"So?"

"So valerians aren't common. James, even *you* didn't know that they were flowers."

"And you're surprised he does? Did you not see that garden out front? Guy seriously needs to get laid."

"He also knew we were going out." She let that hang.

James exhaled deeply. "Well, duh. Of course he does. I invited you, didn't I?"

"So you told him."

Impatience was starting to wear through his words.

"No, I didn't tell him. Not exactly. But he's not an idiot, Val. I'm sure he just connected point A to point B—it's not like I needed to spell everything out for him. What's the big deal, anyway? Why are you so worked up over this?"

"I—" Her voice broke. She wanted to shake him for not understanding what she couldn't put into words, silly and irrational though it was. Why couldn't he see what she could? Was he that oblivious, or was she that crazy?

I don't like those odds.

GM was talking to Lisa now. *She* didn't appear to have any doubts about him at all.

What secret was he hiding behind that flawless facade? GM—who wouldn't tell them his real name, and yet knew so much about the meaning of hers. GM—whose initials happened to be the same as *grandmaster*, in addition to Gavin Mecozzi.

She felt like she'd been splashed in the face with ice water. GM was the abbreviation for grandmaster, she'd seen it used. Three coincidences were *not* a coincidence. They were a pattern. "He calls himself GM," she said aloud. "Who else has those initials that you can think of?"

He eyed her a moment before slowly tilting his head to one side and studying GM. "I'm not sure."

"Well, I think we should leave. Right now."

James spat out his mouthful of cider and his spit-take drew stares from the other guests. *"What?"*

"James—people are looking! What's the matter with you?"

"What's the matter with me? What's the matter with *you*? You're acting completely paranoid."

"Our host—GM—he gives me the creeps. He reminds me of my *stalker*. I don't feel safe. I'm not having fun. I don't want to be here, and I just want to go *home*."

"Val," he said, very gently, "Did you take your medication today?"

It was as if he'd slapped her. *He thinks I'm crazy.*

Without another word, Val stormed to the snack table and helped herself to a California roll. Then two. Then a third. The vinegar sweetness of the rice and avocado made her feel better, but it couldn't take away the bitterness in her mouth.

Am I crazy? She took another look at GM. *I don't think so. But then again, crazy people never do.*

"Good, huh?" Blake said. He was munching on a California roll, too. "I love these."

Val nodded, but kept her mouth shut, not trusting herself to speak. If she did, she suspected she might explode. Or cry. Blake raised his eyebrows pointedly at her silence but didn't press the subject, which she appreciated. She had always liked him the most, out of all of James's friends. Most of them were rowdy, athletic golden boys just like James, but Blake was quiet, calm, contemplative.

I like James, she told herself. Unconvincingly. *I just wish he weren't such a jerk sometimes. All the time. Most of the time.*

But that wasn't completely fair. She had been accusing their host of being a psychotic stalker. That was jerky, too.

Not if he is one.

Everyone thought she was being paranoid. They couldn't see the resemblance; they thought it was all in her head like so much else. Even she was having her doubts. Yeah, the words were a little similar, but GM's behavior was quite different. And he'd mostly left her alone, speaking to her only to deliver an impromptu lecture on horticulture.

He still should have taken me seriously. She glared at James, who had joined Lisa and GM in their discussion. *Traitor.*

"Are you…all right?" Blake asked hesitantly.

"I feel a little sick."

"That cider probably isn't helping then. Here." He handed her a bottle of water, still cold. "Drink this."

She took it gratefully downing a fourth of it in one gulp.

"Better?"

"Yes—thank you."

"No problem." He turned back to the sushi, his face a little pinker than it had been before.

Val hesitated. "Blake, do *you* think—" *Oh wait. He didn't move here until last year. He wouldn't remember Gavin.*

Blake was watching her, his expression curious but guarded. "Do I think what?"

"Do you, um…think GM is weird?"

"Who isn't?" Blake's eyes lingered on the trio on the other side of the room. Something in his face, some niggling suspicion, gave her hope that her own fears weren't entirely unfounded. Then he shrugged. His silence was more receptive than James's casual dismissal.

"He reminds me of someone."

Blake lifted his eyebrows. "Oh? Who?"

"Someone…dangerous."

Blake opened his mouth. Shut it. Val watched him glance over at GM again and frown. She would have given anything to know what was going through his head.

"Are you sure?"

"No."

"Then be careful," Blake said.

It wasn't much, but it was something.

"Has everyone finished eating?" GM asked, noticing the lull in the conversation. No response met his query. He smiled at all of them. "In that case, shall we return to the parlor for introductions?"

His gray eyes seemed to search their faces intently before he spun on his heel and started back into the adjacent room, leaving them with little choice but to follow.

Val was still furious at James. When he motioned for her to sit by him, she sat between one of the other boys—the tall one—and Blake. The former gave her a critical once-over. She looked him in the eye and he turned his attention to the front of the room. *Stiffed again.*

James mouthed something, his face twisted into a concerned frown. Val ignored him and looked at GM. He'd gone too far this time. She couldn't believe he'd all but accused her of being mental in *public.*

"Why don't we start by saying our names, and then something interesting about yourselves? You go first," he added carelessly, pointing at James.

"I'm James." He smiled winningly. *Hi, I'm a Big Fat Jerk.* "I'm good with computers. I'm also an artist. I like drawing but find painting a waste of time, and recently I've gotten into digital art."

"You find painting a waste of time?"

"Well…yeah," said James. "It's messy, not to mention time-consuming. You can finish faster and with much better accuracy using a computer instead of a paintbrush."

"Oh, but James—time is what makes it worth our while."

Very creepy. His eyes started to move in her direction. She quickly looked away. *Don't let him catch you looking.*

The next guest was Lisa.

"Je parle français."

"Comme je l'fais," GM said.

Lisa did a double take. *"Couramment? Votre accent est parfait."*

Not one to be left out, the girl on the white team broke in, giving Lisa a dour look. *"Oui, il est. Je suis d'accord."*

"Non." He gave a modest shrug that wasn't very convincing. *"Comme ci, comme ça."*

"I know it's a lot to ask," the boy beside Val said, "but do you mind speaking English?"

"I apologize," said GM. "Moving on."

The brunette was next. She introduced themselves as Charlene—Charlie—who said her biggest hobby was boys. She looked at GM when she said it, but he didn't seem to notice. Her statement *did* earn her a dark look from Lisa, though. *Probably jealous she didn't think of the line first.*

Lisa would have never looked twice at Gavin, so

maybe it wasn't him. Val almost smiled until she realized it was almost her turn and she had no idea what to say. What *was* she going to say? She wasn't the least bit interesting. She thought about saying she spoke Spanish and wanted to go to Chile, but then it would sound like she'd copied Lisa.

The introductions wore on tirelessly as she fretted. The heavier boy was named Brent and liked sports. No surprises there. He apparently had a scholarship to some prestigious university back East to play football. Gravely, Brent informed them all how excited he was.

The other boy's name was Jason who enjoyed writing. He had won some minor awards in the past for some of his horror stories, about which he was arrogant. He wanted to be a "spook," in his own words, and planned on visiting the District of Columbia this summer to look for possible research or job opportunities for his year off.

Then everyone's eyes went to her expectantly. Color seeped into Val's face. One pair was a pale gray. "Um." She wet her dry lips. "I'm Valerian. Val. I volunteer at an animal shelter sometimes." She winced—*lame*.

"Since when?" Lisa called across several of the guests.

"Since the beginning of senior year. It's for my community service requirements."

"Crap. I forgot all about that."

Horrorscape by Nenia Campbell

"You guys have to do community service? That sucks. At White Oaks we have a job shadowing program. It's basically slave labor, but at least we get work experience," Jason drawled.

"I *like* working at the animal shelter," she said hotly.

"Careful," said James. "If you get Valerian going, she'll start lecturing you on the Rights of Man's Best Friend."

She sent him a dirty look.

"What kind of name is that anyway, Valerian?" Charlie wrinkled her nose. "I've heard of Valerie, not *Valerian*."

Val didn't think girls named Charlie should be all nitpicky about names. "It's my name."

"Latin, I should think," said GM, and this time Val got the force of her dark look.

Blake was last. He took off his glasses to polish them on his shirt and Val wondered if that was so he wouldn't have to look at any of them. "I played trumpet for eight years and violin for nine," he informed his crotch.

"Who is your favorite composer?"

"Holst," said Blake. "For his *Order of the Planets*, Goethe for *Erlkönig*, and Saint-Saëns and Debussy for—well, everything, really. They're great. Really great."

"Fond of the Romantics and Impressionists, are we? And what of the Classicists?"

"Not as much. Though all of it's beautiful. But then, you did ask me for my favorite."

"That I did."

Val looked expectantly at him, wondering if this was some sort of segue into his own introduction. It wasn't. Of course it wasn't—and lose that creepy mystique? Instead, he said, "Who wants to play a game?"

"Strip poker?" said James.

"No." GM's smile was tight-lipped. "I was thinking along the lines of something more familiar. Hide and seek, for example."

He paused, and his eyes seemed to search each of them out individually. Val looked down at her hands before their eyes could meet, so she didn't see his expression when Blake said, hesitantly, "Isn't that a children's game?"

"A *baby's* game," James clarified, rolling his eyes. "Ultra lame."

"Ah, but *this* version has a little twist, you see." He straightened, allowing his hands to rest on his hips. "The principle is still the same, of course. One person will count while the others hide. They must be tagged or they will not be counted out—but, rather than simply being 'out', the first person found and tagged will suffer a penalty round. I call this particular version Hunt and Capture."

The skin on the back of Val's neck prickled in alarm.

Penalty round? Hunt and capture?

"Does that mean they have to sit in the corner?" James again, in another stab at humor. This time, no one laughed.

"Not quite. Don't look so nervous. There won't be any *real* traps involved, my no. It just has a better ring to it, don't you think?"

"What's the penalty?" Jason asked.

"Play well enough and you need not find out."

Val thought it sounded sinister. She thought it sounded like something she didn't want to play at all. She thought she wanted to be at home, in bed, curled up with a book.

Nobody else seemed to share her apprehension. One by one, the expressions of concern had dropped from their faces. James looked amused, Blake mildly entertained, and Lisa…well, Lisa was hard to read and probably resented GM for resorting to something so juvenile, but she had her game face on and so it was hard to tell. As for the others, the ones in white, their reactions varied from interest to boredom, in the case of the girl.

"Who's the hunter?" Jason asked, looking like he wouldn't mind having the role for himself.

And for some reason, Val thought, *No*.

"I'll do it," James said. "Sure, why not?"

"Since you're volunteering." GM gave a decidedly Gallic one-shouldered shrug. "Start counting down from one hundred. The rest of you—I suggest you run. Yes?"

Is he going to run, too? She had a hard time picturing him running from anything.

"Run?" Charlie pursed her lips. Not a good look. The gesture got lipstick on her teeth. "Run where?"

"Away. Any room that is not locked is not off-limits. You may hide wherever you see fit."

James paused at ninety-two. "Are we not starting yet?"

"Technically, the game has been in play for ten seconds. I would get a move on, if I were you," he added, glancing at the hunted, still seated in their chairs. "Nobody wants to be caught. Not usually, anyway."

It is him.

She stared hard at him, but he did not meet her eyes.

Isn't it?

It felt like somebody had stolen her senses. The floors seemed to spin and tilt, making the climb to her feet seem as impossible a feat as scaling Mt. Everest.

What's happening to me? Panic-attack? Oh God, let it not be a panic-attack. Not here. Not now.

James continued counting off from eighty-seven, and Val stumbled along on unsteady legs as the rest of the players scattered.

Horrorscape by Nenia Campbell

Chapter Six

Capture

Val wandered the halls consumed by the childish but pressingly real sense of panic that she was going to be "caught" first. GM had been right about one thing— this variant had a twist, and she didn't like it. At *all*.

Every sound, whether in her head or from the floors above, made her twist around to glance over her shoulder while her ears buzzed with the silence and her pulse throbbed in her ears like shots from a gun.

Beads of icy sweat dripped down her back. With each backwards glance, she was sure she had seen something crawl from the shadows, gliding in and out of her periphery like a phantom...but there was never anything there.

I hate this game. I hate it.

She remembered the series of rooms that GM hadn't really stopped to let them see at the beginning of the tour. Surely there was a hiding place there? Better than running around here, like a chicken with its head cut off. She doubled back, trying to retrace her steps in the dark, and her face brightened a little when she recognized a striking vase perched on the sill of one of the cathedral windows.

Yes. I remember that. I remember this hallway. It leads to the foyer, I think.

Val passed more vases and then, yes, there, to the

right of the front door, was a spiral staircase. Footsteps creaked from further down the hall. For a moment she considered bolting—but no, that really was crazy. Where would she go? It was pitch dark outside and James had the keys to the car.

The bus? No. No, the bus didn't head this far out. *Fuck this.* She tightened her grip on the banister and took the stairs two at a time, grateful that her flats didn't make too much sound on the boards. Lisa had worn heels and Val could only imagine the ruckus *she* was making. *She'll probably be the one caught first*, she thought. *Not me.*

She paused, holding her breath, listening for the footsteps she thought she'd heard.

There's nothing there. Nobody's following you. Stop acting like a loon. She had been so sure about their host, and look how quickly her friends had dismissed that as another of Crazy Val's notion. *Who is GM?* She shook her head as if that could make her see more clearly through shadows and secrets alike. *It's like he came out of nowhere. He practically did.*

Even if he wasn't Gavin, he scared her. Behind that plastic mask his eyes *burned*.

The second story was cloaked in darkness. Her groping fingers located the sharp edges of a glass light-switch plate. She hissed, yanking her had back as though a snake had bitten her, and pinched her finger against her thumb. Liquid caused her two fingers to slip and slide against one another. *Damn it—I'm bleeding.* The house was so dirty and dusty; with her luck microbes were already gravitating to the wound.

It was all for nothing, anyway. She couldn't turn on the lights. If they were all off before and she turned them on she might as well just stick a neon "come and get me!" sign over her head. She clenched her injured fingers into a fist and moved on. The sooner she found a hiding place, the sooner she could try and calm down and see to it that this incoming attack went its course.

Eventually, she found a doorknob at hip level. Breathing out in relief, she twisted it open and found herself in another room. A bedroom—or a study, maybe. Her eyes had adjusted somewhat and she could make out silhouettes of furniture. A long table in the center was covered with faintly glowing outlines suggesting tanks or aquariums. She wondered what kinds of creepy-crawlies they contained and then decided she didn't want to stick around long enough to find out.

She started to back out of the room and came into contact with something solid, mobile, and very much alive. With a hissed scream of fright, Val drew back and ended up falling further back into the room with a heavy thud. She was sure the sound had carried well into the floors below, but her far more pressing fear was that the intruder was now between her and the door.

"Who's there?" Val demanded. "J-James? Is that you?"

"My God, you're noisy," the female voice said irritably, closing the door with a muted click. "Stomping around like a fucking elephant. How have you not been captured already?"

"Ch-Charlie?"

"No. It's the *tooth fairy*."

"Oh—thank God." Val rubbed at her thigh. She was going to have a bruise there tomorrow. "I thought...I thought you were someone else."

Charlie did not comment, though if silence were capable of sounding like it was rolling its eyes, she had that particular talent down pat.

Val felt cold displaced air as Charlie strode past her. The dim light caught on her white clothing, suffusing it with an eerie blue glow before the shadows consumed her once more. She sat down on the edge of a surface—a bed, perhaps, or a couch—crossed her legs, and leaned back in an easy slouch somehow managing to make the gesture regal.

"Um. You really scared me." Her voice sounded too loud in the silence. "Sorry I kind of freaked out there for a moment...but I didn't expect anyone else up here."

"Well, *I* didn't expect anyone to steal my hiding place."

"Steal? How did I steal it? I was here first. What makes it *your* hiding place?"

"I thought of it when he first mentioned the game.

Horrorscape by Nenia Campbell

When did *you*?"

She has me there. Though I wouldn't put it past her to lie. "I don't know," Val said at last. It seemed like a neutral enough thing to say without granting too many concessions.

There was a long silence as Charlie studied her in the dark. It was an invasive inspection that had Val edging closer to the door, halting only when the other girl said, suddenly, "Do you like GM?"

Her tone was different—pleasant, low, confiding. It instantly set Val on edge.

"You're kidding, right? I hardly know him. I have a boyfriend."

"That has nothing to do with it."

And Val supposed that, to a girl like Charlie, it didn't.

"No. I don't like him." She said it a little too vehemently. It came across as defensive.

"You seemed pretty cozy with him earlier."

When he was invading my personal space? "You're wrong. There's nothing between us."

"Nothing?"

(I wanted her.

I still do.)

"Nothing," Val repeated.

"Good. Make sure it stays that way." It sounded more like a threat than kindly advice.

The two of them are made for each other.

"I'm going to find another hiding place," said Val, struggling to keep her own true feelings concealed as old fears bubbled up from her subconscious like monsters from the deep. "You can have this one. Oh, and good luck with GM and all. I think you're going to need it."

Charlie grunted. It was a surprisingly unattractive sound from such an attractive girl. Val carefully shut the door on her. There was another door just across the hall so she wouldn't have to scurry around the giant house looking for another hiding place. Good thing, too, since James was still seeking—*hunting* ...

Was this really an act, a theme party, or was GM actually dangerous? So far, with the exception of the awkward silences, cold guests, and cryptic exchanges, it had seemed enough like an approximation of a normal party. GM could pass as a blasé, world-weary rich boy. Then again, Gavin had, too, at first.

The letter she received had been a convincing imitation of Gavin's style. Too convincing, far better than others. If she didn't know the writer, why was he sending her letters telling her how much he wanted to hunt her? To play with her? Maybe it was a prank—but then why would the letter fit in so well with the theme of the party?

Horrorscape by Nenia Campbell

It didn't make any sense. *None* of this made any sense. She was starting to doubt the other guests' sanity, never mind her own. *Especially that Charlie. She seems capable of anything.*

Val pulled out her phone, trying to see if she could call her mother and arrange for an early pick-up. James would think she was a total wuss but she could fake sick. *Sick in the head.* The bright glare of the phone made her eyes water and she swiped at them, irritated. "No signal?"

"Why, *hello*, Val."

She shrieked, backing away from the door so fast it felt like her feet were on fire. How had he gotten up here so fast, the person she wanted most to avoid? How had she come so close to crashing right into him?

Maybe he's the one who was following me in the hall.

"Where did *you* come from?"

"The door, I believe."

"That's n-not what I meant." She snapped the phone shut, shoving it in the pocket of her jeans. "I meant, w-what are you doing up *here*?"

"It's my house. Why shouldn't I be able to come and go as I please?"

She couldn't find anything to say to that. He did have a point.

"Why aren't you hiding? Do you want to be

caught?"

Val took another step back. "*No.*"

"Interesting."

"Charlie's looking for you," Val blurted. He tilted his head, quizzically, prompting her to add. "I think she's in one of the bedrooms—the one with the tanks. Maybe you should go see what she wants."

"I know what she wants."

"You do? But you—" And then she broke off, horrified, as Charlie's cryptic remarks and earlier jealousies became clear. *Oh…my.*

"Please." He took a few more steps into the room, stretching against the doorway. Blocking her exit, she couldn't help but notice. "If it was obvious to you, then of course it was obvious to me. In any case, I expect she's going to have to remain disappointed, because I have no wish to see *her.*"

He paused.

"But that's not what you wanted to talk to me about, is it?"

"I don't want to talk to you at all." She looked for another exit, but he was blocking the main one and his posture suggested that he'd follow if she ran.

"You seemed rather intent on speaking to me earlier."

"I changed my mind." *Where is everyone? Don't tell*

me *I'm alone with him. Up here. In the dark.* "You're hiding something from us."

"We all have something to hide, don't we, Val?"

"You must have some pretty big skeletons in your closet considering that you won't even tell us your name." She folded her arms, trying to put the focus back on him. To distract him. "Is there a reason for that, GM? Or should I say, grandmaster?"

She wondered if she'd played her cards too soon, too fast. Or was just plain wrong. She wasn't.

"You're good." He didn't look worried or angry—that was what she remembered later, that her obvious discomfort had amused him—"but I'm afraid you're going to have to be better than that." A beat of silence. "This time."

And in that moment, when he had her backed against the wall, her world threatened to burst apart. "It's *you*," she said faintly. "It's you, isn't it?"

He didn't respond, but the corners of his mouth lifted a little. She felt like throwing up. For a moment, she honestly believed she would.

"Tell me your name."

"Ask me nicely—you owe me that much of a courtesy, don't you think?" He rested his arm against the wall. "Or perhaps you'd like to take a wild guess. I won't even hold the first two against you."

No. No, no, no, no, no, no.

"Y-you said—you said your name wasn't Gavin."

"No." His other hand brushed the wall beside her shoulder and her knees buckled. "I didn't. If you recall, I merely said that GM stood for something else. Which you guessed."

"Grandmaster." She mouthed the word. She realized, suddenly, just how close his face was to hers. Her heart lurched, and she said, "You were following me in the hall."

"Perhaps."

"No," she whispered, and the "no" meant so many things to her—and absolutely nothing to him. She felt the stab of tears and turned her face away, unwilling to look at him. Unwilling to watch him watch her cry. "I'll scream."

"Spare me, darling. You will do no such thing." His fingers traced the tracks of her tears. They were rough, warm—real. He lifted her head. "Don't make hurt you," he said softly. "Don't make me hurt your friends."

"You wouldn't…" She drew in a breath. *He* would. "Let me go. Let me go *right* now."

The door opened behind them, sending a sliver of yellow light shooting across the room.

"As you wish."

Before she could protest, he gave her a casual shove that sent her sprawling into the light. The rose in her hair (she'd forgotten about that) came free, and fell softly to the floor without a sound. Val didn't have the same pleasure. She landed on her side—hard, and with a loud thud that shook the boards—causing an immediate, throbbing ache.

She felt two hands clamp down on her shoulders, effectively shooting the last of her nerves to pieces. She inhaled sharply, making a strange noise, like a backwards scream.

"Val? Jesus, Val. Are you all right?"

Val was vaguely aware of her boyfriend's presence as he knelt down beside her. "F-fine," she said, raising the hem over her shirt a few inches. A nasty bruise was forming just above her hip. Her green eyes went to GM—Gavin—who was still leaning against the wall, as silent as death.

Why did he push me? He wasn't the—

Oh no. No. She turned towards James with her heart in her throat. "Did you find anyone else?"

"What?"

"Did you find anyone *else*?"

"No. This was the only place I hadn't looked. I—"

Val let out a sob.

"Val? What's wrong?"

He planned it this way. He planned everything.

She opened her mouth, to tell James, warn him, but she didn't get the chance. A soft sound, like the jingle of bells, drew her attention back towards the shadowed doorway as GM stepped out from the shadows. The faintest of smiles was on his lips as he said, "I'm afraid you lose. Penalty, Val."

Chapter Seven

Hanging Pawn

Penalty, Val.

The words rocked her at her very core.

James's hand squeezed her shoulder. She leaned against him, grateful for his steadying presence. Gavin studied first James, then her, starting at her flats and slowly climbing to her face. He didn't bother with subtlety and the obvious appraisal made her flush with angry humiliation and fear.

(I wouldn't mind if she caught a glimpse of the animal in me)

It appeared he no longer cared whether or not she saw the darker side of him. And why would he? She was here.

When his eyes locked with hers she could read nothing in his face about his intent. But she could guess, oh, she could guess. Without looking away, he spoke to James. "You've served your purpose. Go find the others. Have them assemble for the next round. Tell them I'll be down…presently."

Oh no. "James, please—" *Please don't leave me alone with him!*

"Not now, Val." He twined his fingers with hers too tightly. She winced. "Later."

"But—"

"Later," he repeated. "You can tell me on the way back."

Relief trickled through her. Yes. On the way back. Away from this dark and desperate place. She'd tell him the truth and then they'd all get into his car and leave.

"You may go." With a twitch of his fingers, GM flicked his hair out of his eyes. "*She* stays."

Val's relief dried up, leaving vapors of pure, unadulterated terror in its wake. Whatever he was going to do to her, he didn't want to do it in front of James. She clung to his hand tighter.

"Ouch—cut it out, Val, you're hurting me. *What?*" James said, and while he didn't quite sound scared or uneasy, he was definitely annoyed.

"You heard me."

James glanced at her briefly. "And what if she doesn't want to stay? Who died and made you king?"

I can speak for myself.

But no, she couldn't. Her mouth wouldn't move. Her tongue was leaded down by old memories.

(I think I might hurt her if I get too close)

His voice was in and outside her head, and she couldn't breathe. *Don't make me hurt you*, he'd said, *don't make me hurt your friends*. What had she gotten herself into? What had she done?

A chuckle escaped him, slipping through his perfect

mask like water through cracked stone. Then he straightened, all traces of humor abruptly vanishing from his face before either of them could think to ask what, exactly, he found so amusing.

"Do you want a penalty, too?"

"No." James had released Val's fingers but still made no move to leave. Since he was facing away from her now she could only imagine his expression: haughty, defiant, wounded. Gavin knew which buttons to press. "But—"

Gavin's black boots echoed hollowly against the wooden floorboards as he closed the distance. He didn't look at her, but she knew he was aware of her presence in the same way that a mouse knows that a cat's apparent disinterest is only pretend.

"Go." The lone word dropped like a stone in the darkness. She felt James flinch. Nobody ever told him to just get out—especially not in a tone like that. "Now," he added, adding insult to injury by punctuating the order with James' name. She felt him flinch in surprise.

Like her, his tongue appeared to be iced over by shock. She never had been able to stand up to Gavin. Neither as often, or as well, as she should have. Now she was expecting a boy to fight her battles for her? And besides—that was what he wanted. A fight, before he destroyed her.

The moment of disbelief passed, and soon James's

words were flowing far too quickly. "What did you—?"

"Leave."

James jerked his hand away from her. Val spun around to face him. He was looking at GM petulantly, but to her dismay, the expression didn't fade or soften when he turned towards her.

"James—"

"It's fine. Everything's fine." She could sense the stress behind every vowel, every consonant as he spoke; weeks of annoyances and petty resentments bubbling up behind the force of his words, to the point where it made her flinch at his words as she had at GM's. He was so angry. "Stay. I'll be waiting outside."

"But I don't want to!" James stalked away. "James! James, no! Please. Come back! Don't leave me—"

The door slammed behind him.

"—alone with him," she whispered.

"He doesn't appreciate you, you know."

His words struck a chord deep inside her; an atonal chord that perfectly matched her own secret fears in tone and pitch and echoed dully inside her. "Shut *up*."

She took a quick step backwards, when GM walked towards her but he veered suddenly to the left, forming a half-circle around her. His steps carried him to the wall, which he leaned back against. "Brave of you, speaking to me like that," he said mildly. "Or foolish."

"You planned this," she said. "Everything."

"You're giving me entirely too much credit." He smiled, lowering his arms in a gesture of peace. "Although, now that you mention it, I have been meaning to speak to you—alone—for quite some time now."

"About what?" Her voice came out strangled.

"Oh, I think you can guess."

He was right; she could. She edged closer to the door. "You wanted me to lose this round."

"Close, but no. You don't know what I want." He spoke quietly, but his voice carried in the otherwise silent room, and it carried a hint of threat. "You never did. Because you never asked. Would you like to?"

"What do you want?" Val said, in spite of the fearful voice that was warning her to quit while she was ahead. She stared into his pale eyes, trying to find something to hold onto: anger, cruelty, or perhaps insanity—some familiar danger that took at least some of the edge off her fear for the unknown—but there was nothing there except the shadows of the room.

Instead of answering, GM bent down to pick up the yellow rose that had fallen from her hair—when had it come loose?—and he twirled in his fingers. "I think," he began, "That you're a weak pawn. Impossible to protect and open to assault... I think I need to take you off the chessboard—at least for now."

"Y-you're going to kill me."

"Kill you?" He repeated. "When did you get so morbid?" Though there was no actual physical contact between the two of them, he was still close enough that the breath behind his little speech stirred the loose strands of hair around her face. She instinctively wanted to look away, to break eye contact, and had to fight to keep her eyes level with his. It had been a long time since a boy besides James had been this close to her, and he wasn't stirring up fond memories. "No, think of this as an opportunity to get your priorities straight."

"Stay away from me."

He paused, regarding her face, and then opened one of the doors beside her—perhaps it was the one he'd first come through—and a rusty creak made her look into the total darkness, bracing herself for a push that did not come. "You're terrified, aren't you?"

And then his arms were wrapped her, and she felt him breathe in against her hair. For one long moment, she stood stiffly in his embrace, with her arms at her sides. A picture of a fly came to mind, wrapped in the spider's clutches.

"No," she cried.

"Don't lie to me." A new emotion had seeped into his voice like darkness after sundown. A painful hitch sliced into her breaths like a knife when his mouth ghosted over the place where he'd bitten her, almost four years ago. Marking her, like an animal.

"I can tell," he said, against her skin. "I can taste your trembling. I know you're afraid."

(You should be)

She wasn't sure whether he spoke it aloud, or whether it was in her head. At this point, it hardly mattered. Her good sense returned to her and she shoved at him—hard, angrily, terrified that he had managed to get so close to her again. And that she had let him. Again.

"I'm going to tell everyone what you are," she said. "Who you are. And what you did."

"That would be very unwise of you."

Val edged closer to the wall. "Is that a threat?"

"Only if you make it one." He touched a finger to his mouth in thought. "Besides…I somehow doubt that they would believe you. From what I understand, you have a bit of a reputation for being rather…paranoid."

"What?" The word was ripped from her mouth.

"Hmm, yes. I'm afraid so. Poor traumatized Val. Thinking every gray-eyed, black-haired stranger is her evil stalker. You have changed as much as I, my darling, and not for the better. You've become fearful and weak."

"You made me this way. You made me crazy."

"I suppose I did, didn't I?" he mused. "In a way, it's very becoming. Very Gothic. Suits you, really."

Horrorscape by Nenia Campbell

She hit him in the face with a shaking hand. Now he laughed, and she became furious as well as afraid. He caught her other fist before she could strike a mirror image of the previous blow. He'd been goading her, just as he had James. Purposely coaxing her into fighting back, because he loved it when she did. "You are such a—"

He squeezed her wrist, hard enough to make her gasp.

(*Her wrist is so small, my fingers can wrap around it and still touch. I could feel the fragile bones, and, between them, her pulse beating hummingbird fast*)

"I'm stronger," he said, and the pressure increased, causing her fingers to contract involuntarily. "Stop fighting and I'll let you go."

Val clawed at his hand, feeling sick. "*Fuck you.*"

He took a step closer, boxing her in. His other hand lightly circled her throat, his thumb over her pulse. "Sometimes," he said, at the same volume and in the same tone as before, "I could almost believe you want me to hurt you."

Her eyes widened. She opened her mouth and found she could not say a single word.

(*What would it be like, I wonder, to have such power? To feel a creature beneath you, as beautiful and golden and lovely as the sun, and know that you have her by the throat?*)

"It's very strange. You fall for my traps over and

over, and never seem to learn from your mistakes."

(You may even find you don't want to resist my control)

"You're quite the masochist. Something to discuss with your therapist, hmm?"

How does he know about that?

"Get your fucking hands off me. Stop touching me. Stop messing with my head. Just…just stop."

"But you make it so easy," he whispered, leaning in. "Why bother fighting me at all?"

Val wanted to turn away, but couldn't. Not with the way he was gripping her throat. His eyes were hypnotic. His lips seductive as they fleetingly grazed hers. She squeezed her eyes shut and focused on breathing around the lump which had formed abruptly in her throat.

"You'd think I was going to eat you from the way you look at me." But he took his hand away from her neck, brushing her cheek with his knuckles before letting his arm drop back to his side. "The next round won't start until I give the command. Until then, would you like me to show you what I do want?"

She knew she should run, but her legs wouldn't move. She knew she should fight, but her hands were no longer under her command. She could still resist, but even that was slowly beginning to fade. He left her feeling dead inside; like a neurotoxin, he killed off her senses one by one.

"If you do anything to me," she responded,

Horrorscape by Nenia Campbell

"Anything, I'm going to scream."

"I thought you might say that."

She bit the inside of her cheek and tasted blood. *I have to get out of here—before it's too late.*

Maybe it already was.

"No chance of changing your mind?"

"Take me back to James."

He sighed. "Goodbye, Val."

She felt herself falling. He'd pushed her! She scrambled to her feet and slammed against something solid. Sounding very far away through the thick oak, a lock clicked.

Chapter Eight

Compensation

Power was a valuable commodity precisely because it was so difficult to obtain, and even more difficult to use—effectively, that is. Years of experience, however, had made intimidation second nature. He wielded his with an easy grace that had bled into all facets of his life given time.

Time had not been so kind to Valerian. Those same years which had favored him had poisoned her, and the wild beauty he'd remembered now resided in a cage of her own design. He'd had plans for her, but she had robbed him of the pleasure. It was disappointing, really, how easily she succumbed to such plebeian methods of control, barely fighting him off, playing dead like a frightened rabbit even as her pulse buzzed violently against his palm. Her weak attack had been like a captive butterfly's final shudder as it succumbed to the cyanide in its jar.

Submission was all well and good, but he was none too fond of the "playing dead" school of surrender. He expected reciprocation or, at the very least, participation. He wanted her to fight. Not to run, and certainly not to freeze. Not yet, anyway. Not so early in the game.

And perhaps, eventually, she would learn to please him with no resistance at all.

Until that day, he was going to keep her on a *very*

tight leash. He slipped the key into his shirt pocket, running his hand down the paneled oak door. Very fine craftsmanship, that. Modern doors weren't nearly so thick or well-crafted. They reduced Val's pounding and screaming to a nigh inaudible volume.

Then she found the keyhole. "Help!" she said, louder now, "Help! Somebody, please, *hel—*"

Well, he couldn't have that. He rapped sharply on the door. "If you persist in this fashion, you will force my hand. It's not in your interests to do that."

She cursed at him, with a spark of the old fire, and he felt a stirring in his loins begin in response. Yes, this was much better. He much preferred her this way, hot under the collar. "You can't keep me in here forever!"

He could, actually. In theory. Unless she overcame her despair enough to find the way out. And wouldn't she be surprised when she found out where that led. He grinned at the thought.

"Someone will find me," she persisted. "And then I'll tell them all about you!"

"And then what?" he said pleasantly, stooping down to her level. "What's next in this cunning plan of yours? Are you going to tie me up? Kill me? Put me out of commission, so to speak? Assuming your friends believed you, of course, you would still have to deal with me. And with regard to a physical fight, I think I have you outmatched. That is assuming I let you get that far in the first place. Which I wouldn't. I can't very well have you running around, stirring up terror and fear among my guests, now, can I?"

"You don't care about that," she said coldly.

"But you do. And it would be a pity if any of said guests happened to have an accident, wouldn't it? That would be a terrible thing to have on one's conscience."

"You're threatening me." A note of panic now, behind the anger.

"Just a bit of friendly advice. These houses are so old. There's no telling what misfortunes might befall one if one were to, shall we say, panic."

He heard her breath catch; it made him hard.

"Besides," he went on, "I have secrets of my own. Secrets of far more interest to the aforementioned party, I suspect, than yours. That boyfriend of yours, for example—does he know what you feel like when you're beneath him? How your back arches when your wrists are pinned above your head?" And then, in a more guttural voice, "Does he know what you *taste* like, Valerian? Would he *like* to? I think he would. Perhaps I'll tell him, and spare his curiosity."

"No! Stop it! Stop it, stop it, stop it!"

A sharp sting made him glance down. He'd gouged into the palm of his hand with his nails. He drew in a quick breath and took a moment to compose himself, relaxing his clenched hand. She was *his*. If not in body, heart, or soul, then in mind, at least. And soon, the rest would follow.

"What—what do you *want* from me? For God's sake—Why did you invite us? Why are you back? How are you back? Who are the people on the white team? *How* do you know kids from White Oaks Academy? And why—why can't you just leave me *alone.*"

"Does this all have to be some sinister plot? Can't you take it at face value?"

"No," she said darkly.

That nearly made him laugh again. "Commendably wise. It appears you *are* capable of learning, then. That gives me hope for you."

"Answer my questions, you sick fuck," she said staunchly. He wondered if she would be quite so brave if there weren't a solid oak door standing between them.

"Let's just say that things will be quite different this time around."

"You said that before. What does that mean?"

"What it means, Val," he said, rising from his crouch, "is that this delightful chat will remain our little secret. For now. Understand? In the meantime, I have places to go. People to see. Feel free to make yourself at home. Relax. Enjoy yourself. Because I certainly wouldn't want you to do anything…rash."

She slammed her fist against the door but didn't respond. Not in words. He hadn't expected her to; her actions spoke volumes, and she had never been a particularly good loser. Speaking of which, it was time to see to that galling specimen waiting outside the other door.

His lip curled. *Loser, indeed.*

■□■□■□■

James paced the hallway causing dust to rise up from the ancient floorboards with each movement. He sneezed. Disgusting old house. He glanced up at the high ceiling, scoffed at the dusty rafters, and then folded his arms over his chest as he leaned back against the wall so that the door was in clear view. What the hell was taking Val and GM so long?

GM. His countenance darkened. What a piece of work. Even Val didn't like him, and she seemed to like everyone—not that he thought the guy was a psycho the way she seemed to. And he certainly wasn't about to leave (and not just because that would be letting the bastard win, either).

But he's an asshole. An an egomaniac. Strutting around like he thought he was better than everyone else. *Probably compensating for something,* he thought.

A door to his left opened and he turned towards the sound expectantly. Not Val. The girl from the white team. Cherry. Or whatever her name was. He hadn't really been paying attention. Val's pettiness had distracted him during the introductions. He couldn't figure out what her problem was. She was the one making wild accusations. Yeah, she was on medication. Maybe paranoia was a side-effect of it. But still, why was she getting all pissy at him for being the voice of reason?

Women.

Cherry, on the other hand, looked remarkably composed in comparison—as though she had just stepped off the pages of a European fashion magazine. Damn but she had a fine pair on her. He knew it was wrong to think so, but God, she was practically laying them out on display.

He wet his lips, torn between announcing his presence or waiting for her to notice him. Reluctantly, he tugged his gaze away from her chest and said, "Hey."

Her blue eyes flicked up and down his form before she tossed back a brief, dismissive, "Hi."

Oh, one of those types. James felt himself lose interest almost automatically. Girls like her were like a piece of expensive crystal—beautiful, cold, and costly, and absolutely worthless in the long-run.

Still, Cherry had one hell of a rack. Not much of an ass, though. Too bony. Val had a better body from all that running, but you wouldn't even know it since she practically lived in sweatshirts and baggy jeans these days. That top she had on tonight, though, was something else. He wanted to find out what was underneath it. Five months, almost, and he still hadn't seen his girlfriend shirtless. And when he'd taken his off, James remembered darkly, she'd all but run from the room to hide.

Maybe that was his fault. He'd known she was damaged goods but had still persisted in asking her out. And she'd even seemed fine for a while. It was only recently that she'd started getting worse. Goddamn stalker. James wouldn't mind getting his hands on that ugly creep. He didn't enjoy being the bad guy. He didn't like pushing and prodding his girlfriend to be intimate with him.

Yeah, it was hot that she was still a tight little virgin and all, but eventually, he kind of wanted to fix that.

"Did you find anyone?" Cherry asked impatiently, crossing her arms and drawing his gaze downwards once more. White Oaks kids were supposed to be loaded. Maybe they were fake?

"Yeah, Val," he said.

"Figures. Do you know where GM is?"

"He's busy right now." He wished he could remember her name. He was pretty sure it wasn't Cherry. "Laying out Val's penalty, I suppose."

Cherry blinked. "Val? But I thought—"

"He said we're supposed to meet up in the parlor, or whatever it's called." James jammed his hands into his pockets, nodding towards the closed door. "You can take it up with him, if you don't believe me. That is, if you're not afraid of getting a penalty, too," he added, mocking their host.

The girl looked like was thinking about doing just that. Then she shook her head. "I can wait."

James watched her go, following the sashay of her hips beneath the frilly skirt until she was out of sight, and glanced impatiently at the door. Where the hell was Valerian?

As if in response to the unasked question, the door in front of him opened with a rusty screech and GM stepped through, closing the door behind him—almost slamming it. James opened his mouth, ready to let loose with a barbed string of choice words, but something in the older man's expression stopped him cold. "I thought I told you to find the others."

"I found *one* of them. Cherry."

"Charlie."

"Whatever. I was waiting for Val. Where is she?"

An unreadable look flickered across his face, which James found himself wanting to punch more and more with every minute spent in his presence. "She'll be sitting out this round."

James ground his teeth. "That's not what I was asking."

"You might decide to set her free. I can't have that."

Horrorscape by Nenia Campbell

"I don't cheat," James hissed.

"I wonder," came the cool response. And something in his tone made James wonder if perhaps he was referring to something else—but, no, that was ridiculous. "Regardless," GM continued, "I won't be telling you, in either case. So why don't you run along now, hmm?" He offered a plastic smile which seemed to morph into a feral sneer, but he turned his back before James could be sure it wasn't the shadows or his imagination at work. He suspected it was neither.

"Asshole," he muttered, throwing a quick look over his shoulder before marching over to the door and giving the knob a firm twist. Locked. Perhaps one of the other doors...? James looked at the long hallway dubiously. There was no doubt in his mind that he could find Val, if he took the time to. The problem was that GM had already left. The clock was ticking and he wasn't sure he'd be able to make it in time for the next game. Val had lost and, yes, all right; it was his fault, but there was no point in handicapping the rest of their team for that error. There was no way he was going to lose. Especially not to GM.

■◻■◻■◻■

She could just barely hear voices coming from the hallway outside. One of them was James and the other, judging by the deeper timbre, was GM. "James!" Val yelled, "Get away from him!"

He couldn't hear her, though. Of course. The door was solid paneled wood, as muffling as if it were soundproofed. Gavin had made that painfully clear. Val slammed her fists against it, knowing it was hopeless. She could already hear the voices fading away.

Please, James, don't do anything stupid. He's dangerous.

Sighing, she leaned against the door to take in her surroundings. She could make out that it was a bedroom and if the lack of personal belongings was any indication, it was probably a boy's. A man's.

She banged on the door for a few more minutes, making as much noise as she dared. When it became clear no one was coming, she turned her attention to the rest of the room. The bed was made with black sheets that added to the dark atmosphere. A few posters covered the walls, but she couldn't make out the images in the darkness. Along the far wall was a table with a chess set, arranged and ready for play. The pieces were heavy and cold to the touch—some kind of stone. She picked up the knight, which had been her favorite piece once, tracing the elaborately carved mane. There was little doubt in her mind whose room this was.

She set down the horse-headed piece. What the hell was Gavin getting at by locking her in his bedroom, of all places? Was he going to come back for her? Was that his plan? To lead everyone away and then continue where they'd left off all those years ago? The thought made her feel ill, though it explained his cryptic statements about the thickness of the wood and secrecy.

Val let out a sound halfway between a scream and a sob, falling back against the wall. To her surprise, she felt the wall giving away from her weight. Val straightened, quickly, before she could fall, and turned around to see what had happened. It was a door! A secret door?

No, nothing so mysterious. A normal door. She just hadn't noticed it because it blended in so well with the surrounding wall—he'd even slapped a poster over it. Well. There was nowhere to go but out. She just hoped she wasn't walking into another trap.

Horrorscape by Nenia Campbell

Chapter Nine

Exchange Variation

Panes of glass gleamed darkly in the poorly-lit room. The main source of light came from two antique floor lamps. The weak beams caught and illuminated beads of condensation forming on the windows, and made them glow like silvery-hot metal. It was starting to mist.

Lisa, who was hidden behind a plant, did not notice the weather at all. She would have been hard-pressed to describe the room she was in, either, except that it had windows and plants, and a lack of a thermostat. Her knees and ankles were sore from remaining in a hunched position for so long in heels. *At this rate, I'm going to develop a hump.*

The fact that the room was bitingly cold did nothing to ease her cramping muscles. She regretted lending Val her sweater; low-cut or no, at least *her* shirt had sleeves!

Had I known that I was going to be crawling around on the dusty floors, I wouldn't have wasted forty bucks on this spectacle of a dress—which doesn't even look that good at me.

So much for showing Thomas.

The leaves nearest to Lisa's face rustled as she let out her breath in a huff. Rubber plant, she thought. She recognized the large, pod-shaped leaves; her mother had one like it at home. There were various other potted plants in the nearby vicinity, making it seem as though a jungle had somehow managed to creep into what was otherwise a perfectly innocuous room. *Like that movie, she mused absently. The one with the elephants and the killer flowers.*

Except these were fake, thank God. The leaves had the scratchy texture of rough, woven fabric sealed with plastic to prevent must and mildew. Plants that stayed green and never had to be watered. She snorted. How tacky. Surely, if he could afford this house, he could afford real plants and a real gardener? And some real entertainment, for that matter, instead of stupid old hide and seek.

She could almost hear her anger crackling, kindling like the fiery cinders of a fireplace. 'Hunt and capture' was quickly becoming a total bore. At first she had been mildly intrigued—thinking it was going to be a 'grown-up' game like seven minutes in heaven, or spin the bottle—and then she'd found out that, no, he really did intend to have them running around like scared kids in the dark.

This was just so...so stupid. She was eighteen, not eight, and far too old for these sorts of games!

A sudden creak drew her attention back toward the sole door in the room: a massive slab of solid oak with a shining brass handle. Heavy, too. Lisa had barely managed to open it, and when the damn thing slammed closed behind her with a heavy thud she'd nearly shit herself.

Thrills shot through her, eclipsing the annoyance.

Horrorscape by Nenia Campbell

She became engaged, in spite of herself, as the adrenaline flooded her veins. For several seconds, she was still, poised on the balls of her feet in those tortuous heels, scarcely daring to breathe for fear that the slightest sound or movement would command the attention of...no, not James. Someone else. Someone far more terrifying.

James is the hunter, she reminded herself impatiently. *You're hardly afraid of James.*

No. She was not afraid of James. Because, beneath his hard exterior, he wanted to be dominated by a woman; she knew because he'd told her as much when he said Val wasn't the girl he'd thought she was, wah, wah, wah, this wasn't what he'd bargained for when he asked her out, and was she doing this to spite him? *The jury weeps for you, James*, she thought, unsympathetically.

Val's issues weren't easy on *her*, either, but she certainly wasn't going to complain about it. You could blame the victim and say that she shouldn't have gotten involved with that guy in the first place, but Val had always been a little too quick to trust. When people inevitably ended up hurting her, she'd stare at them with the wounded eyes of a kicked puppy. Lisa had decided that this regression was a result of all that lack of suspicion and cynicism catching up to her at once.

Really, when you thought about it, it was a wonder that Val wasn't even more neurotic than she already was.

But James didn't see it that way; he saw it as a

personal affront. He couldn't forget that Val had originally cast him aside for someone else. Despite the fact that Gavin had terrified the silly girl out of her mind, he'd left a lasting impression, far more lasting than any James could hope to leave, and James resented her for that, too: for making him feel inadequate at all. Yes, Lisa knew far more than she would have liked to know about what was happening between James and Val.

The handle of the door, which she had been watching hawkishly this whole time, did not move. The sound, along with whatever had caused it, had vanished. Slowly, Lisa released her breath. The leaves nearest to her face quivered, releasing pockets of dust. She sneezed and flinched involuntarily, then subsided into a nervous laugh. Hunt and capture, *really*. It led the mind to conjure up all kinds of weird imagery.

And GM, its so-called inventor, was more than a little strange, himself.... He could get away with it, too, looking the way he did. Nice shoulders. Big hands. Gorgeous eyes. He had a nice body beneath that ridiculous white-ensemble of his too, she could tell. This was a man who wouldn't need to constantly assess others to gauge his own self-worth.

Charming, too. She was still grateful that he'd bothered to rescue her from that creep Jason—and after Val flaked out on her pleas for help, too. That girl. She was acting so cagey. When GM had started chatting with her casually at the food table she looked like she'd seen a ghost.

Her own conversation with him had seemed innocent enough. He'd asked her about the game, her friends, where they went to school—the usual. She couldn't really remember much more than that; her relief at escaping Jason had eclipsed her awareness of their conversation, so her recollection of the words exchanged was hazy at best. She did remember that he had remained extraordinarily detached, revealing only the thinnest veneer of polite interest in what she had to say.

And GM had sidestepped each and every one of her attempts to turn the conversation back towards him with a non-sequitur that kept the ball placed firmly in her court. That had been a little strange. The first time, she'd thought it was an accident, or courteousness. After the third time, however, Lisa began to wonder if perhaps their charming host was hiding something.

Maybe Val's right to be wary of him, after all.

As attractive and charming and cavalier as he appeared, GM obviously enjoyed manipulating people. The vague and mysterious invitations were evidence enough of that. Oh, he seemed nice and harmless enough—she didn't think he was dangerous, in spite of the way Val responded to him—but he was definitely very, very strange. Eccentric.

Controlling.

I wonder what it would be like to sleep with him.

Lisa started at that, half-expecting to see him lurking in a shadowy corner somewhere as she cursorily inspected the room. The thought had popped into her head unbidden like a scene from bad porn. Or *good* porn. She laughed again, and sounded a bit less panicked than she had before.

He probably likes it kinky and rough.

She giggled again at how bad she was being and then looked around guiltily. She feared that someone would come running and when nobody did, she got angry instead.

Why hadn't somebody found her yet, goddammit?

■□■□■□■

The bedroom door led to a second hallway, presumably into another wing of the house. Val thought it was odd that a bedroom would open up into not one but two hallways, though she didn't dwell on it. She had other concerns. The lights were off in here, too, and she had to press herself firmly against the wall to keep from getting lost or, worse, falling down a flight of stairs.

The air was colder in this part of the house. Maybe it was the part that faced away from the sun all day—not that there had been much of that, what with the rain and the heavy dark clouds. Beneath her fingertips, the wallpaper was peeling and dusty and slightly bloated with moisture and old glue. Touching it gave her skin a swollen, itchy feel.

It's like dead skin, she thought. *Like a corpse.*

Val yanked her hand away from the wall to wipe it on her jeans and her foot caught on something hard. She hit the floorboards with a heavy thud that made her palms and knees sting. She reached out, running her hand over the wooden panels, but there was no trace of the object that had caused her to fall. *I felt something—didn't I?*

"Great," Val muttered, slamming her hand against the boards. "Now I'm delusional as well as lost." She imagined she could hear faint laughter in the dark.

"Is someone there?"

Stupid. Your therapist was right. You really are crazy. You're hallucinating your very own laugh-track.

Val got up from the floor with more force than necessary and promptly lost her balance. She fell against the disgusting wall and felt a hard object collide against her right hip with bruising force. She let out a hiss of surprised pain. A doorknob. She'd literally stumbled upon another door. A neon line of yellow light glowed at the bottom, in the gap between door and floor.

I don't think that light was on a moment ago. I would have noticed.

Quickly, before common sense could rule her, she gave the knob a quick twist. The door swung open, and she reeled back as her eyes were assailed by a dazzling light. The culprit was actually a single naked bulb, swinging haphazardly from the draft she'd let in, but after the impenetrable darkness of the cold, shadowed corridor, the bulb seemed as bright as a blazing hot sun.

Val turned her face away, eyes watering, blinking rapidly as she waited for her vision to adjust. This "new room" actually seemed to be a medium-sized hall closet, just big enough to be called a "walk-in." When she reached out, she could only just brush both sides with her fingertips. The walls felt strange, though—definitely papery, but far too slippery and sleek to be ordinary wallpaper. In fact, the smooth surface was more like the glossy pages in a magazine.

What? She lowered her hands. *Wallpaper? In a closet?*

She opened her eyes. There was a brief flash of searing pain, but she could make out the closet beyond the blur of her tears. She blinked, her eyes going wider, but the images before her didn't fade. Plastered over the walls were dozens and dozens of chessboards in miniature, each depicting a different position—openings, middlegames, and endgames.

She gasped and whirled around, only to hit the now-closed door as she saw the snarling maw of a wolf looming over her. The fact that it was a picture did nothing to calm her nerves *He's trying to scare me*, she thought sickly.

It was working.

Horrorscape by Nenia Campbell

My God. Predators. An entire wall of predators. Spiders. Snakes. Leopards. Lions. Sharks. Her skin crawled just look at them. She reached out a shaking hand, which she immediately drew back; she didn't want to touch them, lest some remote trace of their lethal nature rub off on her.

Val glanced at the other wall, dreading what she would see. Crude weapons and instruments of torture? Pornography? Some combination thereof?

No.

Flowers, this time. Red roses. Yellow roses. White jasmine. Orange lilies. A couple other varieties she couldn't hope to name. Beside the images of fierce teeth and forced mates, the flowers were disconcertingly incongruous. And yet...there was something sinister about these, too.

Slowly, she turned to face the final wall—the one at her back, the other side of the door. She turned...and she clapped a hand over her mouth to keep herself from screaming. She was staring at her own face.

Pictures of her covered the back of the door, riddled with dozens of tiny holes that went clean through the thin coating of varnish and deep into the heart of the knotted wood. *He's killing me in effigy.* She grew even more pale. The door opened outward—she could easily picture him, armed with arrows or darts, casually firing quarrel after quarrel as he used her image as a dartboard.

"Shit," she whispered. The words tasted like acid in her suddenly too-dry mouth.

Above her head, the light went out.

A horrible sense of claustrophobia and vertigo swirled around her in the darkness, dragging her under the weight of her own panic with all the cataclysmic force of a tsunami. She tripped over her own feet in her haste to get out of that horrible room. She felt the eyes of the paper beasts boring caustic holes in her back. *What if the door's locked?*

She would go mad.

Val yanked the handle. The door opened, spilling her into the hallway with a rush of cold air that felt even colder against her feverish skin. *He knows I'm here. Oh God.*

She couldn't remember which way she'd come. In her fear and panic she had completely disoriented herself. She planted her hand against the wall, weeping silently.

He was playing with her, the bastard. Herding her. That probably had been him laughing earlier.

She gritted her teeth and took small, cautious steps through the shroud of dust and darkness, keeping her hand firmly pressed against the papered surface. Eventually she'd find the stairs. Then she could find her friends and show them that closet. *Let's see them doubt me then.*

Horrorscape by Nenia Campbell

(it would be a pity if any of said guests happened to have an accident, wouldn't it? That would be a terrible thing to have on one's conscience)

Or…not.

Beneath her groping hand, rough paper yielded to soft, pliant fabric. Her fingers twitched. For a moment, she could only stare unseeingly into the darkness, absorbing heat from the warm, breathing body beneath her palm.

Her brain paused, rewound, and spiraled out of control. The delayed shriek burst from her lips and she jerked her hand back as though she'd been burned—and in a way, she had; he'd seared her with a skewering burst of fear, shorting out nerve endings and inciting paralysis.

She took a slow step backwards, well aware that if she ran he would easily be able to follow the sound of her footsteps on the wooden floor. She silently cursed her own foolishness, even as her palms began to sweat and her heart pounded and she looked over her shoulder like a cornered animal that had found itself face-to-face with its hunter and left with nowhere else to run. It didn't really matter in any case; he caught her.

"No," she said in a low moan, when his hand closed firmly around her wrist. His touch was like a brand against her skin. Val was reminded of the way he'd gripped her throat as he kissed her, with tightness only just below the threshold required for the sensation of pain.

"You're shaking. Don't like the dark, Val?"

"Take me back to my friends. I went through your stupid penalty round. I saw that horrible—" she broke off, faltering as she tried to come up with a suitable word to describe what she had seen in the closet; she found none. "What you b-brought me here to see. And guess what? I still think you're a monster."

"That wasn't the penalty round."

And before she could offer a retort or a refusal, she was in his arms and he was spinning her around, twirling her in the darkness and making her lose all sense of direction. She was painfully aware of his hand at her waist, toying with the hem of her shirt with a proprietary air that disturbed her. She started to squirm, and he integrated her pushes and struggles into the steps.

"What are you doing?" she yelped.

He dipped her back and held her there, poised for a fall.

"I believe it's a waltz."

"No. You threw *darts* at pictures of me. You don't get to touch me."

"Wrong again, dearest." He yanked her upright, closing his other hand more firmly over hers. "If I wanted to hurt you, I would not need to do so by proxy."

Val jerked her arm and felt the sharp kick of the wall against her heels.

"I thought perhaps some time in the dark, alone, would cool you off, but I don't believe you've quite learned the lesson."

Her stomach flip-flopped at the sound of his voice, filling her with a deep humiliation that he could still make her feel this way. She could imagine that condescending smile slipping into place, and his eyes, which could shift from tranquil to turbulent, depending on the light. Val wondered what shade they were now. Dark, she thought, *So dark that you had no hopes of gauging the depths—*

Not until you were already half-drowned.

"What lesson?"

"That you can't win against me."

"Lesson learned," she said sharply, giving her arm another tug. He still wouldn't let go.

"I don't think so."

"Then why? If you despise me this much—if you're so hellbent on destroying me—then why did you kiss me? What's with this whole elaborate facade?"

"A facade," he repeated. "Is that what you think this is, Val? Some mere trifle I've put together to amuse myself?"

"It's always a game with you."

"In every sense of the word." There was a snarl in his voice now, and she flinched at the quality of his tone. Bitter as wormwood, deadly as hemlock. He sounded almost as if he were implying that this was all her fault.

"I've done nothing to you," Val said, and without becoming any less fearful or confused, she started to grow angry as well. Who was he to accuse her, after pushing her, threatening her, singling her out? After ruining her life, and betraying her trust, and breaking her heart?

He had no right. None.

He dropped his hand from her waist, like an annoyed cat batting aside a toy being held in contempt. "Do you honestly believe that?" he inquired, and though his voice was calm, affable, even, she felt his hand on her wrist tighten, as if he thought she'd run away. "I think you've done plenty. I think you know exactly what you—"

His voice, which had been steadily rising, stopped completely. He'd made a mistake, Val realized. By raising his voice, he'd let the emotionless mask slip free, betraying his real face.

"What?" she whispered, shaking.

"Never you mind. So you consider yourself innocent, a tragic victim of circumstance. Does that make me the heartless villain? I suppose I shouldn't be surprised. We always vilify what we don't understand.

Plus ça change, plus c'est la même chose. Isn't that right, Valerian?"

"I...I don't know."

"No, not yet. But you will. You will."

And then they were running, tearing through the darkened hallways at breakneck speed. Val felt fear explode inside of her as the dry, cold air whipped past her face. Though a natural runner, she had to fight to keep up. She was so terrified—terrified that he'd lead her down a staircase or straight into a wall.

Please, please don't let him hurt me.

The ground disappeared from beneath her feet and she screamed, only to have it return with a heavy thud beneath her feet that seemed to shake the very walls of the house. Just when she thought she was going to be sick or faint or both, he stopped.

With a shaking hand, she reached out and felt mottled wallpaper scant inches from her face. Her fingers slid down and hit hard, polished metal.

A door.

He'd led her to a *door*.

Right *into* a door, almost.

Pure, dumb shock settled over her like fog. She fell to her knees when her legs gave out, cradling her stomach. "You..." *You could have killed me,* is what she almost said until she realized that the hand around hers

Horrorscape by Nenia Campbell

was gone.

    Besides; it wasn't anything he didn't know already.

Chapter Ten

Wild

The black- and white-clad teens filed awkwardly into the room as they waited for their host, and Lisa had the disconcerting feeling that she was back in grade school, awaiting a reprimand from a teacher. James went to the buffet table to pour himself a drink, undoubtedly wishing there was alcohol. There was a brief scramble for chairs.

She found herself seated off to the side, on the fringe, next to the heavier of the two boys on the white team. James was three seats down, flanked by Blake and Charlie. Jason sat on the other side of the larger boy, trying to catch her eye. Since the chairs were arranged in a U-shaped formation, she could ignore him easily—especially since her friends were nearly parallel to her.

Blake was looking at her with a quizzical, owlish expression. She arched her own eyebrow in return before turning her attention to James, who was staring sullenly at the wall, as if trying to burn holes through the plaster. He was gripping his plastic so hard that it let out a crinkle of protest every now and then. Indulging in a private hissy fit. *And once he checks into the grouch motel, he doesn't check out.*

Val could sometimes coax him out of it. Sometimes. But Val wasn't here. And neither was GM. *I wonder if there's a connection,* Lisa thought idly. Even if there wasn't, James was insecure enough that he might imagine that there was.

"James!" He didn't appear to hear. Or maybe he was ignoring her. Asshole. Charlie shot her a glare. *"James!"*

James started. "What?" If he *had* been ignoring her, he was hiding it well.

"Where's Val?"

His face creased into a sulky pout. He shrugged.

"You don't know?"

How could he not know? More importantly, *why* didn't he know? James knew better than anyone else how high-strung that girl was. Being lost in a dark and dusty manor home was not exactly the best situation for someone in that kind of mindset to be in.

And why, she wondered, is he sitting so close to Charlie? His pants were almost brushing her leg.

"I'm not her keeper."

I can see that. "So you didn't find her," she said, trying to keep her voice calm.

"I did." He looked her squarely in the eye. "Last I saw, she seemed to prefer GM's company to mine."

Charlie stiffened. James—the idiot—didn't notice. Aware that nearly everyone in the room was looking at them now, Lisa growled, "What are you talking about?"

"I found her first so she got put into penalty round. They seemed pretty cozy," he said sourly.

"I knew it," Charlie muttered to herself. *"Bitch."*

"You are an idiot," Lisa said. "She's afraid of him. You didn't see? God, James, how could you do that to her?"

"Hey!" James held up his hands. "I tried to bail her out of it, but, you know."

"No, I don't know. How hard did you try? Hard as in, 'not very?'"

Red crept into his cheeks. He said nothing. Jason laughed meanly; both Lisa and James ignored him.

"You threw her to the wolves because GM threatened to dock you points, didn't you?"

"Shut up."

"You did!" Lisa said. "I *knew* it. What is it with you jock-types and going to pieces in front of authority figures? Are you afraid of him, too?"

"I'm not afraid of him!"

"Well, you could have fooled me."

"That's enough," James said in a low voice. "I swear to God—"

She laughed incredulously. "You are. You are, aren't you? Why else would you get all butt-hurt?"

James was saved from responding as the heavy parlor door creaked open. Six heads turned in that direction. GM walked into the room, looking rather pleased with himself; his cheeks were tinged with a faint but distinct blush and his breathing was quick and light—almost as if he'd been running. *Or participating in some other kind of exertion,* Lisa thought, as he caught his breath.

There was still no sign of Val.

He wouldn't—

"Well," GM said at last, looking at each of them in turn, though his eyes seemed to linger when they met hers. "How did you find the first round?"

He might.

"Long?" Blake ventured. "How much time did it take?"

"An hour."

She remembered with resentment those seemingly endless minutes she'd spent crouched behind the fake rubber plant. Smears of dust were still evident on her dress, try as she might to brush it off. Her knees were still sore.

An *hour.*

Where had Blake been hiding? James hadn't even found him; apart from GM, he'd been the last to enter the room, only coming out of hiding when he heard their footsteps on the floorboards.

"Nobody found *me,*" Charlie pouted.

GM turned one of the chairs around. The wooden legs hit the floor with a crack that made them jump. "The hunter filled his role well." He straddled the seat, folding his arms over the back. "However, this next game will be different in both theme and mode, which should please those who weren't left…" he paused, appearing to taste the word, "satisfied."

That prompted Lisa to jump in with, "Where's Val?"

"*Valerian* is sitting out this round." He turned his full attention on her and smiled charmingly, but there was a cold edge to it that set her on her guard. It was the smile of a man who knew the full measure of his strengths and was not afraid to abuse them. "She'll rejoin us for the next."

"Where?" Lisa repeated, with the slightest bit of emphasis.

He glanced at James and his smile grew enigmatic, and slightly taunting. "I couldn't say."

"You see? He doesn't know, Lisa," Charlie said. "Drop it already."

"He didn't say he didn't know," Lisa said darkly. "He said he wasn't going to tell us."

The expression on his face nearly made her shiver; it was flat with dislike, and yet filled with a kind of appraisal. And then it was gone, making her wonder if she had seen anything at all. But then, without another word, GM slipped his hand into his pocket, producing what appeared to be a small plastic toy. She flinched in her chair when the toy whizzed towards her face, and cried out, "Jesus!" even as it clattered harmlessly at her feet.

There was a very long silence.

Lisa glanced at GM, not quite able to wrap her mind around what had just happened. He tilted his head, his eyes flicking from her to the toy, as if saying, "Go on."

She pulled up the bodice of her dress before bending to retrieve it, aware of the eyes watching her. *He threw it at me.*

The toy turned out to be a chess piece: a white pawn. She frowned. A piece of binder paper was furled up inside the hollow at the bottom. She pulled it out curiously, shooting another look at GM as she did so. The writing was cramped but legible, written in expensive, gleaming ink.

"Time," she read. "Time for what? What is this?"

"I have hidden thirty-one chess pieces somewhere inside this house. Each of them contains a clue that, when assembled, will spell out a message. The importance of it will be crucial—though you won't see why until much, much later in the game." And he smiled again. At her.

"So it's like a scavenger hunt?" James asked warily.

It was a reasonable enough question, but it made GM throw back his head and laugh. "Exactly."

Horrorscape by Nenia Campbell

Val drew in a deep breath and opened the door.

She wasn't sure what she had been expecting—another morbid museum of the macabre, perhaps. After that closet, and the waltz in the dark, nothing would have surprised her.

The room was lit, but dimly. A worn desk that had seen better days was the focal point of the room. It had a computer, though the monitor and the keyboard were both yellowed from age. There were a few oil paintings on the wall, as well, but none of them had human subjects.

Déjà vu swooped down on her like a large bird of pray with midnight wings. She was reminded of a different room, four years in the past, where she had first discovered the depths of a young man's twisted obsession in a leather-bound journal inside an unlocked drawer.

This isn't the way it was before.

But things were going to be different this time. He had said so himself.

She bent to examine the contents of a nearby bookshelf. Charles Darwin, Niccolo Machiavelli, and the Marquis de Sade were included among the authors. Those, she remembered from before. But they seemed out of place here, more like props.

Horrorscape by Nenia Campbell

She bit her lip, staring at a three-dimensional case that held some butterflies. *Butterflies of Europe.* Poor things. She stared at them sadly. They reminded her—of something unpleasant.

(Tell me you belong to me)

Her hand seemed to touch her throat of its own accord. She swallowed nervously, looking around, wondering if this was another display meant to frighten her out of her wits. If he was here, cloaked in shadow, watching her, waiting for the perfect moment to catch her off-guard.

He was good at that. He always had been.

A draft blew in and she spun to face the door, her heart fluttering in her throat so quickly that she thought she might choke. But the doorway was as empty as it had been when she came in.

Or is it?

She looked away from the butterflies as nausea made her stomach roil like a witch's brew. Those had been in his house the first time. *Goddamn you,* she thought, feeling tears jump to her eyes. *What are you doing to me?*

She could almost imagine the response, dark and smooth as velvet. *What did you have in mind?*

Val fell to her knees, clasping her hands as though in prayer. She couldn't do this. Not again. The worst part was, she couldn't even tell anyone—because if she did…if she did…he would do something awful to Blake, Lisa, or James. He'd said as much from before, when he asked her oh-so-casually if she'd sacrifice herself for her friends' sake.

(you would, wouldn't you?)

"No!" she gasped, stumbling to her feet. She turned wild eyes on the bookcase and hurled the books into the corridor, half-expecting to hear a hushed gasp of pain.

But no one was there.

She was alone.

Mostly alone.

His kiss still burned her lips. His voice still whispered in her mind. And all she could think was, *He doesn't kiss like James*. James wasn't that forceful or that thorough. James couldn't paralyze her with a glance. James didn't make her feel like she was standing with her back to an abyss. She wished James was here. Jerky behavior or no, she wanted to curl up in his arms and disappear.

Well, you can't. So suck it up—unless you want to wait here…for him. Val exhaled shakily, turning away from the bookshelf. "Right, then," she whispered. "Suck it up it is."

She pushed the computer's power button. Nothing happened. She peered over the top of the monitor and immediately saw why; the computer's back had been pried off, roughly, probably with a blunt instrument judging by the deep gouges in the casing. Wires and chips and glinting pieces of metal spilled out. The computer had been gutted.

Rain spattered against the shuttered windows, sounding like the pattering of tiny feet and she jumped, throwing a sharp glance in the direction of the window.

It was a dark and stormy night.

She shivered again and turned to go, ready to run if need be, but something about the keyboard gave her pause.

What's that?

Nestled in the groove between the spacebar and the letters was a black queen from a chess set. Not the nice one from his bedroom, but a cheap plastic replica.

(The queen is arguably the most powerful piece in the game)

With a trembling hand, she picked it up. It was slightly warm to the touch. A piece of paper was wadded up in the bottom, folded several times, reminding her of the secret notes she used to pass along to her friends in grade school. There was no question who had written this note. The handwriting was the same as that which had been on the envelope she got in the mail.

A single word was printed in the center of the wrinkled paper. Just one word, but it caused frost to glaze over her skin, crystallizing the air in her lungs and stopping her heart, making her freeze from the outside, in.

The word read: "dangerous."

Deep and unrestrained, GM had the type of laugh that Lisa would have found attractive under ordinary circumstances; there was a bit of the wild in it. But these were not ordinary circumstances and in this present context, it chilled her to the bone.

"What's so funny?" James demanded.

Still chuckling, he said, "You wouldn't understand."

But Lisa thought she might. Scavenger hunt. It was a play on words. Predators again. Blake nudged her and her thoughts dissipated like smoke. "Yes?" She glared at him. "What is it?"

"Are you all right?"

"Why wouldn't I be?"

A faint, pinkish blush tinged his cheeks as he nodded down at the chess piece, still in her hand. She had been gripping the pawn so tightly that it had left a reddish marking in her palm. "He, uh, threw that at you pretty hard."

"Well, he missed."

"Not if it was a warning shot," he said quietly.

"Warning shot?" She snorted. "Don't be ridiculous. He overthrew."

"That's not what Val seemed to think."

Lisa frowned. "You talked to her? When?"

"Earlier. Before the game."

She waited for him to go on, but he didn't elaborate. That made sense if it was something he didn't want GM to hear since he was still in the room. She looked away, then back. Blake was looking at her just as intently, prompting her to say, "What?"

His face reddened further, the flush spreading to his ears and nose. "Uh. Your dress…it doesn't have any pockets. Do you want me to hold that for you?"

What does he have to be so nice for? Why can't he get mad like a normal person? Lisa gave him the pawn, feeling both sheepish and spiteful as she watched it disappear into the pocket of his white slacks. *I wonder what he wants from me.*

"Thanks."

"Well." GM cleared his throat. "I apologize for keeping you all…hanging. I'm sure you all are quite eager to begin the next round."

Because the last game had just been so thrilling she could barely reign herself in. First hide and seek, now a scavenger hunt. What was next? Musical chairs? Lisa scowled. If he decided to initiate a creepy version of Duck, Duck, Goose, she was out of here.

Maybe they should leave anyway. Jason was a creep and she trusted GM about as far as she could throw him.

As soon as we find Val, we'll go.

"I have a question." The boy next to her—Brent, she remembered—said, throwing up his arm.

GM leaned forward on the chair, resting his chin on his folded arms. "Shoot," he said lazily.

"Is there one piece per room? Or do some rooms have more than one chess piece?"

Good question.

"This house does not have thirty-one rooms. Do the math."

Lisa sighed loudly.

"Any other questions?" GM paused a beat. "No? Excellent."

He swung his legs off the chair. His black boots—the only other article of clothing that wasn't white, apart from his incongruously dark shirt—echoed dully as he walked over to the solid oak door, pulling it open with a screech of rusted hinges that made Lisa wince. He leaned back against the door, keeping it from swinging shut.

Holding the door open. Lisa stood up slowly, as if in a dream. *What a gentleman.*

Except … with his current position, he was blocking

the entryway, leaving only the barest amount of space for her to get by. She was the last one in the room. How had that happened? And had he been so much of an obstruction for the other players? She thought not.

"Where's your chess piece?" GM inquired, neatly stepping into her path as she attempted to squeeze by, tilting his head in a vaguely feline gesture.

Lisa was startled into responding, "I gave it to Blake."

GM nodded absently, settling back against the door again.

A heady scent surrounded him, too refined to be cologne, and very familiar. Earthy, somehow. God. He was even more intimidating up close, like some kind of wild animal. "Why did you throw it at me?"

"You were the closest."

"What? No, I wasn't." Lisa hiked her chin up a notch. "Charlie was. She was sitting right in front of you. I'm not even on your team."

"I try to stay impartial."

"Bullshit. I think you're hiding something."

That made him laugh. Not the free laugh, from before, but a deprecating one that Lisa found particularly offensive. "Forthright, aren't you? What on earth gave you that impression?"

She didn't let herself rise to the bait. "I'm going to

find out what it is. It has something to do with why you put Val in penalty round, doesn't it?"

He frowned. She half-expected him to lunge at her and flinched when he raised his hand to push his errant bangs out of his eyes. "You're very protective of her."

"Only when I have to be."

"And you think she's in danger...from me?"

"I know that she's afraid of you. I don't know why. Maybe there isn't a reason. Maybe you did nothing to her. But I'm telling you to back off right now. She has a boyfriend," Lisa said bluntly.

"I noticed," was the dry response. "James, isn't it?"

"Well, then I'm sure you've noticed that she doesn't appreciate the attention, even if she's too nice or too shy to say so. She doesn't really go for psycho stalkers."

One of his dark eyebrows shot straight up. "That's quite the accusation."

She bit her lip, painfully aware of how close they were standing. He had closed that distance; so subtly, that she hadn't even noticed until it was too late. Like a trap snapping shut, she thought. "I think it's reasonable enough under the given circumstances."

"Really." He took a step closer. Then another. Until he nearly had her backed against the wall. He rested his hands on either side of her, casually barring her escape. "Then you're considerably more foolish than I gave you credit for, if you would confront a possible psychopath…alone…"

She stared up at him, wordless with shock and fear. His eyes were as hard and steely as cold hematite, and his skin was so pale, she could see the veins of his throat, like purple striations in pure white marble. There was something unnatural about him, almost supernatural. His smile turned hard, sardonic before her eyes. And she realized, sickly, that in spite of his slender build and deathly pallor, there was absolutely nothing weak about him.

Slowly, cautiously, she took a step to her right, and his hand closed into a fist, slamming inches away from her face. "We're not finished here," he said quietly. Lisa jumped—and hated him for getting to her with these cheap intimidation techniques. Hated herself for falling for them.

What have you gotten yourself into, Val?

Her eyes flicked from his hand to his face. "You're going to hit me?" she said flatly, trying to mask her terror. She wondered if the others would be able to hear her if she screamed.

"Nothing quite so barbaric. I'm merely suggesting you concentrate on the game at hand, before attempting any new ones with me. You won't win; and you might get hurt." He chuckled humorlessly. "But, as I said. It's only a suggestion. You're free to do as you like."

"Val is off-limits."

"I suppose we'll see about that, won't we?"

"You're so not functional," she said. "Stay away from her. Go to Charlie, if that's what you want."

"Run along, Lisa. Your friends are waiting." With that, he gave her a firm push out the door. Caught unaware, she stumbled out of the doorjamb, nearly falling flat on the floor. It slammed shut inches behind her.

Shit.

GM sighed, leaning against the closed door. Everything was going nicely to plan. He had created an obstacle course, leaving doors either locked or unlocked as he saw fit, to keep his little lab rats on the correct path. They were playing right into his hands. Well, mostly. People were slightly less predictable than plastic pieces, but that element of chaos lent an interesting bent to the game.

He always had appreciated a challenge, provided he won.

He could hear them, faintly, talking. Lisa's attempts to bait him had been laughable—almost insulting, really. She was quickly becoming more problematic than he'd anticipated. He had seen something in her eyes—a brief spark of recognition that made his pulse lift in anticipation.

Do you know who I am?

She didn't; it quickly faded. How lucky for her. He thought he really might have killed her if it hadn't. He couldn't have anyone spoiling his plans. He had already waited so long; he intended to see them come to fruition.

And she'd seen part of that in his face. He had scared her, and she was not the type to be easily scared. Yes, Lisa would almost certainly still try to talk to Val. To warn her. But it would be nothing Valerian didn't already know for herself, not that she would say so. His foresight in swearing the red-haired woman to silence pleased him. No. There would be no problems from that quarter.

Val's quickness to give into him made him wonder if he should have demanded a higher price. But he never reneged on a bargain; for now, he was content to take from her what he wanted in small, but ever-increasing increments. For now, the delay of gratification could be edifying.

For now.

He had, admittedly, been hoping that she would try and force his hand, but Val was nowhere near as strong as she once had been. Her frozen helplessness when he pinned her against the wall and kissed her; her broken sobs when he threatened her; her mindless terror when she saw the little surprise he'd left for her in the hall—all of these things concerned him. Conquest was not satisfying if it began with a surrender. He wanted her to fight, to struggle, to resist—

He wanted the pleasure of subduing her.

Perhaps he needed to up the ante a little…to get closer…to confuse her senses enough that she forgot herself. He could be very persuasive, when he wanted to be. All it would take was a moment, just one micron past her defenses—less than the time it took to sigh.

She might try to resist then but it would be too late, merely futile struggle by that point. Because he noticed the way her breathing changed when he got too close, the way her pulse vibrated like a small pair of furiously beating wings trapped beneath the cage of her skin. Whether she knew it or not, Val lusted for control—for being controlled.

Perhaps he would make her beg first, until she verbalized all those desires she wished so strongly that she didn't have. All that ugliness, out in the open where it could break her. Pleasure and pain, so closely intertwined that they were nearly indistinguishable from one another.

Go to Charlie, if that's what you want, Lisa had said. She didn't understand. Comparing the two of them was like comparing two flowers—one strong and proud, cultivated in a green house; the other wilting and weather-beaten, having struggled through fierce storms and frosty winters. Not quite as glowing, perhaps, but wild, lovely, and far more tenacious.

He had come to the remains of the buffet. The table still had some food. He picked up one of the grapes and ate it, closing his eyes as he washed it down with cool water.

Delicious.

Chapter Eleven

En Passant

Had Lisa really expected him to confess to everything, like a murderer in the bad parlor mysteries of which her mother was so fond? No, obviously. But it bothered her that GM hadn't exactly denied her accusation, either. If he was innocent, wouldn't he have been shocked, or even affronted, by her theories and not quite so coldly menacing? There was no question in her mind over the fact that he was completely out of Val's league and possibly hers, as well. GM had deliberately challenged her, and Lisa wasn't entirely sure she was up to the challenge.

He's guilty of something. I'm not sure what it is. In a way, it would have been better if he had threatened her outright. At least then she'd have had some kind of proof.

Lisa hoisted up the bodice of her dress and went over to see what Blake and James were discussing. They were trying to formulate a strategy for how best to go about searching the rooms for the pieces. James wanted to start with the smaller rooms first, which he thought would be easiest. Blake wanted to take them as they came, in case they got lost and missed some pieces along the way.

It's like they didn't even notice I was gone.

James was toying with something incessantly, and

Lisa kept seeing flashes of movement in her periphery as a result. She tried ignoring him, at first, but he was being too distracting. "What is that?" she snapped.

"This?" James stared down at his hands, as if only just realizing the object was there. "A chess piece." He held the chess piece out for her inspection, one of the castled ones.

"A rook," Blake clarified.

"You found one and you didn't say anything?"

James shrugged and went back to rolling the rook over his knuckles and into his palm. "I didn't want to, not with GM there. He might've taken it, penalizing us. You were clearly pissing him off back there."

Lisa made a noncommittal noise, biting the inside of her cheek to keep from insulting him. James, the idiot, did have a point—but he was right for the wrong reasons. She wished she could figure out how to articulate her misgivings, but how can you put into words what you don't understand yourself?

"Look inside it," Lisa ordered. "See if there's a message."

James pulled out the rolled-up paper, somewhat awkwardly because of his large hands. "It says winner." He looked up at them, raising his eyebrows. "Maybe that means we've won a prize."

"I doubt it," Lisa said. "I baited him, remember? He's docked us all fifty points from Gryffindor."

"Oh, for fuck's sake, Lisa—"

"You should talk, anyway. Ditching your own girlfriend because you're afraid of the consequences of taking a stand for her—and for yourself. And for what? Points? A piece of plastic? What did he do, that made you so wary of him?"

"I'm not going to answer that," James said, tightening his fingers around the chess piece.

So something, then. Only the guilty plead the fifth.

Silence reigned between them, broken only by the sound of their footfalls.

Well this is fun. I sure am glad I came. This is so much more fun than making out with Thomas in his parents' hot tub.

Sullenly, James said, "How many pieces are there, anyway? These things are too small."

"They're not the only thing," muttered Lisa.

Before James could offer a retort of his own, Blake said, "Thirty-two." Lisa's head swiveled towards Blake who, mistaking their stares for confusion, went on to add, "Sixteen pawns, four bishops, four knights, four rooks, and two kings and queens, respectively.

"Oh God. Next thing you know, he'll be planting flowers and telling us the meanings of them."

Lisa's brow furrowed. "James—"

A flush crept up Blake's collar. "I don't play. My

mom does—did."

"Just don't go all GM on us, dude. Trust me, one is enough."

"Blake is about as threatening as a piece of lint," Lisa said coolly.

"I wouldn't go quite that far," said Blake, drawing himself up. "I can be quite nasty sometimes."

James rolled his eyes. "Yeah. If you try hard enough, you can make fluffy bunnies shift in discomfort."

Blake slugged James in the arm. Pretty hard, for a geek boy. James winced. "Ow. That—" he sneaked a look at Lisa. "…almost tickled."

Sure, James. Lisa almost smiled at the blatant chagrin on his face but another, far less pleasant, thought had just occurred to her. If Blake was right, and there really were thirty-two pieces, then the task at hand suddenly seemed more daunting than juvenile. The pieces were small and finding them all could easily take hours, even with three or four people to a team. *And what if we don't find them all?*

It's not like he could keep them here until they did.

Lisa wondered if Val was having better luck. Probably not, she thought, and shivered. *Penalty round.* The name alone gave her the heebie-jeebies.

Horrorscape by Nenia Campbell

The computer room led to a long, tapering hallway that gave the unsettling impression that the walls were closing in. An absence of good light gave the illusion of the floor being at a tilt, like the skewed angles of the chase scenes in horror movie cinematography. Val hadn't even realized she had been holding her breath until she reached the staircase and began to gasp like a fish out of water—

And promptly found herself in another labyrinthine hallway that she didn't recognize. GM—Gavin—must have purposely taken her to the opposite wing of the house. So he could put her in another penalty round, no doubt. She slammed the wall with her fist, wishing it was his arrogant face instead. "Son of a bitch," she whispered, finding herself close to tears. She felt like a mouse being tortured by a cat.

Why? Because she had refused his advances in the dark? Because she refused to give into her fear, or into him? *I'm breaking apart. I can't fight him the way I did before—*

And he's counting on that.

"Valerian?"

Val dropped her fist from the wall, whirling around. The voice had been male, and she could make out the speaker's white shirt in the darkness, but his features were a blur of darkness. It wasn't GM, though. The voice lacked Gavin's sense of sureness and the proprietary way he spoke her name, as if he owned her. *Because in his mind, he already does. God, I wish I had a flashlight.*

She squinted, as if that would help. "Who's there?" It wasn't Gavin, and it wasn't familiar. There were really only two people it could be. Brent, or—

"Jason."

Great. The nastier one. She wet her lips. "What are *you* doing up here?"

"We've already started the next round. I'm sure your teammates will tell you about it." His voice oozed smugness. "How's penalty round?"

"It's been a blast," she said flatly. "Because, you know, the name is so misleading. What do you think?"

"I think you're being a bitch," he said, in a deceptively pleasant voice.

Irritation rippled down her spine like a shiver. "I'm sorry," she said tartly, with an attempt at dignity. "I was lost, and it was dark, and I'm not in the best of moods right now—" *What with my psychotic stalker being here, threatening my friends, threatening me if I so much as breathe a word, and he frightens me, and I can feel him watching me, and I can feel his breath on my neck every time I turn around—*

Val swallowed, hard, and added, "It wouldn't be called penalty round if it was fun, right?"

Jason made a noncommittal noise that sounded

farther than before—he was walking away! That asshole! "Wait!" She called, in a panic. "Where are you going?"

"I don't have time for chitchat."

Chitchat? This is life or death. "Do you know the way back to the starting room, at least?"

"It's clear on the other side of the house, Val."

I knew it. Evil bastard. I hate you. "Can you take me there?"

Another pause. "What do I get out of it?"

"E-excuse me?"

"What are you willing to offer me in return for my help?" he repeated, as if she were dumb.

The chess piece, along with its strange message, lay forgotten in the pocket of her jeans, else she might have offered it as a possible bargaining chip. Val's mind raced, trying to come up with some sort of a solution. She found none. "I don't have anything to give you."

"Oh, I think you do." Her stomach twisted unpleasantly as he took a step in her general direction.

No, she thought. *Please, not him, too.*

"You're friends with Lisa, aren't you?"

"Lisa?" It took a moment for her frenetic thoughts to click together. When he didn't correct her, she said, warily, "Yes. Why?"

"Let's call it a matter of personal interest."

That sounds like something GM would say. Her sense of mistrust deepened. If Jason had decided to emulate Gavin that spoke volumes in itself. "What are you talking about?"

"Oh, nothing bad. Just a few questions about the usual. What her favorite music is, and so on."

"You like her." Val felt numbed by this realization, unsure whether it was due to relief or fear.

"That's a pretty infantile way of saying it, but yeah. I like her."

"Then why don't you ask her those questions yourself?"

"Because she refuses to talk to me." He paused a beat. "Besides, this way we have a deal."

"A raw deal." If Lisa didn't want to talk to Jason, she had a reason. He was creepy. But GM was worse. Infinitely worse. And if she didn't get out of here, he'd find her. He always did. She shivered violently, and was grateful the other boy couldn't see it in the shadows. "You're the only one who benefits."

"Maybe." Jason laughed softly. "But it's the best you're going to get, so I suggest you take it. I'm doing you a favor. Think of how easy it would be for me to simply tell your boyfriend what you've been up to behind his back, Val. And I'm making it so you can actually get something out of this."

The air in her lungs deflated like a punctured

balloon. "What I've…been up to behind his back?"

"You go missing, GM goes missing. Could be a coincidence—I think not, though. Charlie doesn't, either."

There's no way—he couldn't have seen—

"That's a load of bullshit," she said hoarsely. "Nobody will believe you."

"Do you really want to put that to the test? Because I think GM would back me up. He seems to have it in for you, grilling you like that in front of everyone. I wonder why he hates you so much…"

If you only knew. Val felt another dizzying headache coming on. *Oh God. Jason, you idiot, you're playing with fire, and I'm the one who's going to get burned.*

But she couldn't say a thing to warn him off the subject. Not if she wanted her friends to remain unharmed. Jason wasn't the only one going around and making deals.

"Just tell me what I want to know," he coaxed. "Trust me, everyone will be so much happier."

■□■□■□■

He hid a smile as he walked away.

Well, well, Jason—I didn't know you had it in you. I had you pegged as a mild annoyance, and yet it seems there's a bit of the predator in you. In any case, you've got my Val backed up right against the wall, exactly where I want her. Thank you for that. It saves me a lot of trouble. Your little bargain with Valerian may well have a place in my plan—just take care that you don't take what's mine.

As for you, my dear, I suggest you get comfortable with the feeling of what it's like, being trapped. Because this time, for you, there will be no escape.

Horrorscape by Nenia Campbell

Chapter Twelve

Sham Sacrifice

There was no doubt in Val's mind that Jason was willing to follow through on his threat, damn him, hurting James in a way she might never be able to repair.

Does what James believe really matter?

Perhaps not. But then, what gave Jason—or Gavin—the right to decide that for her? Val's eyes flashed with a hint of her old fire. None, that's what. She was nobody's pawn. But…nobody could get hurt with a few questions, right?

Oh, Lisa…

"I won't answer anything personal," she said quickly. "And I…I, um, retain the right to veto anything…inappropriate."

"What are you, Ally McBeal?" Jason sounded like he might be smirking. "Whatever. It's fine—I accept your terms."

Val wasn't finished. "If you hurt her, I swear—"

"I get it." His hand fell on her shoulder so casually, so arbitrarily, that she was unable to finish delivering her threat. "But you're being a little over-protective, don't you think? Call off the dogs, Val. Let's not make any threats we aren't capable of carrying out ourselves."

"Don't touch me." She swiped his hand from her shoulder as one would a scorpion or a killer bee. GM had said something very similar to that when he had threatened her friends and mocked her name. Jason hadn't managed that same level of menace, though. Yet.

No, she certainly didn't feel very caring or protective. James had almost ended up in a fight with Gavin because of her, and now Jason was forcing her to choose to condemn one of two people whom she truly cared about.

Jason's grip reasserted its presence on her arm. "So we have a deal, then."

"I said *don't touch me*." She yanked her wrist out of his loose hold. "How many questions?"

He seemed to think about it. "Ten."

"Five."

"Nine."

"Five."

"Eight."

"*Five*."

"I don't think you get how this works," Jason mocked. "You're supposed to go up—don't you know how to bargain?"

"I'm not bargaining. Five, or no deal."

Jason's laughter sounded out in the darkness, horsey and unbearably loud. "Eight, and that's my final offer." At her silence, he went on. "You don't seem to realize the position you're in, Val. Do I need to remind you? Or do you want James to know what you do in hall closets with our host when he's not around?"

Val sucked in a breath. *Hall closets?* "No! I don't—" *Wait a minute.* "Did he tell you something? Did he *lie* about me?"

"Or maybe," Jason continued, as if she hadn't said anything. "Maybe you don't really care about him at all, and this is just the slap in the face he needs to get the message? Huh?"

It's not like that—I'm not like that. What did GM tell him? What did he say? She could almost picture it. The two of them talking. GM dropping hints as though tossing Jason a treat. The thought made her sick with helpless, impotent rage. "Eight is fine," she concluded miserably.

As if she had a choice.

■□■□■□■

Two hours passed and the black team—they couldn't help but think of themselves that way; GM, Jason, and Charlie did not exactly inspire feelings of camaraderie—had little to show for their efforts, beyond the fickle intervention of chance. James found a black pawn ("king") in a soap dish when he went to the bathroom to respond to nature's call. Lisa found a white rook ("the") in the library, sandwiched between a dusty book on

Romanesque architecture and the leather-bound biography of a Russian chess player. Blake found nothing at all.

Two pieces in as many hours, he thought tiredly. Thirty to go. If they kept on at this rate, they wouldn't finish for days. Was the white team having better luck?

"Somebody is obsessed with Italy," Lisa sang, in an entirely too-cheerful voice. It seemed to annoy James, who winced as if her words were an icepick being wedged with slow, painful precision, directly into his eardrum. "I wonder if he's Italian. He speaks French, but doesn't look it. And don't Europeans speak several languages, anyway?"

"Who cares," was James's comment.

"Why don't we start on the second floor?" Blake said, before they could start fighting again and end up giving him a headache.

It was a reasonable idea. They were in the main hallway now with the staircase looming to their left and the door to their right. James leaned back against the wall, just under a painting of a forest. The trees were tall and pointed, like lances, resembling the Black Forest that had inspired the tales of the Brothers Grimm, which Blake had read when he was a child. James stretched, and his hand knocked against the frame of the painting causing it to swing precariously. He caught it, though, before it could fall and shatter.

"Careful," Lisa said unnecessarily, as James straightened it back on the wall. "Breaking his stuff is a surefire way to get him even more pissed off at us than he already is."

"Why don't we call it quits and go home?" James responded. "If he doesn't like us, I mean. Why stay? The white team is a bunch of assholes, anyway."

"As I recall *you* were the one who wanted to stay."

"Yeah, but I changed my mind. Why do *you* want to stay?"

Lisa snorted. "Oh, I want to leave. But I, for one, don't want to let them chase us off like a bunch of schoolyard bullies. Do you want them to win?"

His face darkened and he yanked his arm back down to his side. "Fuck no. But this isn't much fun—and I'm never going to see any of them again."

"We also still haven't found Val," Lisa pointed out, looking at him accusingly. "Or did you forget?"

From the flush on the other boy's face, it seemed that James had. Blake frowned. How could he forget about his own girlfriend? She was pretty, too. Not as pretty as Lisa—in fact, Blake couldn't think of any girls offhand who were prettier than Lisa, except maybe that girl from the white team—but far prettier than anyone Blake felt likely to date. He had always been vaguely annoyed by men who took their pretty girlfriends for granted. Particularly since women tended to flock towards those kinds of men, regardless of their personalities.

The fact that one of his best friends exhibited the very same characteristics of which he was so abhorrent provided a steady source of cognitive dissonance for Blake. Though he would have liked to put in his own two cents, he didn't have the guts. *It's none of my business anyway.* So Blake sighed and changed the subject like the wimp he was. "We don't even know how many pieces the white team has—or how many Val might have found. We might even be ahead, in which case there's no point in tiring ourselves out over it."

Lisa opened her mouth, her eyebrows drawn together, as if to say, *We don't even know where Val is. Period.* Blake shot her a look, raising an eyebrow. A "don't even think about it" look that he'd inherited from his mother—back when she'd still been around to deliver it. A tremor went through his features at the thought, slight but visible. Lisa saw the wavering expression on his face, paused, and then said, "Yeah, you might be right."

There was a pause as each of them calculated how many chess pieces there might be left to find. Four out of thirty-two isn't horrible, Blake told himself. Assuming Val hadn't found more, that was 12.5-percent. It stood to reason that the white team had accumulated a similar amount, leaving roughly 75-percent left for the taking. Pretty good odds. Assuming nobody cheated.

He wasn't sure where the thought had come from,

but once it had, it refused to leave. Blake found himself recalling their host's eyes, how coldly he had looked at Lisa when she'd argued with him. The gaze suggested a man who found the very idea of losing offensive. He'd cheat. Charlie, too. And Jason—if he thought he could get away with it. Brent probably wouldn't, but he didn't seem too bright to begin with. He'd probably go along with whatever his teammates decided.

Crap. Well, it wasn't like they could do anything about that. Worrying wouldn't help, anyway, and Lisa and James would most likely start another fight over it. Blake decided to keep his thoughts to himself. For now. *I'm probably just being paranoid.* It made him feel a tiny bit better.

Not much, though.

"Don't you think it's strange how he seems to know all of us?" Lisa said suddenly.

James blinked. "Who knows who?"

"GM. Our host."

Blake winced inwardly at the annoyed expression that traversed his friend's face. "He's nobody I know."

"Maybe he went to our school before but his parents transferred him out," Blake said tentatively.

For a moment something flickered across Lisa's face. Almost—but not quite—recognition. She shook her head impatiently. "I don't know. I don't think I've seen him before." This, she directed towards James, responding to the insinuated accusation. "But he won't tell us his name, so I can't tell for sure."

Blake had also been wondering about the name thing. That was weird. Especially since the white team didn't seem to have a clue who he was, either.

"He seems to know Val, though," Lisa said, after a pause. "And the way she reacted to him—it was almost as if she knew him, too."

James frowned suddenly. "Yeah. She said he reminded her of that creepy guy who she used to hang around with freshman year."

"Gavin?" Lisa blinked, startled. "She said he reminded her of Gavin?"

"Wow. Now there's a blast from my past. But he looks nothing like—" She trailed off in thought. "Hmm."

"Who's Gavin?" Blake asked.

"Oh, that's right," Lisa said, looking up. "You wouldn't remember, would you? You only moved here sophomore year. Gavin was—"

"Val's first boyfriend," James said.

"Not her boyfriend," Lisa interjected. "A boyfriend wouldn't do what that man did to her." She locked eyes with Blake. "He alienated her from her friends, forced her to lie to her family. I knew he was a loser, but I didn't know how sick he was. I guess I tried to warn her but I was kind of a bitch back then—" she laughed deprecatingly "—a bigger bitch than I am now, anyway.

And I guess I was kind of jealous that a big upperclassman was interested in her, and not me. Even if he was a loser. She ignored me, anyway, and it almost cost us our friendship. And all the while, the son of a bitch was herding her deeper and deeper into this fucking web, toying with her thoughts and feelings by pretending to be something he wasn't."

"And what was he?" Blake asked, his mouth dry.

"A monster." Lisa gritted her teeth. "A manipulative psychopath. He got off on fear, and somehow he came to the conclusion that Val was the perfect girl to play lamb to his lion."

"Oh, Jesus," Blake said, feeling sick. "I think I read something about that when we moved here. I didn't know it was about Val." *Is that who she meant earlier? When she said GM reminded her of somebody dangerous?*

"It wouldn't have her name," Lisa said. "She was only fourteen, and the sick fuck paid her parents hush-money to keep it out of the courtroom. We never talk about it." She closed her eyes, drew in a deep breath. "I'm pretty sure GM isn't Gavin, though. Superficial similarities aside, Val didn't look scared enough. She'd go out of her mind if she saw him again. And besides—"

"He's back on the East Coast, to work through his Freudian mommy issues?" James suggested.

Lisa looked at him, her expression bitter. "Yeah. That, and he would have already done something to her—and us— by now."

■□■□■□■

He was circling, like a wolf deciding where to land the killing strike, and the comparison made Val's tongue wither up inside her mouth. *Like the wolf in the closet. Like the wolf in the closet that he left there for me.* Most of the questions Jason had already asked were impersonal, though, and, in Val's opinion, slightly pointless. Hardly worth blackmailing over. Why would he waste his eight questions on trivialities—unless there was a purpose to them she hadn't noticed. Or he was trying to distract her from the bigger picture.

Val was too tired to give in to the conspiracy theories swarming her head like locusts. She just wanted to be alone, and think…and plan.

"Last question," Jason said at last, much to Val's relief. "How did you and Lisa become friends?"

"What kind of a question is that?"

"A simple one," he said condescendingly. "You aren't anything alike. It must be an interesting story."

Well aren't you just Mr. Observant? Well, duh. Of course he was. Almost uncannily so. He couldn't have trapped her into this situation, otherwise. "It wasn't."

"I want to hear anyway."

Of course you do. "Lisa wasn't always so outgoing," she allowed, shoving her thumbs through the belt loops of her jeans and rocking back on her heels. "She was the new girl back in middle school, and didn't have any friends. Except me. I was her first friend."

"Until she became the social butterfly and you become the wallflower," Jason guessed. "Interesting. And she stayed friends with you out of loyalty? No. Out of…pity, perhaps?"

"Shut up!" Val growled, stepping forward suddenly. "You…you—you don't know what you're talking about. So just shut the hell up right now!"

Jason snorted. "Jesus, Val. Don't get your panties in a twist."

She felt her face color. "You—"

"I have the upper-hand," the utterly repulsive boy continued, "Really, I can say anything I like, do anything I like—within reason, obviously—and you can't stop me. So don't tempt me, Val."

Her eyes had adjusted to the darkness in the last few minutes or so, allowing her faint glimpses of sealed doors and her captor's knowing smirk. When she spoke again, it was not fear that made her voice tremble, but rage. "We had a deal."

"Pissing me off voids it." Jason glanced over his shoulder, and Val thought she saw a shadow shift against the far wall. But it was over before she blinked, so she couldn't be sure. "Luckily for you, I think you're a riot. So, how about getting out of this hallway? You know, before anyone jumps to any conclusions about *us.*"

I could push him down the stairs, Val thought, shaking with pent-up emotion. *I won't, I couldn't—but oh, God forgive me, I want to.*

She waited behind him, but Jason held up his hand. "Oh no, you don't. I'm not having you club me or anything from behind. Ladies first."

"I don't know the way," Val said flatly, shaken that he had read her so easily. *Even he knows how repulsive he is.*

Or maybe she was just that predictable.

"I'll guide you," Jason said. "You don't have to be so sore with me. It's nothing personal. I'm merely using this situation to my advantage. Don't tell me you wouldn't do the same. Left, here."

Val turned grudgingly, not trusting herself to look behind her, not letting herself think about whether or not the creep was checking out her ass. "I'm sure Hitler and Stalin said the same thing."

That made him laugh, much to her annoyance and disgust. "It's a game, not a dictatorship."

"It amounts to the same thing in chess, doesn't it?" It did to Gavin, anyway. Wins and losses, with people as mere pieces to be won—or taken by force. "One person holds all the power. There's no emotional judgment required, either. The logic is reptilian enough that they can teach machines how to play chess."

Jason laughed, and she had a childish urge to cover her ears with the palms of her hands until he stopped. "It's really too bad you aren't on our side."

"Why?"

"Right, then straight. Because you're actually rather intelligent—unlike the rest of your teammates—and yet, you have no idea of the advantage that you have.... And you aren't even using it." He shook his head ruefully, "It's pathetic, really pathetic. What a waste. If you used it correctly, you could go so far."

"Then why don't you use it?" Val snapped. "What's stopping you? Common decency?"

"Biology," Jason said, with an audible smirk.

Before she could respond to that puzzling statement, they had arrived in the parlor. Everything was almost exactly the same as they had left it; the mahogany sitting chairs, the silent TV, the half-eaten food, and the Oriental rug—nothing was out of place. For some reason she couldn't explain, that seemed wrong. "What do you mean? How is biology my advantage?" she asked, turning around, only to find that Jason had vanished. Without a single parting word, he had left her in the beautiful but creepily empty room.

Alone. At last. She was thirsty—her mouth was,

anyway. She poured herself a lukewarm drink, which she sipped as she examined the parlor. A thorough search of the chairs had yielded nothing but lint, and a dime that must have fallen out of one of the players' pockets. Val was a little disappointed—she'd been hoping to find another chess piece or, at the very least, some indication of what she was supposed to be doing in this game—but mostly, she felt relief that she was free from that grim, shadowed corridor. And Jason, too, for that matter.

She would have to be a lot more careful around Jason and definitely avoid the grandmaster at all costs— not that she hadn't been doing that already, but he always seemed to find her when she was alone. As if he was following her.

No, things hadn't been going well for her at all. What advantage was Jason talking about? Surely, he hadn't been referring to the penalty round? *He said something about biology. Penalty round can't be the advantage. Otherwise, it'd be called 'bonus round,' and it'd be a reward—not a punishment.*

Val looked around for a trashcan and, not finding one, simply dropped her cup on the floor, taking spiteful delight in the way the dark, viscous liquid stained the expensive-looking carpet. *Take that, you son of a bitch.* She bypassed the staircase, exploring the first floor. She passed a spacious dining room with a dangling chandelier, a bathroom, and a massive library; the shelves of which stretched clear up to the ceiling. None of the rooms provided any clues, however, and Val continued around the corner.

Val looked up at a framed portrait of an owl moth, and shivered at the large, fake eyes staring out at the observer. Very creepy. She was not surprised. She bit her lip, looking around the room, wondering if the door was open because it had already been explored. But no, a white pawn, barely visible among the tacky plaid pattern of the comforter, was peeking out from under the pillow. Like the other piece, it, too, contained a message. She unraveled the paper inside, revealing the words, "The game." A box enclosed the two words, presumably to show that they were a pair. What game? Val wondered, and then berated herself for it. Chess, obviously. It was always about chess, always about capture.

Then something else fell out, on a different kind of paper. The writing, too, was different. Inkier, hastier. The words they contained made her freeze with a different kind of fear.

Behind you.

The door behind her slammed closed.

Chapter Thirteen

Breakthrough

She knew who was behind her without turning around. Even so, she jumped, nearly knocking over the bedside lamp with the moth-eaten shade.

Gavin.

The flickering light made his angular features look even more menacing and a cold chill seemed to emanate from his body, though that could also be attributed to the draft from the door slamming shut so quickly.

For a moment, neither of them moved, his posture threatening and hers defensively wary. She hated the way her heart seized when she looked up from the lamp she was steadying with a shaking hand and saw him smile, because it wasn't entirely due to fear. The villains were always ugly in books and movies. Necessarily so, it seemed. Because if they were attractive—if their looks matched their charm and their cunning—they wouldn't only be dangerous.

They would be *irresistible*.

She drew in an unsteady breath and took a step back, cursing herself for such thoughts. He matched her retreat with a step forward, letting his folded arms fall to his sides. His face was intent; this was part of the thrill, after all. Better to chase prey that was aware of its pursuit, because fear would make it run faster and fight harder.

Horrorscape by Nenia Campbell

And he loves a good chase.

(Plus ça change, plus c'est la même chose)

Everything had changed; nothing had changed.

"What do you want now?" Val tried to sound defiant, hostile. It came out sounding like a wretched plea.

His eyes shuttered. She watched his weight shift forward, as if he were considering closing the distance between them, and then back again as he relaxed into another one of his lackadaisical poses. But not slouching—never slouching. She had never caught him with his head down. His eyes were watchful, though, regarding her thoughtfully, the way one might look upon a painting, as if he might find some sort of elaborate symbolism there.

The porcelain resisted beneath her trembling hand. She was still holding onto the lamp; it felt like the base might just snap in her hands. Val thought she might snap, too, if she was left with nothing solid to hold onto, left to deal with the figure from her nightmares…alone.

"You needn't look at me like that. I'm not going to attack you." Val went rigid and the smile became a sultry grin. "I might bite you a little, though."

Val opened her mouth to repeat her question, then immediately thought better of it. "Stay away from me," she warned, stepping back. "D-don't come any closer."

"I don't see how I can resist. Not when you look at

me with those fear-filled eyes."

She tightened her hand around the neck of the lamp and hurled it at him—it happened so quickly, she was barely aware of doing it, blinded as she was by the rage and fear that bubbled through her like champagne. He dropped to the floor, throwing up his arm to protect his face as the lamp shattered against the closed door, raining porcelain and glass against his back.

In the small space between them, the crash sounded like thunder. Did one of the others hear it? She remembered the muffling effects of the wall. Probably not.

He took off his white jacket and cravat, tossing both on the ground rather than merely brushing them off. His eyes were as sharp and hard as the gleaming pieces that surrounded him. Val took another step back automatically at that look. She had seen it once before—a cold, determined look incapable of mercy.

"Well. To what do I owe such a violent reception?"

Val jumped when her posterior come into contact with the edge of the bed. Trapped. She dug her hands into the comforter, bracing herself. "I—" She moistened her dry lips and his eyes followed the movement. Her heart thudded in her chest and her blood seemed to turn to heavy sludge in her veins. "I hate you," she said. "I wish you were in *jail*. I wish you were—"

"Dead?" He smiled thinly.

"You've been spreading rumors about me. Lies. To your team." She made herself look him in the eyes. They were even more intimidating in the light—pale, blueless gray, with motes of darker gray and gold caught in the iris. Beautiful eyes, she thought. Deadly eyes. Tigers had eyes like that. So did serpents. "To Jason," she added, viciously. "That we—that is…you…"

"Yes?" he said. Softly. Dangerously.

Her heart gave another warning stutter. But she couldn't bring herself to say it. Because Val wasn't entirely sure what *it* was. All she knew was that Jason had somehow gotten the impression that she and GM had some kind of—well, *physical*—relationship.

And it's not like I can refute it, either, because they'll ask for proof. I know they will. I can't give it without telling the truth—

Because though the truth might set her free, it would imprison her friends in her stead.

"Son of a bitch," she hissed, her anger momentarily overcoming her fear. "You tricked me."

"I beg your pardon?"

"That's why you wanted me to keep the truth a secret. You knew someone would find out—" Val sneaked a look at his face. It betrayed no outrage or indignation, only mild amusement. "What did you say to him?"

"You're acting hysterical, Val."

"What did you say to Jason?"

"Just look at yourself." He stepped closer to catch her by the chin, and their bodies brushed. "On the edge of the abyss, one push away from madness." Val leaned away from him, bracing her weight against her arms to keep from falling back against the bed. GM smiled and leaned closer, until she was suspended at an uncomfortably obtuse angle above the mattress on shaking arms.

"The only one here who's crazy is *you*."

"That means you're trapped with a madman, my dear. A psychopath." He drew out the word. "Your friend saw the fatal flaw in that line of reasoning far more quickly than you." At her expression, he said, "Mm-hmm. She's a clever girl, your Lisa. She suspects something is going on, though she isn't quite sure what. You're going to have to avoid her, if you wish for our little agreement to remain valid. And I am certain you wouldn't want her to see you in this position." He pushed down, hard, using his weight to buckle her arms and knock her into a supine sprawl. "Who knows what wild conclusions she might leap to?"

His fingers wrapped around her throat like a collar.

"No, you had better hope that I am—" he drew in a breath "—the very flower of sanity. If only for your friend's sake. Don't you agree?"

She couldn't breathe; she was forced to back up, to

slacken his grip, sliding against his body and even more firmly into his embrace. His scent, his very presence—all of it was overwhelming. She had to close her eyes to keep from going into sensory overload, from her mind spinning off its axis and out of control. When she was able to look at him again, his face was inches from hers.

"Don't you *agree*?"

"No."

"No?" he repeated, tasting the word, and the defiance of it. "My, but you are determined to vilify me, aren't you? Well. That is a role I can play very well."

"Not a role," Val gasped. She tried to twist away, but his hand was like a vise around her throat. "Real."

Gavin shook his head, letting his free hand trail down her face and she realized that her cheeks were wet with tears. "Don't play with things you don't understand. They might play back, perhaps far better than you." He loosened his collar, then, undoing the buttons halfway as dexterously with one hand as many were with both. "So. Let's *play*."

And then he kissed her.

■□■□■□■

Charlie gripped the black knight until its base formed a reddish imprint in the palm of her hand and her fingers began to ache in dull protest. She paid them no mind. The ache inside was far worse, more bitter than sweet, and tinged with anger as she watched the two fumble on the bed.

Val had said herself that she wasn't interested in GM, that she already had a boyfriend, so just what the hell did she call this? Hypocritical little slut. She obviously just wanted him for herself.

Not that Charlie could really blame her. Well, yes, she could—and did—but she understood the rationale behind it. Because he truly was something else. She stared at him unabashedly, at his half-buttoned shirt, at the tangled dark hair on his chest. Was he that hairy all over his body? He growled softly at Val, tightening his grip on her throat as he bit her lip.

She could have stormed in, made a big scene, and humiliated Val to boot. That alone might have been worth it, seeing the expression on the bitch's face. She could have, but she didn't. It simply wasn't her style.

Her parents were notoriously absentee during her childhood, so she spent the vast majority of it under the care of her grandfather—an avid sportsman whose one goal in life, it seemed, was to shoot an animal on every continent. Sometimes he would take her and her twin brother with him. Charlie had enjoyed these outings, though she had been loathe to go into her grandfather's study where he kept his trophies for fear that the animals would suddenly come to life, glass eyes sparkling with a terrible vengeance, and consume her whole.

But if her grandfather had taught her one thing, it was that the most difficult things to achieve were often the most worthwhile. The fact that he had illustrated this lesson with a lecture about a particularly ferocious Siberian tiger he'd killed in the taiga made it no less pertinent a life lesson.

In fact, if anything, it might make it even more relevant.

A wan smile crossed her face as she pictured their host dropped into a cat-like crouch, crawling, on his knees. For *her*. The image was surprisingly easy to conjure up, and rather striking. With his dark, Roman looks and lean, muscular build, he resembled a jaguar. He was nice and tall, but didn't carry himself with the awkward slouch most boys of his sheer height adopted. Sure, he could pretend to be polite and gracious all he wanted, but nothing about him—not even his walk—denoted subservience.

So why *Val*? Maybe this innocent act was just that—an act. Maybe he liked the idea of a reluctant schoolgirl. Charlie honestly couldn't see the attraction there, unless GM got off on intimidation—which, if the charming scene before her was any indication of his sexual proclivities, seemed to be the case. *Really, GM? How predictable.*

GM glanced up at the door—she'd left it open—and their eyes met. She felt a thrill go through her at the sheer intensity of his expression. He broke the connection and kissed the other girl, long and hard, winding his free hand through her red hair. When we glanced up again, she could read the warning there. It pissed her off.

But he was still glaring at her through those hooded eyes, and the thought of invoking his wrath sent a shiver down her spine of an entirely different nature. *Fine*, she thought, trying to convince herself that she really didn't care. *Let him have the dumb slut, if that's what he wants.*

She would follow her grandfather's advice. She would wait. Charlie nearly felt cheerful when she walked away. She did not even notice the piece of paper that fluttered out of her pocket. The clue was "Queen."

■□■□■□■

Like a fly that had suddenly found itself ensnared in a venomous spider's web, by the time Val detected the impending capture it was too late. She had forgotten how thorough—no, invasive—his kisses were. How, in a time that now seemed to be in another epoch, he had once kissed her so deeply that she could barely remember her own name, let alone stand.

In the heartbeat he gave her to catch her breath, Val could make out the tartness of rose, the spiciness of sandalwood, and the musky, male scent that was inherently his. *We've played this game before—and I lost.*

Val jolted into awareness when he began to unbutton her blouse. She cried out and shoved at his chest, driving a knee upward. He twisted his hips to avoid the blow and repositioned himself so her legs were being compressed by his muscular thighs. He ran his fingers lightly across her bared collarbone.

"Don't worry. I only want to play with you a little."

Her belly corkscrewed traitorously. *Not this again.*

She grabbed his throat, trying to hook her fingers around his necklace. He made a sharp noise as his air supply was abruptly closed off. He grabbed at her hands, collapsing against her in the process as his weight was no longer mediated by the bracing of his arms. Val wheezed as two-hundred-something pounds of Gavin squeezed out what precious little air remained in her lungs. She could feel every hitch of his body as he struggled to breathe.

He'd been so overwhelming when she was fourteen. He still was. Perhaps even more so here, at this moment, because now she knew what kinds of games men and women played in the dark.

But in spite of all that, he's still only human.

She tightened her grip, knotting the metal links around her knuckles to cinch it all the more tightly around his neck.

His eyes narrowed, and he tore her hands away

from the chain with much more force than necessary. She yelped as one of her fingernails caught and ripped. "All right," he rasped, "We can play rough."

He kissed her again, harder, yanking the sleeves of her sweater down her arms to pin her wrists behind her back, forcing her body into an unnatural arch that bowed against his. Even if intimidation had been his original intent, his motives were quickly shifting towards the sexual.

Their teeth clicked together as he prized her mouth open wide enough to get his tongue inside before she could bite. She kept hers firmly pressed against the floor of her mouth. She felt him smile as he levered her tongue up with his, stroking the sensitive underside in a rough caress.

Val strained, trying to work her arms free. The best way, of course, would be to wriggle back and forth using her own momentum to slide the sweater off her hands. It would also involve rubbing herself against him, as he undoubtedly knew. She pulled back, trying to get herself clear to bite him hard and choked in mingled horror and outrage when she felt his hand slide neatly into her unbuttoned blouse.

"You're so warm. Hot almost." His hands were quite a bit larger than James's, rough and unfamiliar against her skin. "And your heart is beating like a little bird's wings."

"Stop. Please, stop."

"I thought I wasn't doing anything to you," he said, his voice rough. His fingers played across the tingling surface of her skin, silencing her retort. With a satisfied smile, he turned from her mouth to her neck. She shivered when he moved down her throat, sucking on her flesh hard enough to break the delicate blood vessels that lay just beneath the surface. He gave her a searing, provocative look and moved lower, holding the fabric of her shirt aside so he could replace his fingers with his mouth. Where his lips touched, her skin caught fire. "Isn't this what you *wanted*?"

Nerve endings sizzled and her brain whited out. "James."

His teeth bit into her flesh rather punishingly at the sound of her boyfriend's name and the resultant sensation shot like an arrow into her breast. She jerked beneath him like a fish caught on a hook. "Yes. *Has James ever touched you like this, Val?*"

She nodded. She would have nodded at anything if she thought it might make him let her go.

In response, he lifted his head with the same stately grace as a tiger and kissed her on the mouth, letting his hips mold against hers until she could feel every inch of him through her jeans. He was breathing harder now, but it did nothing to mask the cold, cruel intentness in his eyes.

"Liar," he said softly.

Horrorscape by Nenia Campbell

She would have screamed at him, if not for fear that someone—James, Oh God—might hear her. Val could hardly imagine a more incriminating situation, both of them half-dressed, on a bed, the room heavy with something too dark and twisted to be mere lust. Her hands were losing feeling, and buzzed with angry numbness that mimicked the panic in her blood.

"How would you know?"

"I know because you're a poor liar, and an only slightly better kisser. He clearly hasn't had you yet. And since he hasn't yet taught you how to satisfy his own pleasures, he has undoubtedly failed to even consider yours."

"Shut up." Her voice was unrecognizable to her own ears. "You're *wrong*."

"I'm never wrong." He pushed something solid into her hand and then got to his feet, giving her the space to free herself. The cold rushed in to take his place, and she fumbled to hold her blouse closed. "I'll be outside, waiting. Once you've composed yourself, meet me there."

Val looked down at her palm uncertainly. She was holding a white king.

The clue was *lives*.

■□■□■□■

Lisa disentangled a spiderweb from her long blond hair with a shudder of disgust.

"Here," Blake offered, carefully removing the wispy thread. "It's just a web. There's no spider."

"Like that matters," Lisa said sourly. "It's still sticky and creepy and disgusting."

Blake shrugged, allowing the web to fall to the ground. "For the spider, it's home."

It had been Lisa's idea to go upstairs. They had already cleaned the downstairs rooms of their chess pieces—the ones they could find, anyway—and Lisa wasn't about to let the *menfolk* make all the decisions. Plus, she was hoping to get a peek at GM's bedroom, if only to get some sort of glimpse into their mysterious host's personality. She was starting to rue her decision.

"I'm going back downstairs," James announced.

"Why?" Lisa looked up from the door she was trying. "You afraid of the creepy-crawlies, too?"

"Gonna look for Val," he muttered. Lisa watched him go with a silent shake of her head.

"That probably isn't a bad idea," Blake remarked. "She's been gone an awfully long time."

Lisa slammed her shoulder against the door. "What is wrong with this thing?"

"It's locked, Lisa," Blake said, in a reasonable voice she didn't care for. "Let's try another."

"He wouldn't lock it unless he had something to hide," Lisa pointed out.

"Or maybe he just doesn't want people snooping around in his room."

Lisa's eyes narrowed. "I am not snooping!" Blake raised one tawny eyebrow but said nothing. Her irritation soared. "Don't look at me like that. I'm not."

"Then what exactly are you doing?"

"I'm…*investigating*. It's because I'm worried about Val!" she added, when Blake affected pointed silence. "GM gives me bad vibes. I want to find out more about him, and why he's interested in her." *I want to make sure he doesn't have any actual skeletons in his closets.*

"And why he won't tell us his name?"

"That, too." *And why he threatened me. And why Val is so terrified of him. And why James refuses to take a stand against him. And why the white team is perfectly happy to act as his pawns.* "I think it's really strange that there's no family pictures."

"Some families aren't into that sort of thing."

"You'd think that there would at least be baby pictures, little league pictures, school pictures, prom or graduation pictures—something. I mean, it's not like he's bad-looking." Quite the opposite, in fact There was a pause, longer than usual, which prompted Lisa to add, "Blake?"

No response.

Horrorscape by Nenia Campbell

Lisa turned around slowly. An empty hallway greeted her. "Blake?" *He was here a moment ago. Where the hell had he disappeared off to?* "Blake!" Lisa repeated, stepping away from the door. "Goddammit, Blake," she muttered, pulling up the bodice of her dress. "This is starting to turn into a bad movie."

The narrow hallway branched off into several doors, lit by a lonely bulb swinging lazily from the ceiling. Something about that image struck her as wrong. It took her a moment to realize why:

There's no breeze.

Chapter Fourteen

Attraction

Lives.

The word stretched across the white paper in spidery cursive—vague and infuriating, just like him. *That's all?* She glanced at the place GM had been standing moments before. He was gone, though he had left the door ajar. Taunting her. Daring her to follow. After all that.... She quickly did up her shirt, feeling a wave of loathing so strong she was unable to stand from the force of it.

Even now, she was overly aware of the feeling of her clothes against her skin: a sweet chafing that buzzed with the hollow echoes of pleasure as yet unfulfilled. *He had done that to her and she hated him for it, because it was never like that with James*—and she hated to think about what that might say about *her*.

Broken glass crunched beneath her feet as she made her way to the door. She wished he'd been cut, that her attack had drawn blood. Just once.

He was leaning back against the wall with one knee bent, his arms folded over his shirtfront, which he hadn't bothered to do up all the way. The light sheen of sweat on her back turned to crystals of rime. *It's like he's reminding me he didn't finish what he started.*

She averted her eyes and realized only too late that might be taken as a sign of weakness. She needed to get out of here. She was afraid of what she might do if she stayed in his presence a moment longer. Tears seemed to be the most likely candidate, and she'd be damned before she let him see her cry again, but violence was starting to look like a viable option, too. When she had thrown that lamp at him, it was as if her common sense had been obliterated by white-hot rage. Part of her had wanted to *kill* him.

If he succeeds in taking away my self-control, he wins. I won't let him be the master of me. I'm *the master of me. Nobody else.*

He still hadn't said anything, so she turned away and began to walk briskly in the opposite direction. She heard a sound that might have been a chuckle but could have easily been a warning. It must have been the latter, because seconds later he grabbed her by her upper arms.

"I don't recall saying you could leave."

"Tell me what you want or fuck off," she said shakily.

"Ah, Val—ever the charmer. But then, you do have such a way with words."

Val pulled away, and he let her. She stumbled several steps away before she hazarded a backwards glance. He hadn't moved, and was watching her with thinly-veiled amusement. There was a flush of color in his face that hadn't been there before. *"You,"* she said, in a shaking voice, *"you* are fifty different kinds of twisted."

"Only fifty? Val, you wound me."

"I want to leave."

"Without your gift?"

"I don't want anything from you. I want to go."

"You don't even know what it is."

"I don't care. With you, *nothing* is free."

GM slipped an envelope from the pocket of his pants, somehow managing to take a step closer as he did so. "How true that is." She eyed it warily, her attention wavering between the bit of parchment and its wielder. It was just like the one she'd received before, the invitation.

This letter—if it was a letter—was sealed with wax, though. Her name was written on the outside in ink that glittered like mica. She started to reach for it, checked the impulse, and folded her arms.

"I said *no.*"

"It's not like I'm asking you to sell me your soul." He chucked her under the chin with the envelope. "Just don't open it until I say so."

"How would you know?" she said numbly, staring at the envelope, weighing it in her hands. How had it gotten there? She couldn't remember taking it from him.

"What was that, Val?"

It took her a moment to realize what she'd said. "I…how would you know? W-what if I just read it when you leave?"

For a moment, he seemed taken aback, as if such a magnitude of defiance was beyond him. But then he laughed, and she wondered if he hadn't been expecting such a response after all. In either case, he regained his composure so quickly, it didn't really matter. "That would be cheating. I think we both know how that fits in with your...moral code."

The envelope crinkled as her grip around it tightened. "I don't cheat," she hissed.

He shot her a meaningful look that made her insides shudder. She clenched her jaw and prayed that her body's subtler movements were not quite so betraying in the dark. "But since you ask, I'd be able to tell if you broke the seal. Perhaps not right away...but soon enough."

She picked at the wax rebelliously, causing reddish fragments to flake to the floor. "So?"

"I don't think it's in your best interests to do that. There will be consequences. Collateral, you might call it, to ensure this arrangement is honored by both sides." He plucked at his necklace and said, "Yours, specifically."

The hand holding the envelope became a fist. "What—"

"If you open the envelope—assuming you do decide to defy me—you have to give me seven minutes of your time."

Seven minutes? "I...I know that game," she said faintly.

"Then I won't need to explain the rules to you."

"But—that's a child's game. You want to play a child's game for—for seven minutes?" She might as well just kiss the bastard now and get it over with. It was no worse than anything he'd done to her already.

"You aren't a child," he said. "You aren't bound by a child's rules—or a child's imagination, for that matter. Yes, now you're beginning to understand," he said, as her features rearranged themselves into something that must have remembered horror. "You still have an imagination, don't you, Val? You're going to need one—to play with me."

Val punched him. And then, she punched him again. And again. It didn't matter that he managed to dodge two of them; it made her feel better. At the very least, it had wiped the satisfied smirk from his lips. "Take it back then," she snapped, in between blows. "Take it back!"

"I don't think you'd like the consequences of that, either." He managed to catch one of her swinging fists, and squeezed absently, making her yip. She felt his fingers wrap around her other wrist and her shoulders sank, prompting him to lean in. "Or perhaps...you would."

She stomped his foot—hard. He hissed in mingled pain and surprise, and his grip loosened. Val slipped out of his grasp, rubbing her wrists. All she could hear was her heartbeat. GM looked at her, his eyes slightly narrowed, reevaluating his approximation of her.

"I'm not opening it." Val shoved the envelope in her jeans. Or tried to. She missed the first shot; her hands were trembling too violently.

"You never know," he mused. "Accidents happen."

And remembering his threat from earlier, she gagged.

■□■□■□■

Bulbs did not just move of their own accord. Not without some kind of draft…or someone to cause said draft. The instant the thought occurred to her, Lisa whirled around, nearly tripping over the heels of her shoes. *As soon as I get home, I'm donating these to Goodwill.*

"Blake?" She kept her voice low. "James? Val?" She hesitated a long moment. "GM?"

Lisa rubbed her bare arms. She felt cold, suddenly, and was beginning to wonder if there wasn't a window open somewhere after all—it was pretty dusty and disgusting in here—when somebody grabbed her arm from behind. She let out a startled shriek. "What the hell? Who's there?"

"Me," the someone said unhelpfully.

She recognized the voice, though. Only one person was so obnoxious, so socially-challenged, that they would think this an acceptable form of greeting "Jackson."

"Actually—" the voice sounded affronted "—it's Jason."

"I don't care if it's Kris Kringle," she said coldly. "Let go of me right now."

He clicked his tongue. It made her want to slap him. Everything he did made her want to slap him. "Why am I getting the feeling that you don't like me very much?"

"Probably because I don't, you utter freak of nature," she snapped. "I swear, if you don't let me go right now—"

"You know," Jason interjected, "You're not as dumb as I thought. When I first saw you, I figured you were an airhead."

"Funny," Lisa said, starting to become frightened in spite of herself. "I had you pegged as a dickhead."

"But you aren't an airhead," he finished smoothly, as if she hadn't spoken. "I overheard part of your conversation with GM, you see, so I know. So why are you pretending to be something you're not?"

Lisa yanked her arm. "Let *go*, Jason."

"You got my name right. That's a start."

Thin tendrils of fear wrapped around the logic

center of her brain. She felt herself on the verge of losing control. She balled her hands into fists, wincing when her long nails cut into her palms. "What do you want?" she snapped, after an interminable silence.

"A partnership."

"Ask your own team."

"I'd love to," was the dry response, "But GM and Charlie have their own agendas and Brent—well, Brent just sits around like a bump on a log. Not exactly the best material to work with."

"My heart bleeds for you." Lisa filed the bit about Charlie and GM away. She wondered what they did, when they went off on their own. Was GM using that time to harass Val? Jason would know, probably. He'd already established himself as residential spy. *Stealing GM's intimidation tactics, to boot.* Too bad for him, he was way too pathetic for it to be even half as effective.

Though half as effective might be bad enough.

"So fuck off," she added. "I have my own team and, unlike yours, they're actually functional."

"Oh really," he sneered. "Val seems to be doing a lot of disappearing herself. James, too."

Something about that needled her, though she couldn't quite put her finger on why. "Doesn't matter," Lisa shot back. "We have Blake, as well—and he's twice as smart as you think you are."

Even in the darkness, she saw his face grow rigid.

And she had time to think *Oh crap* right before he lunged.

■□■□■□■

She had performed a complete roundabout, heading away from the parlor in the process, and now the hallway was beginning to widen as Val came to the place where it branched off into the staircase.

The thick envelope crinkled as she turned to regard the hallways, reminding her of its presence.

Dust hovered thickly in the air, and when Val breathed in next the inside of her mouth was coated with it. She coughed and swallowed dryly, wincing at how loud the sound was in the silence. She wished she'd had the forethought to steal a bottle of water from the buffet table in the starting room, but her mind had, of course, been on other things. She covered her mouth tightly in a futile attempt to muffle the sound, and heard a furtive movement only partially eclipsed by her own.

Her eyes jumped from one end of the hallway to the other, before swinging up sharply at a sound from above. Val froze like a rabbit. From the groans of the wooden boards, somebody was descending those steps. Unlike the stairs in Val's own home, however, this staircase had a slight curve, so that someone on one of the higher steps would be able to view those below without being noticed.

Can they see me? Are they looking at me right now?

"Val?"

The stunned fearful expression slowly gave way to relief. "James?" He stepped into her line of sight. His face was taut, grave, and his hands were tightly clenched at his sides. He looked as tense as she felt, and that pained her. It was like seeing her own misery reflected back at her.

At that thought, Val was overcome by a wave of…something—not quite affection or sympathy, but more of a cathexis, instilled with a sense of duty and emotional obligation. She bounded up to the brown-haired boy, wrapping her arms around his waist, and breathed in the scent of fabric softener and Old Spice on his starched black shirt. It was a little comforting, but not by much.

James didn't respond, but she felt him stiffen beneath her touch. She let her arms fall away as she took a slow step back. The blankness on his face frightened her. "James?"

Very slowly, he turned to look at her. His sea-foam eyes burned with a soft charge that trickled into his features like drips of water from a melting glacier, slowly transforming the overall whole. And, she couldn't help noticing, he didn't seem especially pleased to see her. Then again, he hadn't the last time she'd seen him, either. Because the last time she had seen him, she had failed to defend him properly in front of GM, in spite of her own fears, and in a fit of temper he had left her—*left her*—convinced of treachery before she'd committed the crime.

What if he saw Gavin kiss me?

GM had left the door open. Perhaps there had been a purpose to that. Wound two birds with one stone.

Or maybe Jason had broken his promise, which would mean that she had betrayed Lisa for nothing.

Val swallowed, hard, and sneaked another look at his face. He was glaring, now, and a bolt of panic flashed through her like lightening. *He knows.* The pit of her stomach lurched like a small boat caught in the ebb of the same storm. She ducked her head again, trying to keep from hyperventilating. *Somehow, he knows.*

"James, I—"

"We need to talk."

His words, and the tone they were spoken in, send a wave of coldness through her. "I…I…can explain…"

"I don't want to hear it." James shook his head firmly, and Val thought she might vomit. "I've had some time to think—because this so-called game is pretty much shit—and…well, I'm not very good at this kind of thing, but…" He sighed angrily, and his bangs blew upwards in an indignant puff. "I've been an asshole. There."

This was so far from what Val had feared that for a moment she could only blink rapidly. "But—"

"Before you say anything, Lisa already chewed my ass out," he added. "She thinks I should have been more understanding about your, uh, issues." Then, seeming to realize that this invalidated his apology, he added hastily, "And she was right. About that. GM was being an even bigger asshole and I shouldn't have left you alone with him when he was making you so uncomfortable. Especially with what...with what, ah, happened." He paused. "I feel like a fucking tool."

At his earlier words, Val froze again. James didn't notice.

"I shouldn't have let him provoke me into being a tool, but he's just such a fucking asshole—GM is, I mean—and I don't like the way he speaks to me, or the way he looks at you. I mean talk about goddamn balls—" James glanced at her, seeming to only just realize the depth of her unease. "You're shaking," he said, seeming surprised. His eyes narrowed. "Did he hurt you?"

"No," she said, too quickly.

But he did. And you liked it, you know you did. Because deep down, you're fucked-up. Just as fucked-up as he is. Maybe more so. After all, you know better—you know what he's like.

"Val—"

"No," she whispered.

Horrorscape by Nenia Campbell

Under her boyfriend's penetrating gaze, she faltered a little, the blush draining from her complexion like water down a sewer, leaving her face bleached and pallid. And she shook her head, recalling even as she did so how right it felt to have him on top of her, walking a thin line between dangerous and deadly. How he could do things with his mouth she only thought possible in books, and how she had never imagined that pain could exist apart from agony, and oh, if he could do those things with his mouth, what could he do with the rest of his body?

Val thought all these things, and shuddered so violently that she nearly stumbled, and suddenly she was in James's arms, and her stomach hurt, and her head hurt, and her heart hurt worst of all, and before she knew it, she was crying, even though she had promised herself she wouldn't.

Because she was good at that, breaking promises.

James looked horrified. Or disgusted. Perhaps both. Or maybe she was just projecting her own feelings onto him. She wasn't exactly her own favorite person right now.

"Val?"

"I'm not crazy," she whimpered. "I'm not."

"I didn't say you were." But his eyes said he was thinking it.

Val looked away from his face. "I know…I know the

things I think and say might sound that way, but they aren't. As ridiculous as it might seem, you have to believe me. You have to trust me."

You have to trust me, because I no longer trust myself.

"OK, but why are you crying?"

"I can't tell you."

"Can't?" he said, "or won't?"

"I don't know."

She felt an arm wrap around her, and she burrowed into his armpit, burying her face into his shoulder. "Please stop." She felt him turn, as if he was afraid someone would see them. "Val, please. Don't cry. Not here. Not now."

"But I hate this game. I hate the white team. And I hate GM." Val said, but her words came out muffled.

James bowed his head lower. Even if he hadn't exactly heard her words, he understood the tone. And naturally, he assumed that he was the cause, the star around which his girlfriend's world orbited. "I'm sorry."

His solid warmth was like coming into a safe harbor after a vicious storm. James could be rather childish and annoying sometimes, but it didn't make him dangerous. That required a more calculated, purposeful form of cruelty. *I like being safe*, Val told herself. *I don't like being scared.*

They stood like that for several minutes, and James

was painfully aware of her soft skin, the sweet smell of her hair, the press of her breasts against his chest. And he realized, for the first time since the party started, that they were finally alone. His arm around her tightened, pulling her closer, and his other hand went around her waist, stroking the gap between her shirt and jeans. *She's fucking crazy*, he thought resignedly. He wondered if it was true what they said, that crazy people were better in bed.

"Can I kiss you?"

She nodded. His lips were soft, unobtrusive, and he still tasted vaguely like the cider he'd drunk earlier, though it had soured on his breath. He kissed with an awkwardness that was minimized by his confidence. Val closed her eyes and her heart trembled that the same form of contact could differ so vastly between two men.

I like this, she instructed herself. *I prefer this.*

"Oh, wow. That was…that was…. Minty," James murmured, smiling a little, though he looked confused. Not suspicious, though. Not yet. "Were you chewing gum?"

■□■□■□■

"God damn her."

The chess piece flew from his hand, momentarily transformed into a dangerous projectile—at least, until it collided with the wall across from him and fell to the floor with a clatter, before rolling underneath a table with carefully arranged chessmen carved in black and white.

"Running straight to him." He was breathing hard. "As if he could protect her from *me*."

Anger spiked through him again. When his hand slammed down on the table, the organized ranks of the chessmen dissolved into chaos. "As if she could fight me. As if she could run if she tried."

His face darkened, in response to some private, inner thought, and he sighed.

"No," he said aloud. "That's hardly appropriate." He paused, bending to scoop up some of the pieces from the floor. The set was ancient, the pieces carved out of ivory and ebony, steeped in history—and blood. He found himself holding the queen. "There is," he concluded, "A time and a place for everything."

He sat down on the edge of his bed, his features haggard in the dim light. There was a flash as his pale eyes moved downward, to regard the wooden piece of carved ebony in his hand. His thumb traveled over the well-worn notches, his mind on a very different piece— flesh, instead of wood. Fair, instead of dark. The taste of her was still in his mouth, salty and sweet, the thrum of her pulse like a spicy tingle scalding the tip of his tongue.

His belly clenched like a fist, as he recalled the sensation of rough lace and smooth satin yielding to soft, bare skin. His fingers tightened around the black queen and he leaned back. "There is a time and place for everything," he repeated softly, his anger spent but not exhausted.

After a few minutes he sat up, and let out a deep breath. He let the chess piece drop from his hand as he headed for the door, pausing only to pick up a top hat from his desk.

It's time to play another game.

Chapter Fifteen

Castling Into It

Was it the insult to his intelligence or the mention of Blake that had set him off? Either? Both? It hardly mattered. She cried out when his grip tightened—his arms were surprisingly strong—sending a bolt of pain through her belly and making her feel, momentarily, as if she urgently had to pee. "You think you're better than me," he breathed against her ear, his voice rough with anger.

And something else—something worse.

"I don't think," she snapped. "I *know*."

"Do you want to know what I think?" Ignoring her growl to the contrary, he went on, "I think you're overcompensating for something."

"Shut up."

"But what? Life must be so hard when you're beautiful. Though, perhaps you weren't always this pretty." She stiffened when his other hand sketched down her front. "Are you an ugly duckling, Lisa? Did some guy break your heart by deciding that you weren't fit to suck his dick?"

She drove her elbow into his ribs. Hard. "You bitch." He tightened his grip around her waist. Turning her around. Lisa was ready for this. Blinking away the tears in her eyes, she raised her knee and ground it into his crotch. He released her then, with a gasped, "Jesus fucking Christ," all traces of sleaziness gone now from both his face and his voice.

Jason doubled over, one arm wrapped around his midsection, the other cupping himself. He gagged. Lisa hoped he'd throw up. Hoped he'd choke on it. "That hurt," he whimpered.

"Good." Her eyes were still unnaturally bright. She took a step closer, keeping out of reach. She didn't think he'd grab for her again—not now—but she couldn't be sure. "Where's Blake?"

"How the hell should I know?"

Lisa lifted her foot warningly, spiked heel first, and was gratified to see him flinch.

"All right," he said nervously. "All right. You called my bluff. Hall closet. Two doors down."

She was tempted to kick him anyway. For a moment, they stared at her in mutual dislike, like two animals locked in combat. Her legs were still trembling. She could still smell whatever vile cologne it was that he was wearing. But most of all, she was scared how easily he'd read her, how easily he'd managed to catch her alone. Slowly, Lisa backed away from him. She refused to show fear.

"If you ever touch me again—" almost out the door "—I will make you so—" just one more step "—so sorry. Is that clear?"

He growled and made a threatening move towards

her.

She decided now was as good a time to leave as any.

■□■□■□■

Mint. The bitter taste of it hung between them like a silent accusation. Val held her breath when James opened his mouth but it was only to kiss her again. As if being driven by some primal urge to wipe all traces of Gavin away. She drew in a breath when his hand went up her shirt.

He pulled back, as if he'd been burned. "I'm sorry," he said, lowering his eyes.

"I need to sit down," said Val. "I feel dizzy."

"I'll choose to take that as a compliment," was James's dry response.

You do that. They sat down on the steps, Val holding her head to keep the floor from spinning. James was looking at her; he seemed both worried and irritated. Why, she could only guess. For several minutes they were silent, though he eventually put an arm around her.

("Has James ever touched you like this, Val?")

She must have made some sort of movement—a shudder—because suddenly James moved to the step below hers, nudging himself between her legs, and kissed her again. She didn't stop him this time, and it quickly deepened. He groaned softly, and Val opened her eyes in annoyance.

His were open, too. "You have gorgeous eyes."

She smiled, but only a little.

"And gorgeous freckles."

He moved forward, and began to lap at her face with his tongue. Soon, she was laughing, laughing so hard that it hurt, because oh god, it tickled. She felt James smile against her skin as he gently nudged her backwards. "Stop," she protested.

"Make me," he growled, and an unexpected thrill shot through her.

"Oh." The sharp edge of the step was digging into her back, achingly familiar and excruciatingly uncomfortable, reasserting its presence every time she drew in a gasping breath. "*James.*"

"They all look the same." His voice was husky as he moved down her neck. "Do they all taste the same?"

(*"Does he know what you taste like, Valerian? Would he like to? I think he would. Perhaps I'll tell him, and spare his curiosity."*)

It was as if someone had splashed her with ice water. She realized with horror that she had forgotten to do up one of the buttons Gavin had unfastened. She gave him a nervous push. "Someone might see."

Horrorscape by Nenia Campbell

"Come on, Val. Just a peek."

Val froze, her eyes staring at the second floor, at the shadows cloaking the hallways. *Is someone there? Is someone watching us?*

"Whoa." She felt a tug on her blouse. "Did you wear this for me?"

She slapped a hand against her shirt, pinning it to her front. "James!"

He tore his eyes away from her chest. "What?"

"I...I think there's someone up there."

She was almost relieved for the interruption—and then she saw the expression on James's face.

"There better not be."

Val grabbed his sleeve. "What are you doing? Don't go up there."

"I'm not going to let some creep get away with whacking off to—"

"James." She felt like she was chastising a small but persistent dog. "For once, just *stop*."

"I've had just about enough of this goddamn party. We're leaving. After this round, I'm taking you home."

Val opened her mouth to issue a retort. A slight tintinnabulation startled them both. It sounded, to Val, like the ringing of a servant's bell. Her eyes flicked up to the ceiling again. There was only one person she knew, who would find it appropriate to summon party guests like that.

"Duty calls," James said, in a stuffy voice undoubtedly supposed to resemble an English butler. He fixed her blouse for her and chucked her jovially under the chin. "Come on, poppet."

His voice, though, was tense. Val managed a watery smile that probably looked just as unconvincing.

They ran into Blake and Lisa a little farther down the hall. Val flushed at the thought that one of her friends might have been their hidden observer—but no, a second later, she dismissed it. Lisa would have made a joke, and Blake ... well, his face wasn't nearly red enough.

If there even was a person there, she chided herself. Which there isn't. Wasn't.

Val looked at Blake and Lisa a little more closely. The two of them looked surprisingly grim.

"What's wrong?"

Lisa shook her head. "I don't want to talk about it."

"You hear that? She doesn't want to talk about it, Val."

"I heard her, James."

"Let's try to make this last round pleasant." James pushed open the door. "Ladies first." He smirked at Blake, clearly including him in that category, which earned him a half-hearted punch to the shoulder that fell short of making its target. "Oh, too slow."

"Don't be an asshole, James," said Lisa.

"What? I was just joking."

"The two aren't mutually exclusive," she bit back.

"Are you calling me an asshole?"

"The brownest."

"Quoth the biggest."

"You would know," James said, deadpan, and for some reason—really, it was a little funny—Lisa got mad enough to slap him.

"Lisa!" Val said, shocked. James was staring at her, open-mouthed, one hand pressed to his reddening face.

"That's enough," Blake said. "You're both big, brown… er…assholes. Okay? It's not something to be proud of."

"Here, here," Val muttered.

She surveyed the room nervously. Only Charlie had beat them to the parlor. She was sitting by herself towards the front, her legs neatly crossed at the ankle. Her eyes flicked over them dismissively, a cruel twist to her mouth that made Val's stomach plummet.

Was it her?

Even if it wasn't, she certainly seemed amused enough now. They were putting on quite the little show.

"She started it," said James.

Val quickly sat down, yanking James down with her on her left. Blake sat on her right. Lisa was sitting on the other side of Blake but kept shooting her these meaningful glances. Val looked up when the door opened but it was only Brent. He looked a little dazed, as if wondering how he had come to be in a room full of people. Jason was the last to enter. There was a thin sheen of sweat, and he kept touching his stomach through the fabric of his shirt. Their eyes met. Then he threw a dark look at Lisa, who stiffened.

Val felt a fleeting bolt of panic that mimicked her friend's. What is that? If it was something, it would be all her fault. *What have I done?*

The parlor door swung open and GM walked through, with a smile that didn't quite reach his eyes, reminding her exactly what she'd done. His hair was mussed, and Val realized, with a not-entirely-unpleasant pang, I did that. There were other differences, too, small ones mostly, but the easiest to place was his attire. He was still dressed in the white pants and the black shirt— rumpled now—but sometime between now and his ventures through the halls, GM had managed to acquire a black hat: a top hat, perched at a jaunty angle on his head.

He pulled it off with a flourish and bowed, like a magician performing his final act. He paused, as if expecting applause, before setting the hat down on the table beside him and producing a white envelope from his shirt pocket that was nearly identical to the one in her jeans pocket. Ignoring them now, he tore it open and a flurry of white papers cascaded into the hat's velvet-lined interior.

Was this for a raffle of some sort? For a prize? Advantages in the next game?

"Abracadabra," James whispered.

Val giggled. It was a wild, desperate-sounding gasp, and she clapped a hand over her mouth, glancing quickly around to make sure nobody had heard. She happened to catch Gavin's eyes, and her laugh died in her through when she saw the expression on his face.

Oh God, his eyes. She scooted back in her chair, her heart pounding.

"There are six slips of paper inside this hat," GM said at last, looking away from her to meet the eyes of the other players in turn. "Each of you must draw one. You are to draw your slip of paper silently. Do not discuss them with those around you. There will be serious penalties if you do."

Again, his eyes returned to hers, and she felt herself begin to sweat.

"Only six?" Blake asked, pushing his glasses up. "But there's eight people."

"I'm aware," GM said coolly. "Why don't you go first…Blake, isn't it?" His eyes flicked briefly towards Val again, and he added languidly, "You can proceed clockwise from there."

So I'll be last. He had something planned and he was making a point to drag it out.

With nothing better to do, she watched Blake reach into the hat, his eyes closed, before selecting a slip at random. His brow creased slightly as he read over the words written there silently to himself, before slowly making his way to his seat.

The others had similar reactions—ranging from confusion, to disgust, to boredom—as they mulled over their papers before inevitably crumpling them up into a fist or a pocket. One by one, they went up to the hat, until, finally, it was her turn.

A warm flush crept up her neck when she realized that the other players were staring at her. Lisa hissed, from across Blake, "Go, Val. He's waiting for you."

She clenched her fists and marched over to the waiting grandmaster, her feet seeming to grow heavier with every step. She stuck out her hand defiantly, flinching when he seized her wrist in a firm grip. "So kind of you to grace us with your presence. I do hope I didn't interrupt anything, *Val*."

"You're hurting me," she said. His fingers tightened imperceptibly, the only indication that he'd heard. And that was when her fear turned to terror. Because, clearly, he didn't care.

"That envelope I gave you; when this round is over,

you have my permission to read it. Out loud, if you please."

Abruptly, he released her and dropped something light into her upturned palm. It wasn't paper. Val glanced down at the object in her hand. It was a blackened rose, curling slightly at the tips. Every flower has a meaning, she remembered him saying so. Looking down at the withering blossom in her hands, she wished she knew the meaning of this particular flower.

"I'll deal with you later."

She had to repress a shudder.

It's wrong, she thought. It's wrong that he can still sound calm, with eyes like that.

"A flower," James said suspiciously, when she returned. "He gave you a flower?"

"What I have passed out to you," GM said, ignoring James, "Is the main theme of the game."

"And what is the theme?" Jason asked huskily.

"That you must figure out for yourself."

"Oh please, the theme's obviously chess," Lisa said. "I mean, black, white—it's not rocket science."

Charlie sent the other girl a dark look, "It's not that simple!" Her eyes went to GM. " Is it?"

"It *is* a bit more complicated than that, Lisa. Keep in mind that there is more than one theme," GM continued, "But you are right, chess is one of the themes. One of the most important, by far.

"There are only a few rules you should keep in mind," GM continued, turning away from Lisa. "I'll remind you of them periodically as we get closer to the final round. One; you can't tell anyone who is on your paper, two; you can give one person one clue to what is on your paper. I strongly suggest you start thinking as to who that one person should be."

James rolled his eyes, but even he was keeping quiet.

GM glanced at Val. "And now…I believe you have something you wanted to share, Valerian?"

Her fingers dug into the flower convulsively at the way he pronounced her name.

"What is he talking about?" Blake asked.

"Yeah, Val," James said. "What is he talking about?"

For a moment, she had no idea, either. And then she remembered. She remembered, and nearly drowned in the undertow of her own relief: the letter. She tore open the envelope, scanning the letter impatiently. "The game you have elected to play is a very dangerous one—"

She broke off, staring at Gavin with horror she didn't bother to hide. Smiling, he nodded for her to keep going. She continued, hands shaking slightly as she read, "—One king, one queen, six pawns; winner takes all. There is no time limit…except for the one on your lives."

"What are we supposed to do?" James said, rising from his chair.

"Why, say hello, of course," GM said.

"Hello?" The word rippled across the room, reflecting their unease.

The corners of GM's lips tilted up. "And goodbye …"

Goodbye?

He glanced up at the ceiling, innocently. The lights flickered on and off, before going out with an audible hum that plunged the room into darkness. Someone screamed. Somebody else yelled. Feet echoed on the floor boards as they rushed around like disoriented cockroaches.

In the imminent chaos, only Val had noticed the kiss he had blown at her.

Only he could make the gesture look threatening.

The blackout—if it had been a blackout—didn't last for more than a few minutes. The lights came back on, with a buzz, leaving Val feeling even more dazed and confused than before. A succession of gasps made her turn her attention towards the front, where GM had been standing only moments before. He had disappeared, leaving fresh paint glittering in his place like a spectral reminder:

RUN.

Chapter Sixteen

Trap

"Run," Charlie read.

When her eyes met Val's, Val could have sworn that Charlie sneered. But the blackout had weakened the lights and the lingering shadows made it difficult to interpret something as dynamic as facial expressions.

In any case, Val was far more concerned with the menacing word dripping slowly down the wall like blood.

Run.

Did that mean Gavin was the hunter for this round? It seemed likely. Part of her rebelled at the idea and part of her, a much smaller part but no less present for all that, wondered what he would do to her if he caught her this time.

(I only want to play with you a little)

A little thrill shot through her at the thought, and the memories that accompanied it, and her breasts prickled with gooseflesh. Val squirmed in her chair. Her stalker had threatened to hurt her friends if she tried to out him or leave and she was treating his cruelty like a fetish.

Blake blinked at the ruined wall. The paint was already beginning to soak into the wallpaper. "Shit. That paint isn't water-soluble. Look at the way it's dripping—it's going to leave a permanent stain."

Val got up from her chair and approached the wall, reaching out to touch the paint out of some vestigial sense of morbid curiosity. It gave her something else to focus on besides the letters themselves, and the sum of their parts, and the dangerous man who had inscribed them.

The texture was different from the water colors she was more familiar with. It had a strange smell and was slightly sticky, seeping into the grooves of her fingerprints. She remembered this smell, yes, accompanied by pungent sawdust and the voice of a man who wanted to ruin her.

To *hunt* her.

"Well, that's disgusting," Lisa said.

"I think that's the effect he was going for," said Jason.

Val couldn't believe she had sold Lisa out to this creep. She swiped her hands on her jeans but the color wouldn't come off. It had gotten under her nails, too. Oil-based. She was making mistake after mistake tonight.

"What a warped sense of humor," Lisa said, staring at Val's hands. "I mean, seriously. Rip off horror movies, much?"

"If this *was* a horror movie, wouldn't the airhead blonde be dead by now?" Charlie snapped, folding her arms.

"No, see, usually it's the slut who dies first."

"In that case, maybe Val had better watch out."

What? Val looked at her, startled. "I don't—"

"Excuse me," James roused himself from his pout, "just what the fuck is that supposed to mean?"

"Exactly what it sounds like." Charlie nodded in her direction. "Go on, ask her."

She knows.

"You *bitch.*"

James grabbed Lisa's wrist before she could finish her crushing retort. "Lisa. Let it go."

Lisa jerked her arm out of his grip, raising her hand in a defiant gesture, but it was only so that she could comb her fingers through her hair and flip the golden strands in a practiced, indifferent manner.

"You're right," she said. "She's not worth it. I might catch something."

"Fuck you," Charlie snarled. "Fuck *all* of you—but you, especially, Val. No, wait, you'd like that, wouldn't you?"

There was a slam, followed by a series of angry-sounding footsteps storming down the hall. Val looked up. The door, which GM had left open, was now firmly closed.

(Slut)

"Not again," Jason grumbled, shooting an annoyed look at the door and Brent, in turn, who was nearest. The heavier boy flushed a dark, unhappy pink and for a moment, Val almost felt sorry for him.

Almost.

She felt sorrier for herself. Charlie must have seen her with Gavin. Another sharp pain sliced through her stomach and she sucked in her gut like she was trying to physically wrestle the ache into submission. How much had she seen, and what did she plan to do with the information? A girl like Charlie could come up with something much more harmful than blackmail, she was sure.

Lisa breathed deeply, counting under her breath. "Thanks," she said at last, "I think."

"It's not worth it," James said, leaving little doubt in Val's mind as to whom he was really referring to.

"What on earth was that all about?" Lisa asked her.

Val looked down at her shoes. "I…I don't know."

Another hot flash of guilt flushed through her.

The letter, she thought quickly. *The one Gavin gave me. Did* it *say anything about running?*

She fumbled for her pocket, smearing red on the edges of the creamy paper from the paint streaked on her fingers. One of her clues fluttered to the Oriental rug and Val stared at the spiky handwriting on it without really seeing it.

Horrorscape by Nenia Campbell

Dangerous, her mind whispered. It had been her first clue. *Where have I seen that before?*

There was too much happening at once. She couldn't focus. But she knew that she had seen that exact same word somewhere else recently inside the house. The paper in her hand crinkled in warning.

She smoothed out the note over her knee, combing through the various words until she found what she was looking for. Her other hand was reaching for the small squares of paper, though she was only confirming what she already knew to be true—the clues were all in there.

In the *note*.

Val began arranging the white squares on the carpet. *Yes, yes, this one too, they're all here.*

"Give me your clues," she said to James. Giving her a very strange look, he handed them over and she placed them with her own. She looked up. The other players had moved on from the shock of the writing on the wall and Lisa and Charlie's near-confrontation, and were now discussing other, more trivial things in their segregated groups.

"Give me your clues," she said, through numb lips. "Everyone—give me your clues *now*."

"Why?" Jason inquired, shoving his hands into the pockets of his pants, "Why in the world should we give up our advantage for you?"

Brent had been in the process of reaching into his

pockets but immediately dropped his hand. "Yeah," he echoed dully. As if the stupid little squares held any *real* value.

Lisa and Blake stepped over, setting their clues in the spaces Val indicated while the white players looked on.

"Read the letter again," Jason commanded, frowning down at the jumble of words.

Grudgingly, Val picked up the sheet of paper and did as he asked, watching the skepticism fade from his face as his clues were called out, one by one.

"Some are missing," Jason pointed out.

"Those must be Charlie's," James said, as he got to his feet. He looked around the room. "But it's obvious. The clues definitely form the same message as Val's note."

Jason, it seemed, wasn't to be deterred. "What special significance is that supposed to have?"

In a hollow voice, Val said, "That we run."

■□■□■□■

"—Perhaps it's written in a code of some kind. He mentioned lives and a time limit, though, so the letter could be alluding to a computer game—"

Why did she keep getting paired with Blake?

Horrorscape by Nenia Campbell

Blake was nice enough, and certainly a good deal nicer than most of James's loser friends, who consisted of boys who thought that a girl enjoyed being touched like a football.

So maybe she was a little sore. She'd been hoping to get Val alone, to find out what had transpired between her and GM to make her look at her like that. What had made Charlie *shout* at her like that. Why she had been acting stranger than usual since the very beginning.

Honestly, she was surprised that James had managed to miss it—Charlie certainly hadn't. And it was totally eating at her. Lisa could tell; she would have given a lot to know why.

Then there was that creepy encounter with Jason.

"—And the king and the queen are most likely referring to chess pieces—"

"Maybe," Lisa said, sounding more irritated than she had intended to, "The note was just a ruse. Did you think about that?"

Blake blinked at her from behind the thick lenses of his glasses. "What do you mean?"

"A trick," Lisa said, continuing ahead alone, "A red herring, a false—"

She heard him stumble as he tried to catch up with her. "I know what a ruse is," Blake explained, "You just surprised me, that's all. I stopped talking about the note five minutes ago."

"Oh," Lisa paused. How awkward. "Then what were you talking about?"

He took off his glasses to polish them on his shirt. "I asked you what kind of music you liked."

"Anything that has a good beat," Lisa said noncommittally, "Except for metal and country. Why?"

"Just curious."

"Why, what music do *you* like?" she sighed.

"Classic rock." He replaced the glasses, squinting myopically at the ceiling. "Do you like—"

Blake's words were pushed through her ears, and into her temporal lobes, but the meaning of them didn't fully register. What *did*, in a completely different part of her brain, was Jason was heading for the stairs, not twenty feet away. The sight of him filled her with a deep revulsion.

And fear.

Jason hadn't seen them yet, but he would soon. He was on the prowl. She turned towards Blake, who was still talking about various artists that sounded only vaguely familiar and took a step closer to him. Blake barely noticed.

She let her head loll to the side and regarded him in appraisal. He actually wasn't that bad-looking without the glasses. Nice eyes. His skin was pretty clear, though a bit pasty-looking—probably from spending too much time in front of a computer monitor. And he had nice lips. She found herself wondering if he'd ever kissed a girl before. If not, today was his lucky day.

"—the eighties were seriously overrated. I think the seventies had the best—mpphh?"

His hazel eyes grew wide behind the thick rims of his lenses as Lisa grabbed the collar of his shirt and crushed her lips against his. Blake blinked slowly and then carefully pulled off his glasses, which were beginning to fog up, slipping them into his shirt pocket. Slowly, he began to respond, lifting a hesitant hand to cup the blond's cheek in an effort to correct the awkward angle between them.

Nerd-boy has been kissed before. Lisa wasn't prepared for the wave jealousy that accompanied the thought.

A heavy thud echoed from the hall. Blake started to turn towards the source, but she quickly grabbed his shoulders. He didn't bother resisting.

One brown eye cracked open, slipping towards the staircase just in time to see a white-clad figure heading up the steps two at a time. A bitter smile tilted the corner of her lips as her eyes slipped closed again.

Good.

■□■□■□■

"Hello…Jason, isn't it?"

Horrorscape by Nenia Campbell

Jason turned to see their host leaning against the wall beneath a large photograph. It had been taken at a high altitude—probably the Sierras, or the Appalachians—and made him look as if he were standing on the edge of an improbably high precipice, surrounded by redwoods.

How ironic GM barely even knew his name. "Yeah, what?"

GM didn't move from his casual slouch against the wall as he raised his eyes to glance at the photograph hanging above his head. "Beautiful, isn't it?"

"What?" It took him a moment to realize what GM was talking about. "Oh. Yeah. I'm not really a big fan of nature."

"Hmm." GM nodded absently, without taking his eyes off the granite and the pines. "Pity."

"Did you need something?" Jason asked, feeling himself becoming irritated. GM had disappeared for the last three consecutive rounds and when he finally did show up it was only to talk about trees and mountains? If he wasn't so invested in this stupid competition, he would have left hours ago. "I'm kind of busy. You know. Playing the game."

"Actually," GM said, straightening a little and meeting Jason's eye for the first time. "I am in need of a small favor."

Jason set his teeth. "Another one?"

"I'll make it worth your while."

To which he said, "I'm listening."

■□■□■□■

Val yawned, covering her mouth with the back of her hand. "James, what time is it?"

He rolled up his shirtsleeves obligingly. "Eleven."

"Really?" Val frowned, letting her hand fall to her side. It felt so much later than that. "Are we still leaving? I thought we were leaving. Shouldn't we get Blake and Lisa?"

"Oh. Yeah." James looked around. "I thought they were right behind us. Where'd they go?"

"Call Blake on your cell phone. I'll call Lisa."

She waited until James had gotten his cell phone out before she punched in the familiar sequence of numbers. An image of a satellite dish appeared on the screen. The same message from earlier, 'looking for service,' flickered beneath it. Nothing.

Val tapped her foot impatiently as the satellite continued to rotate. Then it vanished and the screen went white. 'No service.' And she started to get the bad feeling that maybe the problem didn't lie with her service provider.

"It says there's no service."

"Yeah, me, too. Try walking around."

Val moved towards the staircase, waving the phone in a slow arc. "No service." The words mocked her. Without technology, they were *marooned* here. The old Victorian might as well have been a deserted island. "James?"

"Still not working."

"I'm not surprised."

The voice came from somewhere below. GM. It took Val a moment to spot him. He was leaning against the staircase she was currently on, with his arm casually looped through the ornately carved posts. There was a faint smile on his face, which grew as she stared down at him in mute horror.

How much of their conversation had he overheard?

The thought troubled her. If she truly believed Gavin wasn't responsible for the phones not working, it wouldn't have mattered whether he knew, would it?

It's still a weakness, whether or not he caused it.

"Why won't our phones work?" James demanded.

"This house dates back to the nineteenth century. It wasn't built to accommodate modern electronics."

"That's a load of crap considering the goddamn plasma you have downstairs. Why won't they *really* work? What's blocking the signal?"

"A fault in the infrastructure, I'm sure."

"Can we use yours, then? The landline, I mean."

"There isn't one."

"James, let's go," Val said nervously. She didn't like that look in his eyes. She'd seen it before, in the art room four years ago, and then again in his bedroom. "Please—"

"What the hell are we supposed to do? Send a goddamn carrier pigeon? Do you really mean to tell me you have no communication out here?"

"I apologize for any inconvenience."

"You're the host. What do you suggest we do?"

"What I suggest is that the two of you start running."

"Very funny," said James.

"He's not joking."

"She's right, James. I'm not. I'll give you a five second head-start. One—"

"He's joking," James said.

"Two."

Val was already running.

"Three."

"Val? Val—wait up!"

"Four."

"Whatever you do, don't let him catch you."

"Jesus, Val. What—"

"Just listen to me."

"Five."

She swallowed down the scream that was building in her throat when he started to chase them. *Run. Just run.*

GM was surprisingly agile for a man of his height, but she was faster—a fact that hadn't escaped James, who insisted that two would be easier to track than one. "Besides," he added, in a careful voice, "He's after you."

She understood that he was probably still feeling angry and guilty, but that didn't mean he could act like a self-sacrificing idiot, and she said as much. "I meant what I said," she gasped. "Don't let him catch you. *Please.*"

"It's just a game," he said.

"No," she replied. "It's not. Not anymore."

When the hallway split, James gave her a hard shove to the left as he veered sharply to the right, and Val had been forced to continue on her own.

Val stumbled through one of the open doors, struggling to catch her breath. She had done track and field, but it had been years since her last meet and her body could scarcely remember how to conserve energy. She was wearing down.

She let out the breath she had been holding and

looked around. She appeared to be in a games room. A ping pong table sat dejectedly in the corner, cover with years' worth of dust, and she could make out a newer, but similarly dusty game of air hockey in the center of the room.

"So," a slow, drawling voice said from behind her, "Where's the fire?"

Val wheeled around and came close to crashing into an old jukebox. Jason was rested against the back wall with his long legs stretched out in front of him.

"What are *you* doing here?"

"Playing some pinball."

She looked at the pinball machine, then back at him. The machine *did* look a little less dusty than some of the other surrounding games, but still.

"Whatever. If you're thinking about pumping me for more information about Lisa, it isn't going to work." She glanced at the doorway, rubbing at the goosebumps on her arms. "I'm not going to let you threaten me."

GM did not appear. Had he lost the trail?

Jason got to his feet, stumbling a little in his haste. "It's nothing like that."

"Oh *really*."

"Really. I hate to say it, but I'm impressed," he said. "You were the only one who managed to put two and two together. Congratulations."

Val eyed him warily. "I don't believe you."

"Do you really think I'd say something like that unless it were true? I'm not that charitable."

That was slightly more convincing. But she was still cautious. Jason had already proved on multiple occasions that he was taking this game far too seriously, that he was possibly in cahoots with Gavin. Her expression hardened. "You never answered my question. What do you want?"

Jason looked truly frustrated. Was he that good an actor? "I found a clue. I want you to help me figure it out."

"You expect me to help you after you just finished blackmailing me? You can't be serious."

"I know how it sounds, but think about it," Jason said reasonably, "This is a solution that benefits both sides. I come out ahead, you come out ahead—and all you have to do is just…well, decipher. I'm sure you're curious about what GM's master plan is."

Yes. And no. Val took a deep breath. And then another. "If this is a trick …"

"No trick."

"We'll see."

"Just follow me." Jason stepped out of the doorway. Val hesitated. To her relief, the hallway was empty. "Coming?"

Horrorscape by Nenia Campbell

I can't believe I'm doing this. "Where is this clue?"

"It's rather difficult to describe," Jason said, chuckling. "You need to experience for yourself but trust me, you'll know it when you see it. Ah." He had stopped outside of a seemingly random door. "Here we are. Ladies, first."

Val peered into the room, but only pitch-blackness met her gaze. That was an easy no. She responded likewise. "Can't you turn on a light or something?"

"And have the others see and steal our advantage? What's the matter, Val? Afraid of the dark?"

"You first, then," she said, "Unless you're afraid I'm going to club you from behind."

The smile disappeared from his face as she tossed his words from earlier at him. "Just get in the room, Val."

"I'm not going in there!"

"Sorry, Val—but it's for your own good." She started when she felt his hands on her shoulders. He was trying to push her into the room! Val's arms shot out to grip the door frame. Hopeless. She could feel her feet sliding. He was too strong. Gritting her teeth, she dug the heels of her sneakers into the carpet for better traction.

"James! James! Help—"

Jason rammed into her with his shoulder. Val had to let go of the door so she could throw out her arms to break her fall. A burning sensation jagged up her forearms as she slid across the carpet. The door slammed shut and she heard the unmistakable click of the lock.

"Have fun."

Val pushed herself up, grimacing, and fell upon the door. "Let me out of here right now!"

She thought she caught the faint sound of his laughter as he retreated down the corridor. "You'll thank me later."

The hell she would. Val leaned against the door, so that she was facing towards the room, waiting for her eyes to adjust as she tried to ignore the pain crawling up her arms. She could only make out dark shadows and the faintest outline of glass.

Hadn't she been in this room before? Yes. Back in the beginning of the game. The creepy menagerie she had bypassed in favor of better hiding places. The one where she had first encountered Charlie.

A long, oak table was the obvious focal point of the room. About seven or eight glass tanks were carelessly arranged on the varnished surface, shimmering with water. Val looked around the room. Seemed ordinary enough. It was a study. Not a bedroom, as she previously suspected. The furniture was modern—mostly white and black, with steel accents—and there wasn't much of it.

A soft blue light flickered on as she approached, dim enough that it caused no discomfort. The light was coming from the tanks. *Must be on a timer or something.*

They were standard size, filled with brightly colored gravel in blue, pink, and purple. They were also empty. Why on Earth had Jason brought her here? And where had he gotten the key to this room?

Something slid beneath her shoe, nearly tripping her. A piece of paper.

The piece of paper was scarcely visible; she had crushed it in her fright. Val held the paper up to one of the blue lights with shaking fingers. Her sweaty palms had blurred the ink in a few spots but the message was still legible.

And she inhaled sharply, for written in fresh, red ink were the words: *Turn around, Val.*

Val froze, turning around slowly. She saw nothing; only shadows. She was alone.

A sudden scratching sound to her left made her jump, every nerve tingling in anticipation as adrenaline kick-started her body's natural flight-or-fight response. There was a deafening silence. Then Val heard the sound again—softer this time…almost playful.

"Who's the—" She broke off, the inflection in her voice shifting from anger to fear when she felt a finger tap her shoulder. She whirled in that direction and found herself facing the tanks again. Nobody was there. The silence was absolute, except for the steady pounding of her own heart.

"Gavin?"

Horrorscape by Nenia Campbell

And then she heard a voice, level with her ear, say, "Maybe." Her eyes snapped open, but it was already too late. Strong, warm arms encircled her waist, pulling her closer, as that same familiar voice whispered, "Checkmate."

Chapter Seventeen

Domination

Checkmate.

"No—" She slammed against him, and the two of them stumbled backwards. He hit the table and one of the tanks toppled over, landing on the floor with a loud crash.

"The door's locked, Val," he said. "Nowhere to run."

"Where's the key?"

"Not on me. You're welcome to take a look, though. Tell me, how are you enjoying the game so far? I noticed you managed to solve my puzzle rather quickly."

Val twisted around, searching for his necklace. Her finger coursed over bare skin, and she felt the low thrum of amusement vibrate through his throat like a purr.

He wasn't wearing his necklace.

"That isn't going to work again."

Or his shirt.

She lifted her knee, intent on driving it into his stomach or groin, and he kicked her other foot out from under her. There was a thud as they hit the ground.

"You know better than this," he said. "I could almost believe you're deliberately trying to provoke me."

"You did something to the phones. You did, didn't you? Why did you *really* invite us here?" At his silence, she said, "Please. *Please*. Whatever you've got planned, don't do it."

"Hush."

"Don't do it," she repeated. "Don't do *this*."

"We both know that's not what you really want." She knocked her own head back against the floor in shock when she felt his tongue flick out to taste the sweat beading on her throat. "Is it?"

She made a small, pitiful sound more animal than human.

"I didn't think so."

"Gavin—"

"A bit early for begging, isn't it? I haven't even done anything to you, yet."

Yet.

The room was different, but the feeling was the same—trapped, with no escape. She twisted away from his mouth, acutely aware of her pulse racing in her ears. "W-what are you going to do to me?"

"That depends on you." His hot breath tickled her ear. "Valentine."

"You were watching us—?"

"It was such a touching display." He knotted his fingers in her hair. "I could only assume it was for my benefit."

"That's insane," she stammered, even as she wondered. Had she known it was him, on some subconscious level?

"Well, I suppose you would be the authority on that."

The casual insult made her eyes sting. "I'm not crazy. You made everyone *think* I was crazy."

"Actually, that was the lawyer who did that. I merely sat there like a good boy, repentant"—he nuzzled her neck—"brilliant, misunderstood, tortured," he hissed the last in her ear, making her flinch. "Seduced and then vilified by the neurotic Lolita, and her wild claims of persecution."

"You don't really believe that. You *can't*."

"No, I don't." He trailed kisses down her collarbone. "But does that matter?" When he got to fabric he took the lace between his teeth and worked the button through the hole expertly with his tongue. "It's all about control."

Part of her relished it, relished the fact that he was so strong, that she wouldn't be able to fight him if she tried. Relished his fierce sexuality, and unapologetic cruelty. The erotic thrill of his bare skin against hers. The deceptive power of his long, slender fingers. The fingers that were slipping beneath the waistband of her jeans.

She bolted upright.

He covered her mouth with his hand, pushing her

back down. Her chest rose and fell in panicked successions as she tried to draw in enough air to scream. *What is he doing oh no no no no—*

"Think, Val. Do you *really* want James to see this?"

She tried to glare at him over his fingers, even as her lower body began to burn and melt. She inhaled sharply, and he lifted his hand off her mouth to let her breathe.

"No," she whimpered. *This isn't what I want...*

"I thought as much." His teeth brushed the shell of her ear. His other hand was on her breast, and her fingers were around his wrist, digging in so tightly that she suspected she had drawn blood. "How can you live, when you're so repressed?" He flicked his fingers. She shuddered.

But maybe it's what I need.

He squeezed, then, and her head fell back against the floor with a thunk. A strangled, wretched sound filled the air, and she realized, with an ill start, that it was from her.

"I think you find me impossible to resist." He pressed against her cheek, tilting her face back towards his. Unlike her, his breathing was quite slow, composed. She could feel his pulse in his fingertips, as steady as a clock. "Because you know I'm the only one who can make you feel this way."

Maybe they were made for each other.

Maybe he was what she deserved.

"Isn't that right?"

Softly, she cried.

■◻■◻■◻■

The seven minutes were up. A hushed click cut through the silence, and Gavin pulled away. "Time to go," he said. Dismissing her as if she were a whore.

Aren't you? Just look at yourself, at what you're doing!

She stumbled to her feet, heart in her throat. Her clothing felt too rough, her knees too weak. She could feel the sting of saliva like a cold brand burning deep into her skin, and where his fingers had brushed she felt a slow burn.

Jason shot a curious, sidelong look at her. He closed the door—but didn't lock it, she couldn't help noticing— and nodded at her disheveled clothing. "Did you have fun?"

And then, suddenly, Val knew. It was only the briefest glimpse of insight, but she knew. And she lunged. Jason's hands were still in his pockets, though he instinctively tried to pull them out to defend himself, but her palm still struck his face with a sickening crack that echoed through the empty corridor. Breathing hard, she pulled her arm hand back. It was tingling.

The shock only lasted for the span of a few seconds

before it was replaced by anger. "Bitch."

The urge to run came again, stronger still, and she tried to heed it but he was too fast. Val slammed against the wall, rattling the frame of a picture of a pine forest hanging over her head. She cringed.

"Oh, I'm not going to hit you. I don't hit girls."

She wondered if he could hear her heart hammering. "Easy to say when you have Gavin doing your dirty work."

"Gavin?" Jason repeated. "Oh, is that his real name?"

Val sucked in a breath. *Shit*.

"I thought you two knew each other. Hmm. I wonder what James would have to say about this."

"He's not going to believe you."

"I think he will. He's the jealous type."

"If you tell James, I'll tell Lisa. I'll tell her *everything*."

"And then she'll know you were the rat who sold her out, and I'll *still* tell James you let Gavin finger-fuck you upstairs," he said. "Face it, Val—you lose."

Val felt the sting of tears in her eyes. Angrily, she blinked them back. "What do you want from me?"

Jason blinked, as if startled by the question. "Nothing."

"Nothing?"

Horrorscape by Nenia Campbell

"Nothing," Jason agreed, and paused a heartbeat before adding, "From you."

■□■□■□■

James retraced his steps from the staircase, trying to locate that adjoining room where he and Val had separated. The hallway was silent and he frowned—it was a large house, but he still should have run into somebody by now. But he hadn't. The spacious rooms and narrow hallways were as silent as a grave. He made an aggravated sound in the back of his throat. What a waste of time.

He ascended the staircase, studying the pictures lining the walls without really seeing them. None of the pictures were family photos, giving the atmosphere a cold, impersonal feel. A lot of the furniture was in disrepair, looking as though it hadn't been used for a long time...

One picture caught his eye. It depicted a king and a queen, both robed in immaculate white. Most of the colors were cold—lots of blues, whites, and grays. The only spot of color was the woman's fiery red hair. He frowned. Her posture indicated helplessness, perhaps induced by injury. By contrast, the man's posture was aggressive. In his fingers was a wicked, slightly curved blade. James shivered. The perspective was slightly off, stilted like the chase scenes in a slasher film. He felt like he'd seen this painting somewhere before—but where? Without really meaning to, he stopped walking and stared.

A door slammed behind him. James pivoted around, but there were so many doors—open and closed—that it was impossible to tell which one the sound had come from. "Who's there?"

Silenced mocked his query.

"This isn't funny," he added in a warning voice, just as another slam—closer this time—resounded from behind one of the closed doors. "I said, Who's there?"

Slam.

This time, the sound came from just behind him. James automatically turned in that direction, disconcerted to find himself facing an empty hallway once more—with one small difference. A little piece of paper, a post-it, was attached to one of the now-silent doors. He walked over, turning his head to scan both sides of the hallway, before closing the distance completely and removing the note.

He didn't recognize the handwriting. The letters had been inscribed so crudely that, in some places, large gaps separated the separate strokes while others were clotted with ink.

CHECKMATE.

Chapter Eighteen

Vacating Sacrifice

James fell back a step. The paper fluttered from his hands and hit the floor without a sound. He barely noticed. Checkmate? He didn't know much about chess—like most things outside of computers and grades, he found it pointless and a waste of time—but didn't checkmate signify a losing move? The end of the game?

And then he heard the words, "Hello, James," spoken effortlessly from behind him.

What?

The blow was so unexpected, it took a moment for his nerves to respond. The pain came as suddenly and violently as an explosion. He saw stars; hot, white flashes of light in his periphery. Something hard slammed against his knees and he realized that it was the floor. The last thing he heard was a faint ringing sound, and then everything went black.

■□■□■□■

The boards squeaked noisily beneath her feet. Val barely noticed or cared.

She looked down at her feet in frustration, surprised to see a post-it note stuck to the bottom of her shoe.

Horrorscape by Nenia Campbell

Where did this come from?

Frowning, she peeled the paper from her sole and smoothed it out. A single word ("CHECKMATE"), printed in ugly block capitals, marched across the page in glittering blood red ink. The unevenness of the letters, and the smeared blots of ink, suggested a hand made unsteady by some powerful emotion. But for whom? And why?

Val couldn't come up with an answer. She wasn't sure she wanted to. But oh, she could guess.

That was when she heard the voices. They were still faint, but growing closer, and she recognized Jason's annoying bray straight off. Charlie's voice was similarly easy to place. Val shoved the note in her jeans and rounded the corner, one hand on a doorknob in case they came closer.

"...I don't think cozying up to GM is going to help your situation..."

"Jason, fuck off. I don't need your advice."

"I've seen the way you look at him. I'm sure he does, too. But he's interested in someone else. Someone who, by the looks of things, isn't you."

Is he talking about me?

"That's all you've got?" she said at last. "Watch me. All I have to do is get him alone for five minutes and I'll have him on his knees — "

"It's a big house, Charles, but not that big. You know

I'm right. You should have been able to corner him by now, but you haven't. He's a wily one, and he doesn't want to be found. Which, by the way, proves my point."

"What point? You think he likes her? That little girl?"

"Like is the wrong word for it."

"What, you mean you've been talking to him?"

"Maybe," said Jason.

"About what? When?"

"It'll cost you."

There was a slight pounding noise, like a hand smacking the wall. "And what do you want?"

"I want your one clue for the papers GM gave us," Jason added carelessly, "That's all."

"Fine."

"Bottom line is, GM asked me to do a little favor for him earlier this round."

"What kind of favor?"

"He wanted to get Val alone. Then he told me exactly what to say to ensure that she kept her mouth shut."

Oh my God, I knew it. I knew it—

"Why would he do that?"

"I don't know, he didn't say. He's not much of a conversationalist. But I'm sure you can take a guess."

"Fucking *bitch*." Charlie drew in a ragged breath. "I should have known, after I saw her all over him in one of the spare rooms downstairs. That little skank."

"I think they have history together." She could hear the smirk in his voice when he added, "Or maybe chemistry."

"She's about to *be* history," Charlie snapped. "Ugh! I can't *believe* her. What else did GM say? Anything useful?"

"Nothing about you, if that's what you're wondering. Apart from that, no, not really. I know he doesn't like Lisa or James. Now my clue?"

"That was nothing."

"It's the best you're going to get."

Charlie sighed, conveying dissatisfaction perfectly. "She's on the black team, you vampire. Are you happy now?"

For the first time Jason seemed caught off-guard. "Is it Val?" Charlie must have shaken her head because he went on, in a lower voice, "Lisa? The blonde?"

Lisa? She shifted her weight, trying to hear better, and her foot came down on a loose floorboard. *Squeak.* Val's eyes widened in mute horror. She half-turned in the direction of the staircase.

The voices in the other room had fallen silent.

"Did you hear something?"

Val shrank back against the wall.

"Probably the house settling. The boards are old. What's the matter? Scared?"

"I thought someone might be listening."

Val's hand tightened around the doorknob, which slipped against her sweaty palms. She stared at the brass circle dumbly before turning her wrist. Oh god. What if it was locked? She'd never even considered that. Hell, she never imagined that she'd be hunted down in one of the corridors like a frightened rabbit. To her relief, the door opened easily. She slipped inside, hearing Jason's footsteps round the bend in the hall, inches away from where she had been standing moments before.

The footsteps paused. She could hear the rustle of their clothing as they studied the empty hallway, imagine them studying the seemingly endless line of doors. Charlie snorted. "It's empty. You must be hearing things. There's nothing here."

Val took a step away from the door…and landed right on another board.

"I heard it again." One of the doors eased open. Not hers—but close. Too close. "Over here."

"Maybe," Charlie agreed, also taking a step forward.

Val's concentration had narrowed so much that it took her a moment to recognize the room. It was a bedroom; the one GM had locked her in during penalty round. The chess set was a dead giveaway—although it looked like someone had been playing with the board; it was slightly off-center and there were pieces scattered all over the table and floor.

She frowned. She distinctly remembered GM locking the door. No time to dwell on that now.

"Lisa?" Jason called softly, with the menace of a prowling cat. He paused, "Val? James?"

"If it is them, do you seriously think they're going to answer?"

Val walked over to the door, still cleverly hidden by that large poster, and walked through, almost crying in relief as she stepped into that musty old office. Thank you. She made sure to test each board carefully as she eased her way towards the main door, going against all instincts that told her to run, and fast. A desperate little voice told her that she didn't want to get caught.

Not by them.

■□■□■□■

James woke up submerged in total darkness.

Everything looked blurred. He blinked a few times, until his vision adjusted. He could make out a faint, blue light that hurt to look at, even at that very low setting. What happened? He looked around the room, trying to come up with an answer, but it was too hard to concentrate with that constant throbbing...

Wait.

Pain.

He'd been walking through the corridors searching for Val and GM had...had clobbered him over the head with something hard and blunt. James blinked, as the anger came back full-force. That *asshole*.

He tried to reach up, to get an estimate of the damage, but his arms remained stiffly at his sides. Immobile. Understanding pierced through the fog. He'd been tied to a chair. The harder he struggled against his bonds, the tighter they became. Slipknots. Someone had gone through a lot of trouble to make sure he could not get away.

James wet his cracked lips and glanced around the room again. The dim glow revealed the outlines of glass tanks. Aquariums. He knew they contained water because of the shimmery undulations on the wall. He thought he could see small shadows flitting around inside.

He jerked forward against his bonds when something plastic brushed against his neck. The wooden legs of the chair squeaked indignantly as he yelped, "What the fuck?"

A low, humorless laugh sounded from his right. "Welcome to the Inquisition."

Bright light flashed into his face. James yelled again,

in pain and surprise, twisting his face away as purple and green splotches danced behind his closed eyes.

"Untie me, you faggot," James bit out through clenched teeth. "I know this isn't part of the game."

"How little you know."

James let several minutes go by before he opened his eyes. As his vision gradually became re-accustomed to the darkness, he thought he could make out his host's thin, white-clad frame from somewhere to his right—but the figure disappeared, making him wonder if it was simply an afterimage.

There was a strange, cottony taste in his mouth and his head ached worse than ever. James tried again, almost choking on the words, "What do you want?"

"Nothing much," GM said, tracing figure eight patterns on the ceiling with the beam, "Just answers."

James stared at the wavering light. Who would have thought that the flickering beam of a flashlight could be so menacing? "To what?"

"Questions, of course."

"What kind of questions?"

Simple questions." The chair creaked as GM placed a boot on one of the wooden rungs, tipping the chair back a few inches. "I'm sure even you'll be able to answer them."

"Fuck you."

The sole of GM's boot hit the floor with a heavy thud, upsetting the chair's balance, and suddenly James was falling. The air rushed past his body, his stomach leaped into his throat. There was a loud crash. Pain arced up his arms, which were still tied behind the chair, and his head, which was still tender. He heard a ragged gasp and realized, with a jolt, that it was his.

The light stopped moving. James felt the floorboards near him groan as GM walked around him. "James, please, let's not be…shall we say…*difficult*."

"Fuck," he wheezed. James shook his head, and immediately regretted it as pain bolted down his neck. "Where's Val?"

"Ah, yes, Val." The flashlight beam jolted as GM picked the flashlight back up. "She cares a lot about you."

"Where is my *girlfriend*?"

"Do you care about her?"

It couldn't be, thought James. *Hit List?* "You gotta be fucking kidding me."

"I can assure you I'm quite serious." He paused. "One might even say I'm…dead serious." There was a thud, the scraping of plastic on wood, and then total silence. James listened intently. All he could hear was the faint buzz of the filters.

He's insane.

A sudden rush of air, followed by a prickling iciness

was the only warning he got. Seconds later, he felt a hand dig into his shoulder. James jolted upright and nearly cut himself on the sharp edge.

"Well, James? Do you care about her? Or perhaps you're more concerned about yourself? I can't say I blame you."

James opened his mouth—but no words came out.

"I see," GM said, as if there had been no pause, "It appears I have gone over your capacity for reason and logic. Perhaps," and here, the pressure on the blade increased, "a different question is in order."

He didn't dare swallow, let alone release the insult that had risen to the tip of his tongue—hell, he could barely breathe. "Holy shit. It's you—it's you, isn't it? Hit List—"

"Did I give you permission to talk?" He dug his fingers into the fleshy part of James's shoulder, drawing a yelp. His warm breath stung James's eyes. "Do you love her?"

"Go to hell, you sick fuck."

"I don't think so." James felt the hand on his shoulder tighten before he felt the pain; a sharp sting, followed by an immediate burning sensation that made his eyes water as a thin line of blood trickled down his neck. "No, I really don't. But if you don't being a bit more helpful, you will, James. I promise you. And I think I might start by digging out your fingernails, one by one."

"No." James choked on the bile rising in his throat. *This isn't happening. This is not happening.* "Please. Don't hurt me."

"Do you love her?"

"No…no, I don't." It was the first time he had ever admitted it, even to himself.

"Did you have her? Fuck her?" GM—Hit List—growled, the raw emotion in his voice as caustic as acid. "Have you ever made her come?"

James flinched when he felt the knife point come to rest on the damp crotch of his jeans. His penis shriveled up, as though ashamed. "No," he whimpered. "Never. I wanted to but—but she wouldn't let me. *Please—*"

"So you had the other one instead," GM mused. "Lisa?" James flinched. "Isn't that right, James?"

"How…how could you possibly know that?"

The other boy seemed to regard him in the darkness. Silence spanned, broken only by James's choked sobbing.

"Foolish boy." Slowly, reluctantly, he retracted the blade and James could breathe again. A few seconds later, he heard the groan of the hinges, the clap of footsteps, and the muted click of the door. Then GM was gone—and James threw up.

■□■□■□■

Horrorscape by Nenia Campbell

Lisa punched in the seven digit number on her cell phone, frowning when the call didn't go through. 'No service.' She tried pulling out the antennae and then she turned towards Blake, who had gone curiously silent. "Do you have any reception?"

He shook his head slowly. "I don't have a cell phone. How many bars do you have?"

"Two—and I just charged it this morning." She threw down her arm in disgust, letting the jeweled charm whack against the chrome. "I'm gonna try going outside. Maybe it's something in the house. Something blocking the airwaves," she added, in an effort to sound smarter.

"I think that's illegal."

Lisa looked at him sharply to see if he was making fun of her but he simply returned her gaze, with the wide, innocent stare of a beagle. "Whatever," she said, "It's annoying."

The two of them walked in silence down the hallway. Blake was only about an inch or two taller than she was, so it made for a comfortable pace—usually, Lisa had to half-run to keep up with James' brisk, hurried strides. This gave her time to observe the house.

Most of the furniture was made of dark wood, stained oak or mahogany, with candy-colored faces and other impersonal touches artistically scattered around the room. Lisa was impressed, in spite of herself. She'd seen a vase just like that one go for a couple hundred at an antique show on TV.

"So," Blake began hesitantly, "What does this mean?"

"What does what mean?"

Blake took off his glasses and started polishing them on the hem of his shirt. Lisa winced. That fabric would only smear whatever gunk he had gotten on the lenses. Blake seemed satisfied with the results, however, and replaced them, pausing to give her a pointed look over the frames.

The two reached the main doors shortly after, distinguishable by the thick oak panels and inlaid glass windows. Lisa tried the polished brass handle. Click. "What is wrong with this door?" she growled, giving the handle a ferocious twist. "Open!"

A line had formed between Blake's tawny eyebrows. "Is it locked?"

"No—just—*jammed*. How could it be—*locked*? It worked well enough when we—*uh*—came in!"

"Well, if it is locked, we can ask GM to open it for us," Blake suggested, though the line hadn't disappeared. "We should probably leave soon, anyway. Val has an early curfew, right?"

"Yeah, one." Lisa turned back towards the parlor. She paused. "I think GM might be stalking Val."

"You might be on to something there. She told me she thought he was dangerous, right before the first game. Seemed scared stiff about it, too, though she hasn't said anything since. Have you talked to her about it?"

"No, and that's the thing. I think that's why I haven't been able to talk to her. I think GM purposely—"

Blake shook his head slightly. Lisa cut off midspeech, slowly turning around, brown eyes rooted to the door. Or, more specifically, to the man leaning against its frame.

"Hello, Lisa," he said, nodding briefly at Blake, "What a nice surprise. I was just about to call everyone back for the next round." He paused. "Perhaps you'll assist me."

Blake exchanged a look with Lisa. It was clear he wanted to do no such thing.

"No, that's all right," she said quickly, "We're actually still looking for James and Val." *Perhaps you've seen them?*

As Lisa watched, his face shifted from halting politeness to the flat, calculating look of a raptor.

"Yeah," Blake said slowly, grabbing her wrist. "So we'll just be going now…"

GM swiftly blocked their exit with one graceful movement; his smile was like poison.

"Oh, but I *insist*."

Horrorscape by Nenia Campbell

■□■□■□■

Val leaned against the carved banister, pausing to catch her breath. *That was too close.*

She took one last giant breath and headed for the parlor room. She'd wait in there until the next round started. That "secret" doorway in the grandmaster's bedroom had allowed her to double back to the main hallway and beat Jason and Charlie to the staircase. The two white players were probably still looking for her…she hadn't heard their footsteps. Maybe they'd gotten lost.

No, her luck wasn't that good.

Val opened the parlor door, pausing when she heard the voices. She could make out Blake's tenor and Lisa's soprano—taut and thin, like the bowstring of a violin. She sounded strange. Val pushed through the door and froze when she realized who Blake and Lisa were talking to.

"Why, hello Val," GM said, with a curved smile. She forced herself not to watch his fingers as he smoothed out the creases in his shirt. "How nice of you to join us."

"W-what's going on?" She was looking at Lisa but it was GM that answered.

"We're just starting middlegame."

"But I haven't found James, yet."

"What a pity that is," he said.

Val stared at his departing back, with the bitter taste of dread lingering in the back of her throat. Before she could think of an appropriate response, though, the door burst open and a breathless Charlie and Jason stumbled through.

Brent arrived a few minutes later. He'd seen Charlie and Jason tearing through the library and decided to follow. "Am I late?" he asked, studying the assembled teens nervously.

"No," said GM. "You're right on time."

Val turned around in her seat, meeting Lisa's eyes. "Where have you guys been?"

"We were about to look for you and James when he burst through the door," Lisa said, nodding at GM, "He scared the hell out of Blake and me. The look on his face—" She shuddered delicately.

"It was as if he was considering how our heads would look hanging over his mantle," Blake said.

"I'm really starting to get freaked out, Val. I tried to call my mom, and couldn't get any reception. So I decide to go outside and see if my phone worked there." Lisa looked around, then added in a hush, "The front door was *locked*."

"Locked?"

"I think Lisa's right," Blake said, sitting up, "We're alone here, in case you haven't noticed. The fact that our cell phones don't work could be chalked up to architectural flaws"—his tone suggested he doubted this "—but the locked door, and the fact that there isn't a telephone in sight, is another thing altogether."

"And James is still missing."

Oh no. So it was already too late; her friends were in danger. Gavin hadn't bothered keeping his word. *Then neither will I.* "Guys—there's something I need to tell you—"

"Welcome back," GM said, and Val hastily stopped talking. "This next round is called middlegame. In chess, this signifies the beginning of the end."

The beginning of the end? How sinister.

"Do you still have your papers from the last round?"

There were some hesitant nods and yeses as the players checked their pockets and purses to recover the crumpled slips.

"I wasn't," Jason snapped, quickly passing the paper along to Charlie, who rolled her eyes and dropped the papers in GM's upturned palm.

Val was sitting on the end of the row, so she ended up with the slips for her team. They were about the size and shape of Chinese fortunes, except more crudely formed, and she found herself turning over one of the slips for a quick look. Really, since she hadn't even gotten to draw a paper, it shouldn't even count as cheating...

She turned the paper over, and a hand seized her wrist, with just a bit more force than friendly contact allowed for. Val looked up, mouth dropping open, as she met GM's eyes. "That will be all," he said, letting his eyes drop to her parted lips as he took the slips. "Val."

She jerked her now-sweaty hand out of his hold, shooting a nervous look at Blake and Lisa to see if they had noticed. They hadn't. But Charlie had. Her expression was thunderous. She looked down at her lap, and wiped her palm on her jeans.

(Say my name)

"Is this all of them?" GM asked, redirecting their attention to the front of the room. Without waiting for an answer he said, "Good." And, to their shock, he ripped the papers, allowing the shreds to fall to the floor.

"What did you do that for?" Jason asked, staring at the remains of his paper.

"Having them around will only make your next task more difficult. You have until dawn," GM continued. He rolled up his sleeve, revealing a black watch, "It's a little past midnight now, so that leaves you with a six hour deadline. The rules are simple. No one is allowed to find out what was on your paper except, of course, for the person you gave your one clue to..." He studied his rapt audience with approval, "If you fail to meet these terms or forfeit, the game is drawn and you hit checkmate."

"What do we need six hours for?"

"It's quite simple. You have to kill the person on your paper."

Chapter Nineteen

Trebuchet

Similar words sprang to mind, a passing threat from years ago that had taken root and was now blooming into vines with venomous barbs. She recalled them as if Gavin had spoken them to her yesterday.

(What if instead of going after you I went after someone you hold dear? Would you resist me then? Or would you play my way in exchange for their well-being?)

Val sucked in a breath. The pain seared as though fresh.

No.

(You would, wouldn't you?)

His eyes locked with hers. She wondered if he, too, was remembering. From the satisfied smile playing about his lips, like a cat that had devoured cream and canary both, she had trouble believing the answer to be anything but yes.

She had made her move all those years ago. And now, four years later, he was making his. Playing her as if she were one of his chessmen. *It's all my fault*, she thought. *Everything—it's all my fault. It's all because of me.*

They will all die because of me.

"You're joking," Lisa said. Her voice sounded small.

"I don't think he is," Val whispered back. The lump in her throat had returned with a vengeance as she watched his gesturing hands and remembered what those same hands had done to her body in the dark.

Her breathing constricted, her throat tightened, and the lump seemed to weigh down the back of her tongue. *You are a monster.* Even now, his every glance sent an attentive thrum shooting down her spinal cord which teased her every nerve. *You may not be the one holding the knife at their throats, but you are the one who signed the warrant.*

She wished she would choke on that lump—choke on it and *die*. The thought that Gavin should, perhaps, be the one who ought to die failed to cross her mind, because at this moment, with his self-appointed power over life and death, he had taken on nearly godlike proportions.

What am I going to do?

"The game you have elected to play is a very dangerous one. One king, one queen, six pawns; winner takes all. There is no time limit—except for the one on your lives."

The players stared at him in horror, recognizing some of their clues from the previous round. Lisa twitched, as if readying to bolt, and Gavin said, "I wouldn't, Lisa. You know what they say about running from a predator—it tends to trigger the instinct to chase."

Lisa went white.

Horrorscape by Nenia Campbell

Gavin cleared his throat. "As I was saying. You must figure out who is who before the allotted time runs out."

"And die," Jason said flatly.

"Yes."

Val jumped at the shriek of a chair scooting back. "I don't want to play," said Blake. "This is horrible—*barbaric*. You're talking about killing people—hunting them for sport like that book, *The Most Dangerous Game*."

Blake looked at Gavin, as if giving him a chance to refute his instructions. To laugh it all off as one big, terrible joke. But he was silent, serious—*dead* serious, Val thought a bit hysterically—and Blake went on in a halting voice threaded with a tremulous sort of bravery, "I won't kill anyone—I *refuse*."

"Then you forfeit?" Gavin took a step in Blake's direction. "Is that what you are telling me?"

Blake stumbled back. "I—I guess. I won't do it; I don't care what you call it. It's murder, and I won't—"

"How very chivalrous of you." GM swiftly cut him off. "However, if you do choose to forfeit, you will die. Instantly. I suppose I forgot to mention that," he said absently, as Blake stared on in horror. "The way I see it, you have two choices. Choice one; sit down and play the game, or choice two; die where you stand. Which will it be?"

Blake sat down looking dazed.

"I thought so. Any other questions?"

There were many questions, weighing down on the air like toxic fumes, but nobody said a word. They were too afraid of the answer, and too afraid to waste the time it would take to receive it. This time, GM didn't have to tell them to run; they were the hunter and hunted, both.

I have to stop him.

■□■□■□■

9-1-1.

'No service.'

She redialed, fumbling in her haste. The same two words blinked out at her, taunting her. 'No service.'

"No. No, no, *no*. Goddammit, *no*."

"I could punish you for that, you know."

Val jumped, her grip on the phone slackening with her surprise. It was pulled out of her hand and she heard a loud crunch, flinching when the pieces dropped to the floor a few seconds later. Slowly, she raised her head to meet the stolid gray stare of the grandmaster. GM.

Gavin.

"*You.*"

His mouth opened, but Val launched herself at him before he could speak. There was nothing more to say, and even if there was, she had no interest in hearing it.

Horrorscape by Nenia Campbell

The two hit the floorboards with a heavy thud. He grunted, and a dark pleasure uncoiled in her that she could do that, make him feel pain.

It reminded her he was mortal, visceral, and, as such, could die. "You sick creep," she snarled, grabbing him by the collar. The knuckles of her hand were pressed against his throat and she could feel his pulse. "You fucking psychopath." Every beat was a taunt, every breath was a mocking laugh. "I'll—I'll kill you!"

"I'll gladly suffer a little death at your hands."

"Don't talk to me!" she screamed, digging her nails hard into his shoulder. Hard enough to make him wince. Because each honeyed word that poured from his lips was corrosive, and gnawed away at her resolve. "You bastard!" She clawed at his face. He caught her wrist before her nails could graze his skin. "Let me go!"

She drove her knee downwards. He twisted his hips, and the momentum of it sent her rolling onto her back. "So eager to have me back on top of you. Val, you're insatiable."

Val let out a frightened wail. She couldn't kick. She couldn't punch. She could barely move; she was trapped. The knowledge of this resounded in her body with a deeply satisfied *yes*. "Let me *go*."

"You've had your fun. Now I suggest you quit while you're ahead." He flicked out a knife; the blade was coated in blood. He waved it at her, watching her eyes track the movement. "I don't want to have to use this on you."

She froze, and after a long moment he folded the knife back into the unseen pocket from whence it came. She shuddered, wondering whose blood it was that was on the blade. *James? Did he do something to James?* "You're—you really are going to kill us."

"Not personally."

He was splicing hairs now, for no reason other than the fact that he could. She set her teeth and demanded, *"Why?"*

"You put me through a lot of trouble with that nasty court case. I almost went to jail because of you. I lost time, money, business, my art," he said silkily. "All because you were unable to come to the terms with the fact that you are mine. By all rights, you still are."

She bucked. "What about the others?"

"Hmm?"

"Jason. Charlie. Brent."

"Oh," he said, "them."

"What *about* them? They have no part in this. You think they're just going to go along?"

"I made sure they had ample motivation. Five million dollars' worth, to be exact. If they win."

Where did he get that kind of money? She shook her head, trying to clear it. That wasn't the important issue here. "So it's revenge you want," she said.

"No, Val. It's so simple, I'm surprised you haven't figured it out already. I want *you*."

"Why?" she asked again, harder this time.

"Because, my dear, you have something that I want." He tapped her breast, over her pounding heart. "In here."

Stall him. "There's a major loophole in your game."

"Which is?"

"You're assuming the others are actually going to kill the people on their papers."

"And you don't think they will? Why not?"

"Because my friends are *good people*."

"Ah, but my players are motivated by something much stronger." He released her hands, reaching up to unfasten his necklace. "Mere greed. It binds them to me."

The cold, steel necklace slithered over and around her wrists, drawing them tightly together. "Just as this binds you to me." Her eyes widened in understanding.

He bound her ankles with the cord of the broken lamp, tight enough to make her wince. "I must say, you do look very toothsome." He produced a roll of tape. "If I didn't have so many errands to run, I'd be very tempted…to stick around—" he tore off a length of tape "—and play."

Val backed up, and a shard of glass pierced her palm.

"You're going to hurt yourself." He smoothed the tape over her mouth, letting his fingers trail down her jaw. She jerked against her restraints, hatred and fear coursing through her in equal measure. His eyes fell to her clenched fist, leaking blood. "Oh dear. You already have."

She cursed at him through the tape.

"Let me see." He opened her hand and prized the shard free by touch alone. "There." He let the glass fall to the floor with a tinkle. "Isn't that better?"

Val shuddered in revulsion.

"When you struggle like that, I don't know what I'll do." He licked his bloodied fingers. "You make me feel things I didn't think possible. I could have appealed to your romantic sensibilities, you know. You were so innocent. So naïve. I could have lured you to me with empty lies and you would have come to me willingly."

Val allowed her expression to say what she thought of that. He wiped his dampened fingers on her jeans and patted her cheek. She flinched.

"I didn't, though. And do you know why? Because I want you to know exactly what I am. So that when you make your choice, there will be no doubt to you, or to anyone else—" he leaned in closer "—that Valerian Marie Kimble knew exactly what she was getting into when she allowed me into her bed. Which of us will be the monster then, hmm? Beauty, or the poor beguiled beast? You won the battle last time, my dear, but ultimately you lost the war. This time, you win nothing. I'll make sure of it."

She heard him get to his feet. Then he was gone.

■◻■◻■◻■

The skin of her shoulder prickled, eliciting a hushed screech from Lisa. With infinite patience, Blake reached over and brushed something off her back. "What—what was it?"

"A spider."

"Ugh!" She reached around, clawing at her skin. She could still feel its little legs crawling…

"Lisa, it's just a spider. We've got bigger problems."

"I know. I'm just…scared, okay?"

Blake sighed. "We have to stay calm—"

"Oh, right. Calm!"

"GM wants us to be scared. Fear narrows concentration and overrides logic. He's probably counting on that to make us stupid and slow. We can't give him what he wants."

"Aren't you scared?"

"Of course I'm scared."

"How can you be rational at a time like this?"

"I'm trying to think of it like a puzzle." Was that a crack in his voice? "That's what it is, isn't it? The clues? The chess pieces? The message on the wall? It's a game and he's not going to make it easy to escape — not with all the effort he's put into this."

"Blake? Who's on your paper?"

A line creased his brow. "I'm not supposed to tell you that. Remember?"

"Screw GM," Lisa said, "And his little rules, too—they're going to get us killed anyway." She thought he might have smiled, but it was too dark and too brief to tell. "Blake?" she said, after a long moment, "who was on your paper?"

"Charlie's on my paper."

Lisa exhaled in relief. No one on their team. Not that she wanted to kill anyone, but—but she didn't want to die. She'd just finished writing her personal statements. She'd just gotten the confirmation from UW. She didn't want to die! She *couldn't* die.

"Out of curiosity, why do you ask?"

Lisa faltered. "I was just…wondering if you were going to…you know."

"No." Lisa flinched. "No," he repeated, in a slightly calmer voice, "No. I'm not killing anyone. I thought I made that quite clear in the parlor."

"And I thought GM made it quite clear that your chivalry doesn't matter to him. This isn't one of your computer games. There are no extra lives. No bonus points for bravery. He'll kill you. Do you not see that?"

"I do." His voice was flat: emotionless.

"Then why are you doing this?"

"I refuse to sink to his level."

"*Blake.*"

"Lisa, trust me. It's personal. I have my reasons."

Tears stabbed at her eyes. She brushed them away impatiently. "Yes, and they're going to get you *killed*."

Who cares? He's just a geek. Save yourself. Run.

This nightmare was bringing out a side of her she hadn't known she possessed; it was a side of herself that Lisa didn't feel comfortable with. "Blake?" *Run.* "Blake?" she hissed, louder, trying to drown out the panicked siren in her head. "Blake are you there?"

He wasn't. She was alone. Again.

How had Blake disappeared? And when? She'd been talking to him seconds ago. Lisa considered doubling back to look for him, but there was no guarantee that she wouldn't run into a prowling member of the white team instead—and there were so many doors. But Blake couldn't have gone too far and if he wandered the halls alone, he might be killed.

"Blake," she groaned, "What am I going to do with you?"

Swallowing heavily, Lisa reached for the knob of the door in front of her. Unlike the front doors, it turned easily in her hand, and she jerked it open, exposing the room that lay beyond. Lisa could make out a dim, blue glow, but couldn't identify its source.

"Is there anyone in here?" she ventured timidly, gripping the doorknob so hard that her fingers began to ache. "Hello?"

Yes. There, in the shadows, she could make out the silhouette of someone sitting in the darkness. It was James. She nearly laughed—*James*. Oh, thank God. All this time they had been worried sick, and he had been hiding out here all along. *Silly, dependable James*, she thought, *who'd have ever guessed that he was such a coward?*

"James, come on, we have to get you out of here."

Silence.

"James? You're scaring me. Please, say something. Anything." Lisa released the doorknob and took a series of steps forward, until she was standing just inches away from the chair. She smelled something strange, unpleasantly familiar, but couldn't put a name to it.

"James. Listen to me—" She grabbed hold of his shirt, "I know it's a lot to deal with. Believe me, I do. I'm freaking out. But we can't—"

Her fingers slid against something wet and slick

against his collar. Slowly, she raised her hands. In the dim light, her fingertips looked almost black. *Blood?*

"Oh my god," Lisa gasped, "Oh my god, no. Please...no."

But she knew. Even as she pressed her shaking fingers to his cooling skin, she knew. James hadn't answered because James was dead. She had been talking to a corpse.

And she recognized the smell now. Piss. He had soiled himself, before or after he had been killed. She retched as she stepped into the hallway numbly, resisting the urge to wipe her hands on the folds of her dress. There had to be a bathroom around here somewhere so she could wash away the memory of his stiff, unyielding flesh...the congealing blood....

James.

She bent over, and emptied the contents of her stomach on the floor with such violence that she began to think that she might never stop. But she did, eventually, and then she found an old bathroom at the end of the hall.

Oh god oh god oh god.

Sniffling, she scrubbed at her hands until her knuckles were red and every last trace of red had been eradicated from her nails and skin. There was a soap dispenser beside the sink but it looked ancient, practically an antique, judging from the congealing crust sticking to the pump.

(You have to kill the person on your paper)

She wasn't sure her hands would ever be clean again.

■□■□■□■

How could Lisa play into the grandmaster's hands like that? It made him so angry that he couldn't see straight. For a second, just for a second, she'd shown herself to be more than one of James' giggling, popular acquaintances and then she'd just…

"Lisa?" he whispered. Then, in a louder voice, "Lisa?"

Something heavy slammed downstairs.

He paused uncertainly, his hand on the ornately carved banister. It could be a trap, but the members of the white team had mostly proven unexceptional so far—*except for Jason*, Blake thought, remembering how he had roughly shoved him into the linen closet before he could recover his senses. *He's a bad one.*

Blake took another cautious step. "Lisa?"

The pounding grew louder. Probably not the white team then; it was too risky, making that much noise without knowing who was coming down the hall first.

Unless it's some kind of distraction.

There was a loud crunch. He looked under his sneakers. Broken glass. Behind the wire frames of his glasses, his hazel eyes widened in alarm. It was all over the place. His eyes lingered on an empty lampshade lying on the floor, beside an old, mahogany end table. Was there a struggle?

"Oh my god," he breathed, "Val."

The red-haired girl was leaning against the wall, on the fringe of the mess. She was conscious, but bound, gagged, and slightly dazed. Blake dropped to his knees and reached around her. Metal. It felt like a bike chain.

"Jesus Christ," he muttered, "I'm no good at knots—can you lean forward at all?"

Val did and said something incomprehensible. He stared at her, flushing with comprehension when her eyes went pointedly to the tape covering her mouth.

"Oh, right. Sorry." He ripped off the tape and Val let out a hoarse scream that made both of them jump.

"Sorry! Sorry!"

She smacked her lips together several times. "It's...oh God, that hurt. It's okay. Th-thanks. The chain isn't knotted. It's a necklace—there's a clasp."

"I see it." Blake forward, sliding the clasp back. Being so close to her, he could feel her shaking, and see the sweat beading on her skin, magnifying her freckles. "Who did this to you?"

"Gavin."

"Who?"

"GM. His real name is Gavin, and there's not one game there's two," she babbled, "he's trying to kill you all and I'm supposed to save you. That's why he tied me up. So I couldn't…he thinks I…Oh god, *James*. I think he might have done something terrible to James."

"We'll find him." The necklace hit the floor with a clatter and he kicked it aside, giving her an awkward pat on the back. "Come on, it'll be all right."

"He blames me," she said. "It's all my fault—"

"We'll talk about that later. Let's go. Now."

And that was when they heard the scream.

Horrorscape by Nenia Campbell

Chapter Twenty

Counterplay

Silence burned her ears. Only the goosebumps on her arms and Blake's bleached face made her sure that the scream had actually happened. Val shivered, unable to tear her eyes away from the darkened landing. She could still hear it reverberating shrilly in her ears, like a track on loop.

Her hand tightened on the banister. "Did you hear that? Blake?"

He nodded mutely, looking up at the staircase. "It sounded like…Lisa. Come on."

Val saw him move forward in her periphery—a slight, black-clad figure—and felt the talons of fear sink deep into her heart. "Wait a second!" He just looked at her, with the glare of the bulb reflecting off his glasses. That expression on his face chilled her; he looked too jaded, too wise. She grabbed his shoulder, adding, in a hushed voice, "You have no idea what's up there!"

"Actually," Blake said, in an unsteady voice, "I do."

(it sounded like Lisa)

And she had sounded like she was in pain.

The saliva in her throat dried up. Val's hand slipped from Blake's shoulder but she didn't notice. Would he dare? Yes, came the answer, he would. That look in his eyes had been so empty, so unstable.

"No," Blake stated, "A trap wouldn't make sense—why risk it, after all? It would only work if they were one-hundred percent positive that the right person was nearby and even then; if the wrong person comes running, too, they could die."

He's really thought this out. Val nodded absently, but inside she knew differently. Because there was one person in this house that the rules didn't apply to; one person who had already proved himself to be quite ruthless—

"Are you all right?" he asked, so carefully that she almost flinched. "You looked…disturbed."

Val wrung her hands nervously. "It's the game," she said, "This *stupid* game, and I can't—" she shook her head. "I guess I'm starting to let it get to me. I can't think of anything else."

Liar.

Blake seemed to think this over. "Is Gavin that boy? The one from your freshman year? The one you're so afraid of?"

"What are you talking about?" She winced. Ouch. That sounded weak and defensive to her own ears.

"Lisa told me. She told me everything."

She wanted self-righteous anger but could only manage to say, in a hurt, snippy tone, "And when were you having this discussion?"

"Right before middle game."

So, in other words, seconds before she had found them in the hallway, when she had been terrified that Gavin would say some small phrase intended to provoke her in front of her friends. They had known.

We could have run.

"But even if she hadn't," Blake hurried on to say, "I could have guessed. The way you looked at him, at the very start—you were so afraid. Why didn't you *say* anything?"

"He told me he'd hurt you all if I did," she sobbed.

"*Shit*, Val."

"I'm sorry, I'm so, so, so sorry. I thought you would hate me. Just like everyone else. You, and James, and Lisa—you guys are all I have, and I couldn't bear it if something ha—" Val froze, and several emotions passed over her face in quick succession, like clicking slides. "Oh my god," she said in a low voice, "that bastard."

Blake had halted at the top of the stairs. He looked alarmed. "Val?"

"This way." She pulled his sleeve in the aforementioned direction. "I think I know where Lisa is." She drew in an unsteady breath, still wracked with the sobs it took so much strength to suppress. "I think Jason has her."

■□■□■□■

Horrorscape by Nenia Campbell

It took several minutes for the water to go from icy to scalding. It took a few more minutes for her body to register this change in temperature Lisa knew she was acting ridiculous but every time she tried to rationalize, an image of James and his slashed throat and inanimate face flickered before her eyes and she thought she might vomit again.

Finally Lisa shut off the tap, gripping the marbled counter with white-knuckled hands. He was killing them one by one, like clay pigeons in a shooting range. She was so terrified that next time it would be Blake's or Val's or, worse, her own corpse that was found.

She didn't want to die. Who was Blake to hold that against her? Who was he to judge?

Slowly, wiping away the thin string of saliva that dangled from her lip, her eyes rose to the gilded mirror and her conviction immediately began to dwindle as she glimpsed the face in the glass. She drew in a quick breath, taking an unintentional step back. Jason moved quickly, catching her wrist in one hand and clapping the other over her mouth, abruptly cutting off her scream.

"I didn't have you down as the obsessive compulsive type," he said casually, ignoring her muffled, outraged cries, "But then again, I suppose you can't be too careful when it comes to blood. You could catch something."

Lisa froze. How did he—

Of course. He'd been following her.

Jason manhandled her out of the bathroom, into the labyrinthine hallway, pausing to shoot a meaningful glance towards the room where James had been killed. In her panic, she had left the door wide open, like a gaping mouth.

It was closed now.

Somebody else had come along—somebody else who had seen what she had seen—and they had chosen to reseal the evidence; to hide it away from prying eyes instead of raising the alarm. Who else would do that, but the killer?

The killer—Jason.

And he was going to take her into that room.

She kicked against the banister—it was thick oak—and slammed against him. Jason crashed into the wall, effectively pummeling the air from his own lungs. With a growl, he grabbed her arm and yanked it behind her back, at an angle that didn't normally occur in nature. Lisa screamed.

And this time, it was perfectly audible.

Jason cursed. He transferred her wrists to one hand, so that he could cover her mouth. "Be quiet." Lisa shook her head furiously, indicating that she would do no such thing. "I'm not going to kill you, you stupid bitch," he hissed, with so much resentment she had difficultly believing him. "If I was, I could have done it while you were hunched over the sink like a drunken sorority girl."

Lisa inhaled through her runny nose. He had a point.

To her surprise—and relief—he went through another door. In fact, it was the door she'd stubbornly tried to open during the scavenger hunt. It had been locked then but the handle opened easily in Jason's grasp. Another bad feeling hit her bloodstream hard, like a drug.

It was a bedroom. A boy's bedroom, judging from the dark wood and steel accents. In the corner of the room was a wooden chess set that appeared fairly old. The pieces were scattered, as if someone had swept their arm across the board in a fit of anger. GM?

Gavin, she corrected herself. *Gavin. It has to be.*

Lisa spun around, turning to face the tall boy. "Did you kill James?" she demanded icily.

"I don't have a death wish," Jason said, shaking his head, "Though I can't say I'm sorry he's gone."

"He's not on your list," Lisa said dumbly. She wasn't sure whether this news brought more relief or more terror. Even if he hadn't killed James—and he could have been lying about that, although Lisa didn't think he was—he was still dangerous. Her eyes flicked to the closed door.

"You're not, either," he said calmly, "I'll be honest with you. One of my teammates has your name on your paper and, if I remember the rules correctly, that means they have to kill you."

"Who…who's going to kill me? And how the hell do you know?"

"I cheat," he said silkily, and it took her a moment to realize that he'd just answered her question.

Half of it, anyway.

"Sounds like you do have a death wish. I don't think GM is going to appreciate that."

"GM is the one who made it all possible. I did him a couple of small favors."

"What kind of favors?"

"The rules have changed, Lisa," he said, "I can do things pawns can't do, go places pawns can't go—like this room, for instance. You may have noticed that it was locked earlier."

This time, she wasn't so subtle about backing away. "Why would he help a scumbag like you?"

Jason grinned. "You mean you haven't figured it out yet? Really? Your friend did."

"No, I haven't," she snapped, "So why don't you spell it out for me, before I break your face?"

He chuckled, seeming positively delighted with himself. "The next time you see Val, ask her."

The anger rose up in a torrential flare, eclipsing her fear for a brief moment. "Ask her what—"

Too late, she realized that the question was intended to distract her. Jason lunged.

He was not particularly strong but he was big and the force of his charge sent them both to the floor. Her shoulder the base of the chess table, sending a shock of pain down her arm. She gasped and hitched up her dress just as Jason's fingers grazed her ankle. She lashed out with her foot, heart in her throat, and managed to pull herself to her feet just as Jason was getting up.

"Stay the hell away from me, you freak," she said warningly. "Or I'll scream."

"Go ahead," Jason said, "And then your hunter might hear you and kill you straight off."

She flinched. Oh, god. He was right—she'd forgotten all about that in light of this new problem.

He grabbed her arms, keeping her in place against the wall. She glared at him. "Despite the details, it is a game." His breathing was heavy from their tousle on the floor and stirred the wispy hairs around her face. "Like any game, it has rules. There's a pattern here, Lisa, and I've figured it out. All this—the players, the pieces, you, me—come down to one central factor."

"Which is?"

"Revenge."

That makes sense.

His sharp blue eyes rested on her face. "It's still not too late for you. I can help you."

"Out of the kindness of your heart, I'm sure," she said, in cracking sarcasm.

"I don't understand why you dislike me so much," he mused, "If my teammate found you, she'd just kill you, straight off, no questions asked."

"So my options are, join you or be sold out."

"Something like that."

When Jason leaned in again—in anticipation of her agreeing to his horrendous deal, no doubt—she shoved against him. Hard.

"I'd rather take my chances with the killer."

She ran out the door, skating past him. His heavy footfalls were right behind her, like thunder in her ears. Gasping from fear and exertion, she selected a door at random and shut it as securely as she dared, nearly sobbing in relief when he rushed right past her. She let out the breath she'd been holding in—

—and ended up sucking it all back up when a hand clamped over her mouth. Had Jason found a short cut or, worse; had he been acting as an accomplice to her true killer? She made a strangled noise in the back of her throat as she clawed at the hand, trying to get free.

"Ouch," said the owner of the hand, in a strikingly familiar voice. "Lisa! Cut it out!"

No, no, no.

"Lisa! Lisa, stop." The hand fell away. "It's us. It's

me."

"Blake?" Lisa opened her eyes. "Val?"

"We saw that guy chasing you," Blake said. "Jason—wasn't it? I didn't want you to scream and alert him. I think he's gone, but I don't want to stay here and find out." He hissed through his teeth, staring down at his hand. "Ouch," he repeated, staring at the three lines of blood she had drawn.

The apology was on the tip of her tongue when

(blood)

she remembered how Jason had managed to catch her in the first place—James's inanimate face, the blood, the terror. Everything started to grow black around the edges as the walls fell away with a dreadful roaring noise…and then Blake's worried face was blocking her field of view.

"I…I think you just fainted, Lisa."

"Oh god." She squeezed her eyes shut, gripping her temples. "The white team…they killed James."

She heard Val stiffen. "What?"

"Are you sure?" Blake asked, sounding shaken. Lisa nodded stolidly. "Where?"

Reluctantly, she opened her eyes and pointed out the door. Blake turned in that direction. No, she didn't want him to go; didn't want to be left alone. She wanted to cry out the words that would make him stay without making her sound utterly pathetic but, lucky her, Val saved her from making that choice.

"I'll go."

Blake was shaking his head. "That's a really bad idea, Val. What if Gavin— "

"I said I'll go." She cleared her throat. "I'll meet you guys in the parlor, okay?"

"No. Not until we watch you go in. To make sure you're safe."

Safe, Lisa thought. *What a strange word.*

■□■□■□■

Val stared at the door, willing herself to open it. She could feel her friends watching her.

Go on.

The taunt, spoken at her ear, was not her own voice. Val whirled around, heart pounding.

It was in my head. There's nobody there. He's not really there.

Slowly, with a shaking hand, she turned the handle and gasped—it was the room with the aquariums.

Val swallowed thickly and forced herself to study the room. The luminescent outlines of the tanks provided just enough light for a cursory inspection.

Horrorscape by Nenia Campbell

Val bit her lip, searching the darkness. The only sign of disturbance was an upturned chair that she didn't remember from before. Frowning, she stepped closer, righting it. As she did so, her hand brushed against something course and rough—like frayed rope.

"There's no one in here," she said, feeling like her head might float away with relief. "It's empty."

Maybe Lisa had imagined it—maybe the fear had caused her to hallucinate. She'd fainted, hadn't she?

But the chair bothered her enough that she scanned the room a second time. Then she heard something. A soft, pattering sound like somebody trying not to be heard.

She raced to the door, only to have it shut in her face. "What the—"

She tried the handle. Locked.

"Open the door, GM," she said, "I know it's you."

She could almost imagine the mocking reply. *Do you?*

Val rammed her shoulder against the door, "And I know what you did."

There was no response. Of course. She wasn't really expecting one, but it still annoyed her. But she thought it sounded like a curious silence, if emotions could be ascribed to a lack of sound.

"Did you really think I'd let you get away with

torturing my friends?" She gave the doorknob a harsh yank, with each word, "In case you were wondering, I won't. I think it's really sick. I think you're really sick. You can't toy with people like this, you sa—"

The door creaked open and Val, not expecting this, fell into the hallway.

She took an unsteady step forwards and nearly crushed the gold pocket watch lying on the floor. Frowning, she picked it up examining the face. The face was crystal clear and polished, the painted roman numerals glistening like mica, but the watch itself looked quite old.

Shooting a sharp look down both sides of the hallway, she turned her attention to the envelope beneath the watch. He hadn't bothered sealing it and the words written inside were rushed.

Greenhouse, it said, 3 o' clock.

The time on the watch was 2:46.

Chapter Twenty-One

Threat

She took the stairs two at a time, clutching the watch. The letter, she left behind. It wouldn't fit into her pockets and she wanted to leave behind some sort of clue that would tell the others where she was just in case.... Val swallowed and shook her head.

Just in case I don't come back.

Where was the greenhouse? How was she supposed to find it in less than fifteen minutes? Once again, he was skewing the odds, setting her up for a fall. Frustrated, Val looked scanned the hall, searching for clues. She thought her efforts might be in vain until she spied a post-it on one of the doors just outside the parlor. She peeled it off.

It was blank.

But maybe that's the point? Hesitating, she opened the door and stepped through. A blast of cold air hit her like a cannon and Val froze, still on the doorstep. She was outside. She was *free*.

The door swung shut behind her with a heavy slam, shaking her back to reality with a grim, *Not quite.* She wasn't too surprised to find it locked. *I guess it's one-way.*

To her left was a swimming pool. It was lit, and she could see thin curls of steam rising from the jewel-like surface. To her right was a small pond surrounded by exotic plants of both the flowering and nonflowering variety. A fence enclosed the yard, concealing it from view from the street. She could see the greenhouse directly ahead. The glass panes glimmered darkly, reflecting the clouds above.

I should have brought Blake with me.

And...what? Put him in danger, too? It was clear that GM had no qualms about playing them off each other.

There was another post-it on the door of the greenhouse. It said, *key under flowerpot.*

She picked up the key and opened the door. The first thing she felt was the heat. Hot, oppressive heat that provided a sharp contrast against the chill outside. And it was humid. Moisture clung to her skin, her hair, her clothing. Val pushed her hair back from her face; it was already starting to frizz.

Two ferns were placed on either side of the door and one of the skeletal fronds brushed against her leg, eliciting a scream from the red-haired girl. It echoed brightly off the glass, chilling her straight to the marrow. Nobody had tended these plants in a long time. She glanced down at the watch. Seven minutes now.

Val took a few more steps into the room. Her foot hit something soft and pliant. She looked down. James.

It was *James*.

And he was dead. She dropped to her knees, reaching out to take his pulse, already knowing what the result would be. His skin was so stiff, so cold. So *pale*.

And wet.

A gash encircled his throat, gaping open like a screaming mouth. With a cry, she frantically wiped her fingers on her jeans. The blood had congealed and stuck to her fingers. She could detect the thick, cloying smell of old pennies. Gasping, she backed away from his body trying not to breathe in that smell. It clung to the back of her throat like a thin film.

"Oh god," she choked, "James. Oh, no. Please, God, no."

A cold space formed in her stomach, as if something vital inside of her had died along with him. She shook her head. How could he be so cold when, two hours ago, he had been warm and breathing?

"What has he done to you?"

But she knew the answer to that, too. Gavin had slashed his throat like some kind of barn animal and now she'd never see his eyes light up again. A line had been crossed with James's murder. Before, Gavin had been merely dangerous. Now, he was a *killer*.

Tears brimmed in her eyes, spilling down her cheeks. "I'm sorry. I'm, so, so sorry, forgive me—"

"It was all your fault. Why should he forgive you?"

Val jerked around to see Charlie leaning against the door, watching her. There was a strange half-smile on her face, and she felt her stomach lurch that someone could be so cruelly indifferent in the face of death.

"Shut up!" Val sobbed, "You have no idea what you—"

She froze, suddenly dry mouthed, as Charlie held up a fire poker. Holy hell. "That's right. Come any closer and you'll be reunited with your boyfriend sooner than you think."

"What are you going to do with that?"

The brunette shook the makeshift weapon in Val's direction, causing the other girl to take a wary step back. "What do you think? Surely you aren't that stupid."

Val walked right into one of the metal tables holding a tray of potted plants. She stepped around it trying to put any barrier between her and Charlie that she could. "I'm not on your list."

"I know. I've got your bitchy friend." She smiled, taking a leisurely step forward. "And I'm going to take care of her as soon as I've finished with you."

Val took another step back, jumping when one of the pots shattered on the ground with a crash that echoed through the greenhouse. "You can't do that," she said shakily, "GM said—"

The other girl shrieked, swinging the poker out in a wild arc, sending several plants crashing to the floor. "Don't you dare talk to me about him, you bitch. Don't even say his name. That's right," she added, sneering at the shocked girl's face, "I saw you kiss him. If you hadn't been leading him on, he never would have killed James. So you see, it's all. Your. Fault."

"He told me he didn't," Val said hoarsely. It occurred to her, too late, that she should have denied everything. Charlie growled and lashed out again. Val had to drop to her knees.

"He told me he didn't," Charlie mocked, "Oh, Val. You're so precious. I thought it was just an act, but you really are sweet as fucking pie, aren't you?

"I tried to bide my time. But no, GM decided he was going to go through with his stupid middle game. I'm nobody's pawn, not his—and not yours. The only reason he made you queen is because he wants to fuck you. But of course, that idea probably never even occurred to you, did it? No, not you. Not sweet little Val. Everything's just fucking *Disney* with you."

Val clapped her hands over her mouth. The smell of earth filled her nostrils. It made her feel sick. She focused on crawling, keeping low, avoiding shards of smashed terra cotta pottery. *I have to get out of here. I have to warn Lisa.*

"But he made a mistake. He thought he could get rid of me—that I'd just take this lying down and be a good little pawn. And that's why I'm going to kill you," Charlie finished savagely, "Because I'm not. With you out of the picture, he'll see that and realize we're perfect together."

Horrorscape by Nenia Campbell

She could barely hear the girl's words. Her heart was pounding too loud.

"My grandfather was a hunter—did you know that? He used to track frightened little animals in the forest, in the jungle, in the tundra—and that's precisely what you are, isn't it? A frightened little animal. There's no use hiding, Val...I'm going to find you. And when I do, I'm going to—"

Suddenly, the table flipped over. Val instinctively raised her arms to cover her face as pottery smashed and wood splintered around them. "Well."

"Charlie, please don't do this—"

"Shut up," the other girl growled. "Shut the fuck up, you stupid little whore." She pressed the sharp end against Val's chest, driving her backwards. "You have no right—none—to tell me what to do."

"I didn't...I didn't mean to..." Val thought quickly. "Couldn't we...talk about this?"

"Sure. What do you want to talk about? What a scheming little bitch you are for trying to worm your way out of what you deserve? Or do you want to talk to me about how I'll never get away with this?" She laughed deprecatingly. "Do you think he's going to come save you?"

Good lord. She was absolutely insane. "No! Jesus Christ, you can have him already!"

"Val, Val, Val." Her voice sounded so much like the

grandmaster's that, for a moment, she almost forgot who she was talking to. "Don't you get it? That doesn't matter."

"It…doesn't?"

"No," Charlie added, shaking her head. "He's not yours to give. See, as long as you're alive, he won't give up. I know, believe me. Because I'm the same way."

Val's back hit a shelf full of gardening supplies. Seed packets fluttered to the floor. "Oh god." She was right, only she had no way of knowing how right.

"And now, I'm going to jab this thing straight through your weak, pathetic heart."

The watch fell out of Val's hand with a soft clatter. The time was 2:59. And then, with a soft click, the hour hand moved to the three. Val closed her eyes when she felt the heavy point press against her left breast.

"On second thought…maybe I'll do a number on your pretty face first."

"Don't even think about it."

Val's eyes opened. She knew that voice; there was no other in the world quite like it. Gavin was standing in the doorway. From the floor, he seemed impossibly tall.

Do you think he's going to come save you?

Charlie jerked upon sighting him, tearing the lace of Val's blouse, drawing blood. Val gasped, clutching at her chest, but Charlie didn't appear to notice what she'd done.

"GM," she breathed, as if in a trance, letting go of the metal rod. The poker hit the floor with a clang. Val grabbed it, quickly, before the girl could think to reclaim her weapon.

"What the fuck do you think you're doing?" he snarled, in a tone she'd never heard him use. "She isn't on your list."

Clearly, this wasn't the warm welcome she'd expected. Charlie suddenly looked lost. "I—I wanted—"

"I know what you wanted," he said. "The only thing more transparent than that...ridiculous getup is your futile attempt at lying. This is not what we agreed upon."

A long, terrible silence ensued broken only by Charlie's sobbing.

Charlie couldn't possibly believe that GM would buy this act. But GM said nothing not even when she leaned into his chest, though Val thought she saw him stiffen. "Don't hate me. Please...please don't hate me—I did it all for us. For you."

"For me," he repeated. "You thought that was what I wanted?"

Still crying, Charlie nodded.

"Oh, Charlene." Slowly, almost mechanically, he placed his hand on the small of her back—but somehow, the gesture didn't seem particularly comforting. No, Val thought, It looks like he's holding her in place.

In fact, that looked exactly like what he was doing. Val's eyes widened. "Wait," she screamed, "Gavin! Don't!"

Gasping, Charlie stumbled away from him. A red stain was visible on the front of the girl's pristine white shirt, spreading around the splayed fingers of the girl's right hand. Her eyes went to the hole in her stomach, and she choked, "Gavin?"

He shook his head. She collapsed in an ungraceful heap.

"You killed her," Val said sickly, turning away from Charlie's crumpled form. There was something so sad and vulnerable about her in death. So *used*.

"She would have killed you." GM looked down, frowning. Charlie's blood had left a slick trail on the front of his shirt. He started undoing the buttons. "That wasn't part of the game."

"But you killed her."

He glanced up, pinning her with that icy gaze. "She's expendable."

She couldn't believe he could be so blasé. "And what about James? Was he?"

GM tossed his stained shirt aside, revealing a white wife beater. "Yes, he was."

This was more than she could bear to hear. An

agonized wail escaped her mouth. "I can't…I won't play this game anymore—not when people are dying!"

"So Lisa and Blake…I suppose they mean nothing to you?"

Val froze, her features twisted with panic. She pointed the poker—which, until now, she had forgotten about—at his chest. "Stay away from them you monster or…or I'll make you stay away from them."

GM took a step closer and touched the end of her makeshift weapon. "Are you threatening me?" He didn't sound angry, only amused. And she realized, with a lurch, that his body wasn't quite as slight as she'd initially thought. He could easily overpower her—and he knew it.

Her grip on the poker tightened. "Stay back."

"Could you do it?" he said. "Kill me in cold blood?"

Yes. Do it. Kill him.

"Let go of the poker, Val. You're not a killer. You never will be. Give it to me."

She drew in a shuddering breath and except for her shaking, which she could not control, Val did not move. With a single pull, the metal rod slid easily from her hands.

"I hate you so goddamn much," she whispered.

"I know."

Tears continued to roll down her face. She swiped at

them angrily. "Why are you doing this to me?"

GM looked down at the poker and then back at her tear-streaked face. "You have something inside of you—something the others are lacking—that makes you a formidable adversary," he drew back, searching her eyes for something she wasn't even sure she had, "It also makes you more vulnerable.

"That's why I made you a queen." GM waved the poker loosely in her direction. "I can't always predict what you're going to do and your conscience won't let you desert your friends, despite all the things you do to further the danger they are in." He paused. "I can make things very unpleasant for them if you choose not to participate."

She saw him glance at her clenched hands.

"But that is not what I wanted to see you about. No, I've decided to let you ask me one question—any question—as a token of my good faith."

"You'll cheat."

"And if I give you my word?"

Val took a deep breath. Her eyes went to Charlie's body and she had to look away, quickly, as her stomach contracted. "What's the catch?"

"Nothing Faustian, my dear. Only that I get to ask one question of my own."

Horrorscape by Nenia Campbell

Chapter Twenty-Two

Overloaded

As Lisa and Blake relocated to the parlor to wait for Val, Blake couldn't help noticing how utterly quiet the large house was, devoid of the usual house sounds, such as the whir of an electrical appliance or a ticking clock. Hazel eyes shifted to his left, focusing on the blond girl walking beside him. She had been uncharacteristically reticent and stiff ever since their unpleasant encounter in the hallway.

"We're going to die here," she said tonelessly, startling him.

"No, we're not." He put his hand on her shoulder, careful in his restraint. "We have to be rational—"

"Rational!" A clotted laugh escaped the blond. "No offense, Blake, but I think rationality stepped out of here, oh, about five hours ago!" She shook her head and took a series of quick steps forward, causing his hand to fall away. "This is a game created by a killer who's already shown that he has no regard for his own rules. If there is a method to his madness, I certainly don't see it!"

In a way, Lisa was right: GM didn't play by his own rules. He threatened some players, harassed others, and kept disappearing during the most crucial moments of the game—and that filled him with despair. However, in spite of his erratic behavior patterns, there was a pattern to his games: a common theme that each one revolved around. Chess, in some cases. Predation, in others.

Blake pulled out a straight-backed chair and Lisa collapsed into it, burying her face in her hands. "I'm sorry Blake. I'm just…so goddamn tired," she whispered. "I want to sleep." Her voice increased in volume. "I just want to fucking sleep! Is that too much to ask from that bastard?"

"Lisa. Please."

"Everything is wrong. Everything! Jason keeps bothering me"—he frowned deeply at this but Lisa kept going—"Val keeps disappearing, and now James shows up dead. I didn't think GM was serious. I mean, he scared me, but I didn't think he actually meant to kill us. I don't know what I was thinking. Maybe I wasn't thinking."

None of us were. We all fell for his trap, not just you. But he kept quiet and allowed her to speak.

"I wish I had never come to this stupid party. If I get out of this, I swear I'll—I'll never break curfew again. Back by four, each day, from school and back." Lisa glanced down at her hands and then up at his face. Her eyes were red. "Jason made one mistake," she said, "He told me who my killer was."

Without speaking, he pulled up a second chair and sat across from her. "Tell me," he said gently.

"Charlie." Lisa made a face. "Can you believe it? Of all the people I could have gotten—"

"Did he actually say it was Charlie?" Blake asked, leaning forward. "Did he say her name?"

"No." She frowned. "All he said was, 'if my buddy found you, she'd just kill you straight off—no questions asked.' I almost didn't catch it, he was so subtle. But he definitely said *she*."

Blake exhaled deeply. "Okay. Let's assume you're right and she is your killer. That just leaves Brent and Jason for me." *If it truly is white versus black.*

He still wasn't quite sure how far GM intended to run with his little chess theme.

"It's Jason, obviously," Lisa said, sounding annoyed that he'd even questioned it.

"You're only saying that because you don't like him." Her eyes flashed dangerously and she opened her mouth to protest. Blake quickly pressed on, "There's a fifty-fifty chance, which drops to thirty-three and a third if we're wrong—or if Jason was lying—and Charlie isn't your killer after all."

Her eyes were still too bright. "And if we're both wrong, and it's neither?"

"Twenty-five percent chance," Blake said grimly, "Or…less."

Not terribly good odds. Especially with their lives on the line.

They exchanged a look.

"I don't think Jason was lying," Lisa said, adjusting the bodice of her dress. "When he said she, I'm pretty sure it was inadvertent. I don't think he realized what he was saying." She shuddered. "Plus, he's a total creeper."

Creeper. Blake's lips twitched. So Lisa.

She was right about one thing, though. Jason was definitely the most ruthless of the three white players. His smile faded as his eyes swept the room, landing on the few empty soda cans and paper napkins strewn around the room. It was hard to believe that they had started out in such high spirits. Eat, drink, and be merry, he thought, For tomorrow we shall die.

His mouth hardened.

His father would be worried sick. Though Blake had no official curfew, he never came home later than midnight; it was an unspoken rule between them. According to his watch, it was a quarter past three.

What had GM said earlier? You have until dawn? Maybe that was good. It meant he wasn't counting on them dying right away. If they played their cards right, they had a shot—however small—at survival.

"Just out of curiosity," Blake said, pushing those thoughts aside, "Who is on your paper?"

"Brent. The missing link," she added, wrinkling her nose.

"Really? Because I'm beginning to think he k-killed James," his ears flushed and he prayed fervently that she hadn't noticed the stammer in his voice, "I mean, they both went missing around the same time. Jason, on the other hand, keeps popping up. In fact, I've been seeing him and Charlie a lot with no traces of the other two."

"You mean GM? But James was missing for a while—anyone could have gotten to him."

"Speaking of missing, where's Val?" Blake asked slowly, "She should have gotten here by now."

"What time is it?"

Blake looked down at his watch. "After three. Do you think we should go after for her? I don't think she should be left alone for too long."

"I'm sure she's fine." Blake shot her a look and her cheeks flushed. "Blake! I didn't mean it like that!"

Blake just shook his head, rolling his sleeve back over the watch. "We never should have let her go in that room alone. One of us should have gone with her. This Gavin guy is messed-up."

"She said she wanted to go alone."

"I don't think she did."

Lisa's face grew pained.

Blake been referring himself, since Lisa had obviously been in no condition to go, but she was already standing with a hard, determined set to her jaw. "Fine," she was saying, "I'll go look."

"Be careful."

"Of Val?" She arched an eyebrow, but Blake didn't smile. "Blake? What do you know?"

"Jason said *she*. Apart from you, Val's the only other girl. Be careful."

■□■□■□■

The door was gaping open again, like a hungry mouth waiting to devour all who entered.

Unwilling to step inside, Lisa poked her head through the doorway, surveying the dark room. She imagined that she could see a dark stain on the floor that might have been blood. With effort, Lisa tore her eyes away from the spot. "Val? Are you in here? Are you…all right?"

Could Blake be right? Could Val be my killer?

To her surprise, the room was empty—James was gone and so was Val. It was as if nothing had happened, although even Lisa wasn't too far gone to overlook that, so what the hell was going on here?

"This just keeps getting creepier and creepier," she whispered to herself, shutting the door securely.

When she moved, her shoe slid on something. An envelope. With shaking fingers, she pulled out the letter. As her eyes read the single phrase printed on the smooth, grainy surface, they widened.

Horrorscape by Nenia Campbell

Greenhouse. 3 o' clock.

No. Val wouldn't play the self-sacrificial martyr, not in a game like this. Would she? Lisa closed her eyes wearily, pressing the paper against her chest. Deep down, she knew the answer to that.

■□■□■□■

A soft rain had started to fall, hitting the glass rooftop with a sound like polite applause. Though the greenhouse was quite warm, Val felt as though her body was encrusted in several layers of ice, rooting her to the soft, earthen floor. She already had several questions in mind, each more tempting than the last—but this game, like all his others, was terribly one-sided.

Two people had died in this room. If she wasn't careful, she could just as easily become the third.

"Why me?"

"Because I lie awake at night, dreaming of all the things I want to do to your body, of leaving marks on your skin so that everyone knows that you are mine. And only mine."

He leaned back against one of the larger metal tables.

"But you fight yourself even as you fight me, and I love that, too. I love watching you squirm, because it gives me some idea of how you'll look when I'm inside you. I want to be your last thought at night, and your first taste at dawn. I want to teach you, own you, control you."

Val could not speak; even if she could, she doubted she would know what to say.

"My turn," he said, leaning forwards. "What is it that you are most afraid of?" An odd smile. "Besides me, of course."

This new terror eclipsed the old one so completely that she simply moved from one into the other, like changing gears. Val choked, undiluted fear flooding her bloodstream like venom. For a moment, she forgot how to breathe. She was afraid of so many things—losing her friends, not getting out of here alive, of him.

And that fear was ever-present, malingering, and threatened to consume her with every growing moment, because she knew she couldn't control herself—not completely—when she was around him.

He knows me too well.

"Why do you want to know that?" she asked, unable to keep the panic out of her voice. Would he be above using it against her?

No.

"Curiosity. Personal…interests."

On the other side of the tinted glass panes, she could make out his spacious backyard. Large mulberry trees shaded the rear of the house, their leaves dripping water, and on the far side, she could just make out the lit, aquamarine swimming pool shrouded in curls of mist and illuminated, silvery rain.

"If I refuse to tell you?"

He just looked at her.

She plucked at the lace of her shirt and said, "Water. I don't like water." And then, in a faltering voice, she added, "I can't swim."

"You never learned?"

"I almost drowned in a lake when I was six. It killed any interest I had."

That was when she saw Lisa. Their eyes met through the glass. Her friend's eyes widened in panic and she started to reach for the door. *No*, Val mouthed. *Run. Get back to the house.*

A furrow formed between Lisa's tawny eyebrows. She frowned, comprehending, and backed away from the door—but GM had seen Val's lips move and started to turn around. "What was that?" he asked curiously but not, she thought, without suspicion. Or was she imagining it?

Disgusted with herself, and with what she was about to do, she grabbed him by the neck of his wife beater and kissed him—hard. *Please understand, James. I did it for them. Forgive me, if you can.*

His eyes opened comically wide and he took a

startled step backwards, hitting the edge of the table he had used as his perch only moments before. His gaze shifted to his right and cold, cynical amusement swept over his patrician features like an ice storm.

With a smile as cool as the night-chilled glass behind them, he cupped her face, returning the kiss with equal heat. But the hands on her face were taut with restraint and when she looked up, his face could have been chiseled from stone. "Very good," he said. "That was very convincing."

"What are you talking about?"

That jaded expression on his face disappeared, replaced by a flat, dispassionate look as he let his hand fall back to his side. "Are you suggesting that you weren't trying to…distract me just now?"

She choked, taking a quick step back from him, horrified that she'd been so transparent.

"As I thought."

Val shook her head repeatedly. How had he known? What had given her away?

"Don't look so shocked, my dear. We're in a room of glass. I saw her reflection cast in your shadow."

■□■□■□■

Blake bit his lip. Half past three. The girls should

have come back by now—both Lisa and Val knew what was at stake here. He pursed his lips. How long did it take to comfort somebody, anyway?

Not this long.

Maybe Val is the killer.

He stepped into the main hall, taking the path Lisa had taken scant minutes before, though in the opposite direction, when he heard an unpleasant voice say, "Blake, right?"

Blake spun around. A tall, thin boy was perched on the edge of the rail, one arm wrapped around the ornately carved wooden banister. For a horrifying moment, he thought the boy was GM—perhaps it was the sheer disregard for safety, or the insolence in his posture—and then he realized that it wasn't.

It was Jason.

"Yes," he said cautiously, taking a subtle step back, "What do you want?"

Jason swung his legs off the rail, hitting the floor in a movement that was, if nothing else, threatening. "Nothing much."

Blake edged back. This was starting to look bad. Jason was blocking his access to the hall, to Lisa, and the only other way down—Blake cast a nervous glance at the stairway, knowing that he would have to turn his back on this boy in order to safely descend the narrow steps.

"Oh, don't even think about it," Jason said easily, "If

you make a break for the stairs, I'll push you."

"It's not very far," Blake heard himself say.

"That's true," Jason agreed, scratching his chin, "But even so, I have this." And he produced a knife, which glinted in the light. Blake was surprised, though he couldn't say why. Perhaps he had assumed that the other players shared their qualms about taking a human life—or that they were too sane, too composed, to be dragged into the grandmaster's sick little games.

Clearly, he had thought wrong.

Blake wet his lips.

"I'm on your list."

"That's right, rabbit."

Horrorscape by Nenia Campbell

Chapter Twenty-Three
Relative Pin

The rain was coming down in sheets, pelting the blond girl with water and soaking her long, blond hair. Wincing a little, she leaned one of the books from the library against the frame to keep the heavy door from slamming shut behind her. She stepped off the stone porch, which gave way to mud that sucked noisily at her shoes. Cold, persistent wind chilled her wet, bare skin and Lisa shivered violently wishing, not for the first time, that she had thought to bring a jacket.

Luckily, the greenhouse wasn't very far. She could glimpse the silvery edges against the darkness of the trees from where she stood. The backyard was surprisingly spacious. Trees bordering the property provided a discomforting sense of being penned in.

Was there a possible escape route out here? It was definitely worth looking into.

For now, she focused on getting to the greenhouse. The windows were slightly misted from the condensation inside. Dead, spindly plants blocked her view from the front door, so Lisa made her way along the side to get a better view of the interior. Val, how could you be such an idiot? she wondered. Val was just naïve enough to let herself be lured out here, for a chance to play the heroine.

Or maybe she's just devious enough to lure you out here

to kill you, hissed the dark voice she'd only recently discovered. *Who would suspect her? Not you.*

Lisa teetered on the edge of the concrete ringing the greenhouse, peering in through the glass. No use. The glass was too dirty to see through. With a disgusted groan, wiped away the grime coating the window with her palm. Her resultant gasp was lost amid the hiss of the rain. She never expected to see the grandmaster in the greenhouse, so far away from all the action, in spite of the letter that he had left behind.

She relaxed a few inches when she realized that he hadn't seen her, yet. His back was facing her and she noticed that he'd discarded his white button-down shirt for a wife beater of the same color. That was odd. Why had he changed his shirt? Whatever the reason, if there was a reason, he still looked intimidating as hell, and Lisa wasn't going to wait around for him to discover her peeping.

But then GM stepped to the side, revealing Val. The red-haired girl was hugging herself and saying something. Lisa couldn't make out the words but she obviously wasn't happy. With a flash of green, her eyes cut away from GM towards the window, where they promptly widened in shock.

What are you doing? Lisa mouthed.

Val went rigid.

Lisa reached for the handle and that simple

movement seemed to jerk Val out of her paralysis. She shook her head—only slightly; it could have been mistaken as a hair toss—and mouthed, *No! Run! Get back to the house!*

That sounded like a very bad idea to Lisa and she was about to say so, when GM started to turn around. Lisa's heart stopped beating. *Oh god, oh god, oh god.*

And then her best friend, whom she had known since middle school, pressed herself against that sadist and kissed him. Lisa could only stare, her face heating up in spite of the chilly rain. When Gavin's fingers slid up her friend's shirt, she glanced away.

She's distracting him. That's all.

Except—that kiss had been a little too convincing. Val had never kissed James like that. She didn't even know Val *could* kiss like that, because kisses like that led to one thing: a thing she knew for a fact that Val had never done.

Or thought she had.

What if whatever was between Gavin and Val wasn't entirely one-sided? What if she had that—what was it called?—Stockholm Syndrome? Shaking her head, Lisa turned and did as Val had asked.

She ran.

Val heard the rain pick up in its intensity as it drummed against the glass roof. The grandmaster's pleasant smile turned ironic before her eyes. She'd been caught and, worse, she'd exploited him; an offense she doubted that he would take lightly, given his sense of pride.

"If you knew, why did you kiss me?"

"I am not particularly easy to fool," GM spoke casually, as though he weren't impeding on her personal space, but there was a snarl in the otherwise seamless quality of his voice, "And it isn't wise to try."

Her arms brushed against the cold glass, causing her to jump. "Those are part of your rules," she protested, rubbing at her arms and trying to hide her unease, "You—"

"Did you know, you always bite your lip whenever you're about to do something reckless?"

A protest was halfway to her mouth when she realized, with no small amount of mortification, that she currently was biting on her lip. Heat crawled up her neck and she hastily unclenched her jaw. A half-smile appeared on his face as he glimpsed her reaction, but there was no real humor in it and that scared her—a lot. Strangely enough, it made her angry, too.

Angry that he had called her bluff, angry that he had killed James, angry that he scared her so badly, angry that he didn't scare her enough. The anger was comforting and she wrapped herself into it like a warm cloak. "At least I'm not reckless with other people's lives," she spat.

He grabbed her wrist when she was two meters away from the door and, with a not-so-gentle pull, twirled her around so she was propped against his chest. Lacing his fingers with those of her free hand he said, in a dark voice, "I wouldn't say that."

"What the hell is that supposed to mean?"

"I think you know very well what it means." GM slid her hands down, so they were resting on the slight curve of her stomach. "I tire of these games. It's all I can do to keep myself from taking you right here…against the wall."

And then Charlie's cruel words came fluttering back, like birds of prey.

(the only reason he made you queen is because he wants to fuck you)

Val made a strangled sound of disgusted horror.

"It doesn't have to be this way, you know. If you swear yourself to me, forever, I will end the game right now."

She could keep the others from being killed?

"What exactly would that entail?"

"Use your imagination," he said. "You know what I

want from you. You know exactly what I want."

He was right. She did.

"I might renege. I might run. What could possibly make you think that's even in the realm of possibility?"

"Because there is a very good chance one of your friends is going to die within the next half hour—if they haven't already." He turned his back on her. "Think it over, Val. Then come find me once you've made a decision. I'll be waiting."

■□■□■□■

Blake took a very large step backwards, colliding with the wall. A picture frame behind him wobbled dangerously, nearly coming off the nail, but he barely noticed. "You're going to kill me."

"Eventually," Jason conceded, startling the other boy. "I have plenty of time before the game ends and there are a few things I intended to ask you before I checkmate you." At Blake's pointed silence he added in a less pleasant voice, "The longer you talk, the longer you stay alive."

His heart thudded against his ribcage, as if trying to break free. *He's trying to talk himself into it*, he thought wildly. *He can't quite bring himself to kill me yet, those last vestiges of conscience are holding him back, but they're fraying fast....*

"So," the tall boy finished, studying his reflection in the blade for a few seconds before turning back to Blake, "What do you say? Shall I kill you now, or are you feeling chatty?"

Blake closed his eyes, feeling himself on the verge of panic that he couldn't give into. Jason was right on several counts; he was trapped and talking did appear to be the wisest course of action, although not for the reason he thought. Fine. If Jason wanted him to talk, then he would—at full-length—and possibly, if he was really lucky, an opportunity might arise.

Jason's arrogance might just lead to his downfall.

Aloud, he said, "I'll tell you anything you want to know."

Jason blinked, but his surprise at such cooperation was quick to fade. "Then why don't we start with why you think you're so much better than everyone else."

This startled him enough that he blurted out, "What?" without thinking. "Better than everyone else? Me?"

"Don't deny it," Jason said, pointing with the knife. Blake flinched. "You were awfully quick to go against the grandmaster when he announced the new rules for middle game—" Blake's face darkened, but Jason was speaking too quickly to notice "—and you're obviously not the confrontational type."

"What's your point?"

Jason looked irritated. "Obviously, you must have had a reason for doing so."

"I did," Blake said tightly.

The blond boy made a forwarding gesture with his hands. Blake shoved his hands into his pockets and looked away. Painful memories started to bubble over, like a pot left over the fire for too long. "I don't want to talk about it. Ask me something else."

"Oh no," Jason said, "I'm afraid it doesn't work that way. You don't get to pick which questions you answer. I do. And if you don't answer, you die."

"Why do you want to know so badly?"

"I didn't, until you started kicking up such a fuss about it. Now I'm curious. That's the price for staying alive," Jason said, so quietly that Blake almost didn't hear him.

"Fine. My mother—" He paused, choking a little. "My mother died when I was seven."

Jason paused, glancing up. "How?" he asked, sounding interested for the first time.

Oh, Jesus. Blake brushed his eyes with his sleeve. This was hard enough already without a bastard like Jason goading him along, with his goddamn morbid *curiosity*.

His lips tightened and he pulled off his glasses to clean them so he wouldn't have to see the other boy's face. "Car accident," he said finally. "She was hit by a drunk driver on her way home."

"Some teenager?" Jason wondered, "Driving around stoned out of his mind?"

"Close. Some rich big-wig driving around plumb drunk out of his mind. He was going fifty miles an hour, heading into oncoming traffic. She never—" he drew in a breath. "She died before they could get her to a hospital."

Jason blinked. "What about the other guy?"

"*He* got a fractured collarbone and a sprained wrist. The asshole couldn't have cared less about what he'd done," Blake said, remembering. "The jury and the judge convicted him like that." He snapped his fingers. "It should have been an open-shut case. He didn't want to go to AA, didn't want to change his ways, but he didn't even have to because he had rich relatives willing to bail him out of jail."

Breathing heavily now, Blake replaced the glasses on his face, where they quickly fogged up again. Jason's expression was unreadable. For a moment, Blake thought he saw a flash of—something—in the other boy's face but it quickly disappeared. "So that's why," he said.

"No," Blake found himself saying, "That's not why. It's because of my dad."

Jason sighed in a put-upon way, but his eyes were rapt.

Blake continued, "My dad didn't take her death well at all. Once someone dies, it's over—for them—but the people left behind continue to grieve. My dad started drinking, started to gain weight. He got fired from his old job because he stopped showing up…and I had to go away for awhile."

Blake swallowed.

"It was awful, living under that shadow. Of grief. Of pain. I could never…make somebody else suffer the way my dad or I did. Not after that. I'm sure even you have someone who must care about you," he added flatly. "Someone who will miss you when you're gone."

Jason's eyes narrowed. "I think that satisfies that question."

Blake took a deep breath. He felt curiously lighter, though mentioning Jason's death had been a mistake. It had brought the blonde boy back to this moment and the subject of Blake's own pending death. "O-okay."

"What, exactly, is your relationship with Lisa?"

The loaded question was meant to intimidate but Blake didn't rise to the bait. From what Lisa had implied about Jason, and from what he had inferred, that hardly seemed prudent. It would only lead to a fight, and unlike Jason he was unarmed. "We're acquaintances—good acquaintances—and that's all."

"Who do you think you're fooling?" Jason asked heatedly, "I saw you two kiss in the hallway."

Blake's face turned a deep shade of red. "You…you did?" he stammered. Okay, that was creepy. Lisa was right, he thought, there was definitely something off about Jason.

"Yes, and do you know why? She *wanted* me to see."

Blake blinked, startled. The possibility hadn't occurred to him. At the expression on his face, Jason snorted.

"Yeah, you were used, pal. Did you really think someone like you had a chance with someone like her?"

He had been asking himself a similar question all along—it really did seem too good to be true, Lisa falling for a nerd like him, especially with death looming over both their heads like a constant shadow. Despite all efforts not to, Blake kept wondering if Lisa stuck with him for convenience's sake.

Aloud he said, "And I suppose you think you do? Have a chance, I mean."

For one horrible instant, he thought Jason was going to deck him one. Then he laughed. "GM is right. You are more than you look. Perhaps you think you're noble, indirectly avenging your mother's death. But honestly? She was just a statistic," he took a menacing step forward, wielding the knife, "And now you're about to join the ranks."

If he looked the other boy in the eyes for much longer, he doubted that he would be able to control himself. Blake averted his gaze. That was why he saw Lisa holding one of the candy-colored vases from the hall. He hadn't even heard her enter the room.

Did she overhear us?

She motioned with a sharp jerk of her chin for him to look away, to not draw attention to her. Quickly, Blake focused his gaze on some other point. "Any other questions?"

"No." Jason's expression was hard. "I'm actually getting really sick of your voice."

He raised the knife as Lisa brought down the vase.

■□■□■□■

Lisa wasn't quite fast enough.

She realized that when she heard Blake cry out in, animal pain and saw his hand clap over his right side to instinctively stave off the bleeding and prevent further injury. Luckily, Jason wasn't able to drive the knife in very far because seconds later, the vase smashed over his head, sending pieces of colored glass tumbling to the Oriental rug, and Jason collapsed in an ungraceful heap at her feet.

"Thanks," Blake said weakly. His face was pale. "I was starting to get really worried."

"Blake! Are you all right? You're bleeding!"

"At least, I'm alive." He tried to laugh but laughing hurt too much, so he settled for a wavering smile she hesitantly returned.

"Let me see the wound."

He lifted the hem of his shirt and Lisa couldn't hold back her moan of disgust. There was so much blood, she suspected that it looked worse than it actually was, but still…. "Oh god," Lisa muttered, shifting her eyes away. Then, in an unconvincing voice, "Maybe it's not so bad."

"It definitely hurts." Blake took a deep breath, bracing himself, and knelt down beside the fallen boy.

"What are you doing?" Lisa asked, "He just tried to kill you and now you're taking his pulse?"

"He wasn't on our paper," Blake reminded her grimly, digging his finger's into the Jason's thick neck, "Remember the rules? If you kill the wrong person, you die."

"Oh," she said in a small, chastened voice.

"It's all right, he's still alive. And so are we…for the moment." He tried to get to his feet. His legs buckled when the muscles in his side moved. Lisa could only imagine what kind of pain he was in. She rushed to support his good side.

He gasped, barely managing a taut, "Thanks."

"If Jason had your name on his paper, does that mean you're safe?"

Blake shook his head. "From Jason, maybe."

"You think we're still in danger?"

"There's no way Gavin's going to let us live. Not willingly. Not if he's as violent as you told me he is."

That possibility hadn't occurred to her. "He is very distinctive looking, isn't he?"

"Yes, he is." Blake shot a nervous glance down the hallway and then nodded at the stairs. "Let's get out of here. Did you find Val?" She felt her face tightened. "Lisa? Did you—"

"I did," she said in a tight voice that betrayed her fear, "She's with GM."

"What?" he fairly exploded. "And you left her there?"

"No," Lisa said, "I mean, she's *with* GM."

"Actually, she's not," came a dry voice that sounded as if it were right behind them. The two teens whirled around to see GM leaning against the wall, with his arms crossed. The white shirt was gone; he was wearing a wife beater now, and his posture emphasized the muscles in his arms.

Shit.

"How long have you been standing there?" Blake asked.

"Oh, not long." His eyes flickered over them. "I didn't realize you two were together."

Blake looked as if he were about to deny it. Lisa stepped forward and answered readily, "I didn't realize you and Val were together."

GM straightened from his casual slouch, letting his hands fall to his hips. "You appear to have a penchant for situations that don't involve you."

Her unease did not go unnoticed by Blake. When he spoke again, his voice was cold and bore no trace of the grudging respect he typically used to address people he didn't like. "Did you need something, Gavin? Or did you just come here to threaten us?"

Lisa kicked at him to tell him to shut up but he sidestepped her foot. GM—Gavin's—face underwent a strange transformation upon hearing his name from Blake's lips, before settling on a grudging smile.

"As for you," GM continued, turning towards Blake, "I underestimated you. That doesn't happen very often, by the way, and it certainly will not happen again. That's a compliment, by the way."

And a threat? Lisa couldn't help noticing the obvious size different between the two, given their proximity. Blake was a good four inches shorter than their tall host who probably had fifty pounds on them both, most of it muscle.

As if reading her thoughts, Blake turned and gave her a carefully composed smile, but there was a tightness in his face and a weariness around his eyes that reassured her.

GM cleared his throat. "Anyway, I merely wanted to congratulate you, just in case I didn't get the chance later. Oh, and to give you this, of course." Blake flinched when GM reached out and seized his wrist, slipping a small square of paper in his palm. "Good luck," he said, in a soft voice.

Then he released Blake and walked off, with both pairs of eyes on him, leaving that thinly-veiled threat hanging in the air. "At least that wasn't weird."

"What did he give you?" Lisa asked, eying the doorway warily.

Since her gaze was directed elsewhere, she didn't see the subsequent blanching of Blake's face as he scanned the paper scrap. "Nothing," he said quietly, shoving the white square into his back pocket, "Just…trash."

Horrorscape by Nenia Campbell

Chapter Twenty-Four

Passive

Jason got to his feet rubbing at his head, which was throbbing painfully. *What happened?* He looked around, wincing at the pressure behind behind his eyes. Shattered pieces of pottery surrounded him, a few tainted by the red of his own blood. The last thing he remembered was Blake—then the sound of footsteps—and then pain—

Somebody had attacked him from behind.

He had failed. He had been so close to killing that little fuckwad with the glasses and getting the five million dollars—and he had *failed*. But if he hurried, there was a chance he might be able to catch him whoever had decided to get creative with the décor.

Jason started for the staircase, only to find that exit blocked by his so-called host. *Probably wants something*, he thought. *That's the only reason he ever shows up.*

"Going somewhere?"

"Trying to," replied Jason, injecting just enough annoyance into his voice to show he meant business.

GM's eyes landed on the broken remnants of the vase. *"Well.* What happened here?"

"Someone attacked me from behind," Jason said flatly. "I think it was that bitch Lisa."

"I see."

"Aren't you going to do something about it?"

"Do?" GM repeated with a slight laugh. "You mean, you wish me to kill for you. But you are still alive, so I'm afraid there is nothing I can do. No rules were broken."

"Somebody hit me over the head with a vase!" Jason shouted. "What do you mean no rules were broken?"

The amused look faded from GM's face. "Let me put it simply. There is a chess term, *j'adoube*, which allows someone to 'touch' a piece and not move it. It means to adjust. Let's just say, for lack of a better word, that you've been adjusted."

Jason swore. "Then let's make another deal. You get me Blake, and I'll get you Val."

"I've already got Val precisely where I want her. I appreciate the gesture, Jason, but unless you have something better to offer I'm afraid we don't have a deal."

"Okay—how about this?"

"I'm listening."

"If you *don't* bring me Blake, I'll kill Val."

GM tilted his head. "I really don't think you want to do that."

Jason folded his arms and put on his fiercest scowl. "That's my offer. No Blake, No Val."

"If that's how you want to play it."

That's more like it.

"Oh—one more thing," GM said casually, as he stepped aside to let Jason pass on the stairs.

Suddenly, he felt a quick bite of cold metal and a painfully contrasting warm, tearing sensation in his chest. He looked up at the grandmaster, mouth opening wordlessly, as GM said, softly, "You lose."

■□■□■□■

As Val moved further down the hall that led back to the parlor, she heard her friends' voices. Her heart surged with relief. *They're still alive.* Then she remembered Gavin's words from the greenhouse and doubt curled around her like a noose. *They're still alive for now.*

Lisa was the first to spot her. She tapped Blake, who was holding tightly onto his side. His hand was stained with blood. Both of them stared at her as if she were a ghost.

Maybe I am, she thought, *Maybe part of me is already dead.*

"Val," said Blake. "You're all right."

There was a question in it, half-buried.

Lisa was more blunt. "Where is Gavin?"

"I don't know." Val closed her eyes. "But Charlie's dead."

"She is?" Lisa tightened her grip on Blake's arm. "There, you see? She's dead. You don't have to kill her."

"Charlie was on your paper?" Val bleated.

"That doesn't matter. We still have a problem," Blake said. He sounded beaten.

The tone of his voice alerted Val. "Blake? What is it? What's wrong?"

Slowly, he reached into his pocket and pulled out a slip of paper. The edges were dog-eared and the charcoal was slightly smeared but that didn't keep her from being able to read Lisa's own name neatly printed in the center.

"Oh *no*," Val heard herself say. "Where did you get that?" But she knew, she *knew*; she recognized the handwriting.

"GM," Lisa answered for them both as he folded the square of paper back up into his pocket. "You just missed him, actually. I'm surprised you didn't have a run-in."

That's his plan.

If Blake didn't kill Lisa, he would be killed by GM. But if he killed Lisa, then, well, Lisa would be *dead*—and so too would Blake, on the inside, at least.

There's a chess term for this, she thought, *forced mate*. "Which way did he go?" Val said, dry-mouthed.

Wordlessly, Lisa pointed. She didn't seem surprised Val had asked, and neither of them questioned her intent. She remembered the way they had looked at her, the way that Blake had flinched back from her approach.

They think you're a traitor.

That couldn't be true—she had suffered as much as any of them. He had designed this game specifically to hurt *her*.

They blame you.

It wasn't her fault.

Isn't it, though? She inwardly mocked herself. *Consorting with the enemy. Letting him catch you alone. Just what, exactly, do you think you're doing right now?*

What she had to, ending this the only way she knew how. On her way down the hall, her flats crunched on pieces of broken glass. Jason was dead, his white shirt stained through the chest. She sucked in a breath and picked up one of the larger pieces of glass, the only shard that didn't have blood. Carefully, she tucked it into her jeans.

It sliced at her with every step, just like her conscience.

She found GM pacing the hallways like a wraith, or a leopard. There was a strange smell here, almost like gasoline. He turned before she could open her mouth, and she wondered when he had sensed her approach, what had given her away. She wondered if he had known she would come. "You win," she said. "I give up.

I surrender. You win."

"I always win."

His smile broke her heart. It was like freshman year all over again, listening to him denounce her at his trial. He only won because he had no qualms over who got hurt in the process. "You promise you'll let them go?"

"Of course, darling." He twined his fingers with hers, and dusted a kiss across her knuckles. "When have you ever known me to break a promise?"

Val looked away. "I don't know." She tried to pull her hand back, but Gavin squeezed her fingers more tightly.

"I don't think so."

It was a warning; it was a threat.

Lisa and Blake were still huddling where she had left them. Her stomach cramped at the condemning looks on their faces.

"You're in luck," Gavin said. "There's been a slight change of plans."

Blake blinked, noncomprehending. "What?"

"You can leave."

"Just like that?" Lisa asked tremulously.

"Mm-hmm. Just like that." He wrapped his arm around Val's waist. "You have Val to thank." His fingers stroked her side possessively. "She was most persuasive in begging for your lives." She stiffened, face aflame, and could not meet the eyes of her friends.

"Stop it," she whispered.

Blake and Lisa looked at each other. "The front door is still locked," Blake said cautiously.

"Observant as always," Gavin said. "I'll get the key. Excuse me."

The moment he was gone, her friends pelted her with questions. She didn't register any of them over the sound of her own heartbeat. Only the tone they were asked in: suspicious, hurt, betrayed, frightened.

"Listen to me—he's not going to let you go. He's going to kill you both. You have to get out of here."

"He said we can leave," Lisa said.

"Yes," Val replied, "but he didn't say you *may*."

"How do you know that?" Blake asked. "That's splitting hairs. It's semantics. It's—"

"It's the way he works," Val snapped. "You don't believe me? He carries a small knife. I...I saw him kill Charlie with it. Back in the greenhouse. I'm pretty sure he killed Jason, too. I saw his body upstairs. He'd been stabbed."

Lisa covered her mouth. "Oh God—"

"Lisa—remember the greenhouse? There was a back entrance, I think. I was trying to find a way out and then Charlie showed up—" she cut herself off. "You found it. Try that way. If he's locked it, smash the glass. It's far enough away that he might not hear it."

"But not the front door?"

"I smelled gas. I think he's going to torch the place."

"Oh God," Lisa said again. "This isn't happening—"

"And what are you going to do?" Blake demanded.

"I—" She fingered the glass through her jeans. "I'm going to try and distract him."

"Distract him? This isn't a movie, Val," Lisa warned, shaken from her hysteria. "He might really kill you."

Not if I kill him first. She turned away, before they could see the sangfroid in her eyes, the blood lust in her veins.

"I'm willing to take that chance. Now run."

Chapter Twenty-Five
Checkmate

GM pretended to look surprised when he came back and found Blake and Lisa gone. "Where are your friends, Val? I was under the impression they were dying to leave."

"I don't know."

"You're a poor liar, Val. They're trying to escape, I suppose? Leaving you here—to distract me, like a lamb to the slaughter." He grinned. "Welcome distraction though you are, I'm afraid I can't have that."

"Can't—or won't?"

"Touche."

He took her by the wrist, yanking her out of the house. Her feet were slipping and sliding on something wet, and the sharp smell of gasoline burned her sinuses.

"Where are you taking me?"

"You'll see."

At the door's threshold, he struck a match and tossed it on the boards. A river of fire erupted through the halls. It was terrifying, akin to glimpsing the hell that awaited her into the afterlife. "Wait." Her throat was coated in grit from the smoke. "The others—" Had they made it out in time?

"I agreed to spare their lives. I said nothing about preserving them."

That's splitting hairs. It's semantics.

This must have been how Cassandra felt. She dug her heels into the dirt. "We have to go back."

"No," he said, with cold finality, "Have you learned nothing? Survival of the fittest, my dear. Only the strongest are capable of living on to reproduce and flourish."

"Is that right?" Her voice sounded raw.

"Two million years of evolution seem to indicate so."

GM led her off the porch—not that she had much choice; his hand tightly gripped her wrist, tighter when she tried to pull away one last time. She could scarcely breathe, and only barely resisted the impulse to check that the glass shard in her pants was still secure. It was like ice against her sweaty skin; a grim reminder of what she was going to have to do.

"Then why do people exist who aren't like you?" she spat, to take her mind off the blade.

"That's a simple case of mathematics. It takes many sheep to satisfy one wolf."

"Is that what this was? Some sick, Darwinian experiment?"

"I suppose you would see it that way. No, my intentions were slightly less grandiose. I merely wanted something that would ensure your good behavior. And it worked."

She let her silence speak for itself.

"Don't be that way. You know I'm right. You would never have come to me alone."

They were by the swimming pool now. Spirals of steam rose up from the water to mingle with the morning air. Val could smell the chlorine. The water lapped at her feet.

"I'm here now," she said quietly, bowing her head so he would not see the hatred there. Or the fear.

He moved her down with him until she was lying flush against the second step of the pool. The chemicals of the pool water stung her many cuts and scrapes. At her hip, where the glass had gouged her, was a steady, painful throb.

"You look like Ophelia," he said huskily.

"She killed herself."

"Only because Hamlet was foolish enough to let her. You are mine. As long as one of us still breathes, that won't change."

Exactly.

She yelped when he lowered his hands to his jeans, and got into position over her. "Wait—"

"What is it?" He didn't sound human. Where his white clothing was damp, she could see right through. Leaning over her like this, face blackened with smoke, wet, and unkempt, she realized she had never seen him look so wild.

"I...I want to touch you." She thought frantically back to the movies she had seen with James. Action movies, where the heroine tricked the villain. "I want to, um, g-get used to you a-and your body."

The blush that colored her face wasn't feigned.

His face didn't change, but she thought she heard his breathing quicken. For a moment, he seemed about to refuse, and the glass burned like fire against her hip. *He's going to kill me, if he sees it*, she thought, her heart pounding.

"All right."

He backed up off her, and she was free. Well. Not quite. Even as she rose to a sitting position, she knew he was tensed and ready to spring if she tried to run. She kept that in mind as she straddled his waist, letting her fingers slide through his dark hair that had the texture of coarse fur.

He remained still at first, letting her touch his face, his eyelids, his lips—though he bit her fingertips when she ventured too close. His willingness shocked her; was he that trusting? Or did he simply believe her to be so weak that she was incapable of betrayal?

Which would be quickest? She wondered, as their lips met again. His throat? Her fingers played over the supple skin, the rigid tautness of his Adam's apple, as she let her hands fall down his body. His heart? But she wasn't sure she'd be able to find it—the ribs were in the way, and a wound to the stomach wouldn't kill him fast enough.

"What on earth are you looking for?" he whispered, as her hand slipped down his soaked shirt. And—perhaps she was imagining it—but he sounded perhaps the tiniest bit suspicious. The way he had sounded when she'd kissed him and he'd seen Lisa's reflection in her own.

"This." She bared her teeth in a mangled attempt at a smile, and grabbed him through his pants. He inhaled sharply, as though his breath were a knife slicing through his throat and lungs, and his hips bucked beneath hers involuntarily.

The crotch of his trousers was under the water, seated as he was against the steps, and the tight fabric was plastered to the skin because beneath it, he wore nothing else. She looked up from the hard, corded flesh she clutched in her hand and gasped at the expression on his face. With a splash, he tackled her, and they fell down a step, forcing her to sit upright to keep her head from being submerged.

She waited until he was over her, until his hands were on her hips and out of the way, and then she let the glass shard fly. But she hesitated, and he'd sensed the flash of silver in the corner of his eye. He whipped his head back to look at her. Instead of slicing the arteries in his neck, she merely grazed the skin with the teeth of the blade. A crimson collar blossomed on his skin, studded with garnet drops of blood.

He stared at her, eyes wide with disbelief.

And then he was wrestling her for control of the blade. She slashed at his hand, and he let his weight settle on her belly, keeping her hips pressed against the ground—so she couldn't crawl away. She let out an angry yowl, holding her hand as high above her head as it could, trying to keep the blade away from him. Just when it occurred to her that she should toss it he tore the knife from her hand and poised the blade at the hollow of her throat.

"You are quite a bit more ruthless than I gave you credit for, my hellcat." His voice like clotted cream, disgustingly thick. She moved her head back, trying to put space between herself and the blade, and water flooded her ears, lending a strange, robotic quality to his voice. "I had no idea your claws were so sharp. Or perhaps you merely wanted a bit of blood-play?"

She spat in his face.

He pitched the shard into the water. Then he yanked her to her feet, so her back was to the pool, and kissed her so hard that her head tilted back. His long fingers wrapped around her throat, and his other arm kept her bent at an acute angle over the water. She had never seen him look so angry, even before. His kiss was bruising, and she clutched at his hand desperately to keep him from choking her. He gave her a cruel smile and slid his hand down her pants.

"I knew you were up to something—though I never imagined it was premeditated murder. You always have been able to surprise me, though." She felt the caress of his fingers against her underwear, as gentle as his smile was hard. "I admit, I was curious…to see how far you'd go," he said softly, sliding his fingers deeper. Her knees buckled, and she felt her grip on his neck slacken. He studied her for a long moment before slowly withdrawing his hand. "All the way, apparently."

Val stared at him, and her heart seemed to tear in two.

"What should I do with you?" he whispered, and if it were not for the rage that held his words in their choking grip, he might sound seductive even now. "Oh, I *am* furious. I could easily strangle you. And yet…I find your daring quite arousing. Which would you prefer? To be my consort—or my kill?"

"You're insane," she whispered. "Really and truly insane. Delusional."

"That's not an answer," he responded.

"Go to hell, you sick, twisted fuck."

His lip curled. "You first, Valerian."

And then he threw her into the deep end.

Horrorscape by Nenia Campbell

Epilogue

A black sheet of rolling fog seemed to encase the red-haired girl as she stared up into nothingness, wondering what had happened. Her chest hurt in that tight, constricting way that sometimes followed a severe flu, except, unlike the flue, she couldn't ease the tension there by coughing. She couldn't even breathe. Val turned her head to the side, wondering why her cheeks felt so cold. Why there was so much pain?

(Because you drowned, a small voice said.)

Had he been planning to kill her all along, or had it been spontaneous? An act of passion? In the black fog, Val wondered, bleakly, whether she was still at the bottom of the pool.

A feeling of warmth broke through the cold barrier that had woven its way around her like a cocoon, wrapping itself around her like a blanket, and she felt the firm but reassuring pressure of someone's mouth on hers. The feeling wasn't exactly pleasant, and Val wanted to turn away, but she couldn't move. Just leave me alone, she thought wearily.

The pressure disappeared and, following in its wake, a horrible pain exploded in her chest like a cannon. She gagged, wincing at the disgusting sensation of chemical-laced pool water rising in her throat. The tightness eased and she found that passageways previously blocked were open, allowing her to breathe again, roughly, as she rolled on her side to spit the water out.

Horrorscape by Nenia Campbell

Her eyes opened slowly, and she found herself staring at the grass. There was an unfamiliar woman leaning over her, with an expression of concern etched on her youthful face. Confused, Val's eyes drifted down from the woman's face to the symbol of the red cross on her stark white uniform. Oh. "Are you all right?" the woman asked. "Can you talk? Do you know your name?"

"I.... Yes," Val said, wincing at the light. It was sunny now and possibly warm, but the heat of the sun didn't reach her cold, unresponsive body. Someone had stripped off her wet clothes and wrapped her in a fuzzy blanket, which she now wrapped more tightly around herself. "Val. W-what happened?"

"You almost drowned," the woman said, answering the question which Val had asked in what felt like an eternity ago, point-blank. "You have mild hypothermia. Just a few minutes longer, and you would have been a goner."

Oh, Val thought again, more faintly this time.

Her words had an undesirable effect, and the girl's eyes widened, remembering: *Suicide Chess*.

Val shot up, ignoring the woman's anxious suggestion that she shouldn't, and winced at the fiery pain that coursed through her (she later found out that the painful Heimlich procedure had resulted in a few broken ribs), but she'd seen what she'd needed to see.

Horrorscape by Nenia Campbell

The massive white house was now swarming with men in uniform, the driveway packed with police cars, two ambulances, and a fire truck. There were a few other cars as well, but a bar of yellow crime scene tape kept the curious onlookers from coming any closer. Her eyes shifted up to the second story, and the single shaded window that faced her.

So Lisa and Blake had managed to escape after all, and they'd called the police, too.

We won, she thought weakly. Funny, I don't feel much like a winner, right now.

An old quote drifted to her, from a place long-forgotten, but it's meaning was still fresh: "You may have won the battle, but you've lost the war." Yes, that was it. She'd lost the war.

"I lost," Val murmured quietly, which the paramedic heard as 'I'm frost', and she gave Val an odd look.

"Are you cold, honey?"

Acknowledgments

There are so many people to thank that if I went through them all I'd have a miniature book in and of itself.

But let's start with:

- Louisa, for her beautiful covers, and even more beautiful personality.
- The PH whoars (I love you, skanks! <3).
- The Goodreads community for being so supportive and wonderful about helping out a little indie author like me.
- My original readers who read my first (admittedly not-so-great) draft of this story, and who enthusiastically supported me on the subsequent revisions.
- My family, for their tongue-in-cheek support.

Printed in Germany
by Amazon Distribution
GmbH, Leipzig